# LIGHT AFTER DARK

## GANSETT ISLAND SERIES, BOOK 16

## MARIE FORCE

Light After Dark
Gansett Island Series, Book 16
By: Marie Force

Published by HTJB, Inc.
Copyright 2016. HTJB, Inc.
Cover designer: Kristina Brinton
Interior Layout: Isabel Sullivan, E-book Formatting Fairies

ISBN: 978-1946136046

"Smells Like Nostalgia," Lyrics by Emily J. Force. Used with permission. All rights reserved.

"Can't Stop," Lyrics by David Sardinha. Used with permission. All rights reserved.

www.marieforce.com

*For Relmond Van Daniker, boss, mentor, dear friend.*
*Rest in peace.*

# The Gansett Island Series

Book 1: Maid for Love *(Mac & Maddie)*
Book 2: Fool for Love *(Joe & Janey)*
Book 3: Ready for Love *(Luke & Sydney)*
Book 4: Falling for Love *(Grant & Stephanie)*
Book 5: Hoping for Love *(Evan & Grace)*
Book 6: Season for Love *(Owen & Laura)*
Book 7: Longing for Love *(Blaine & Tiffany)*
Book 8: Waiting for Love *(Adam & Abby)*
Book 9: Time for Love *(David & Daisy)*
Book 10: Meant for Love *(Jenny & Alex)*
Book 10.5: Chance for Love, *A Gansett Island Novella (Jared & Lizzie)*
Book 11: Gansett After Dark *(Owen & Laura)*
Book 12: Kisses After Dark *(Shane & Katie)*
Book 13: Love After Dark *(Paul & Hope)*
Book 14: Celebration After Dark *(Big Mac & Linda)*
Book 15: Desire After Dark *(Slim & Erin)*
Book 16: Light After Dark *(Mallory & Quinn)*
Book 17: Victoria & Shannon (Episode 1)
Book 18: Kevin & Chelsea (Episode 2)
A Gansett Island Christmas Novella
Book 19: Mine After Dark *(Riley & Nikki)*
Book 20: Yours After Dark *(Finn McCarthy)*

# CHAPTER 1

The slap, slap, slap of running shoes on pavement was the only sound in the otherwise tranquil morning on Gansett Island. No cars, no bikes, no mopeds, no airplanes overhead. Nothing but wide-open road before her as Mallory counted down the miles on her usual circuit around the island.

Slap, slap, slap. *Laid off.*

*Escorted from the premises after twelve years.*

*Disposed of like yesterday's hazardous waste.*

*Galling.*

*Humiliating.*

*Infuriating.*

It'd been ten days since Mallory Vaughn, RN, director of emergency nursing, had been given a pink slip. With hindsight, the handwriting had been all over the wall for months, with every management meeting focused on the hospital's increasingly dire budget situation.

Naturally, they were cutting the highest-paid employees and in many cases not replacing them at all or with people so new they were still trying to tell the difference between an ass and an elbow. Oh to be a fly on the wall the first time the Emergency Services Department didn't have enough nurses on duty to cover a shift. She hoped it was utter chaos. That was the least of what the hospital deserved after treating her like a common criminal when she'd given them everything she had for a big chunk of her professional life.

*Thanks a lot for nothing.*

Although, the severance package *had* been generous, she'd give them that much. They'd given her a year's salary, a one-time, lump-sum payment for all her accrued sick and vacation time and health insurance coverage for a year. It definitely could've been worse, but it would be a very long time, if ever, before she got over being escorted from the building by security as if she were a common criminal rather than a faithful, dedicated employee.

She understood why they had to do that. Disgruntled employees had been known to leave with a flourish by deleting critical files from computers along with other malicious activities, but did they honestly think *she* would do something like that? The incident was particularly galling in light of the fact that she'd sacrificed so much for that job, including any semblance of a personal life. Who had time for a personal life while working eighty hours a week, doing a job that needed two people to get it done properly?

*Good luck finding some other schmuck willing to work like a dog.*

More than once since it had happened, Mallory had thought the layoff might turn out to be a blessing. The tight knot of stress in her gut that she'd lived with for years was gone. She woke up now unencumbered, with the whole day ahead of her to do with as she pleased. It'd been years since she'd had a real vacation with no one calling or texting or emailing for answers only she could provide.

And best of all was unlimited time on the island that had become her second home in the last year, since a letter from her late mother had finally given Mallory the name of her father and told her where to find him.

*Big Mac McCarthy.*

All she had to do was think about him and she smiled. After she'd lived her entire life with a giant question mark where her father should've been, Big Mac had more than made up for lost time by wrapping his big, burly arms around her and welcoming her into his life. He and his wife, Linda, had made her feel like a part of their family from the minute they learned she existed.

Like everyone else who knew the big, jovial, generous, affectionate man who'd fathered her, Mallory was madly in love with him as well as with Linda and their amazing family. Mallory had gone from being completely alone after her mother died to having parents, five siblings, four sisters-in-law, a brother-in-law, two nephews and a niece, as well as uncles and cousins she already adored and the wide circle of friends that came with the McCarthys. Sometimes she still couldn't believe the twisting turns her life had taken since she lost her mother.

Over the last year, she'd tried to reconcile and make peace with the secret her mother had kept from her and her father for nearly forty years. She'd run the gamut of emotions from anger over what she'd missed, to sadness for what could've been, to elation over her new family.

Though she knew that raging against her late mother wouldn't change the past, anger simmered just below the surface of her newfound happiness. Her mom had sacrificed a lot to bring her into the world, including her own parents and siblings, who'd turned their backs on her when she became pregnant out of wedlock.

Diana had done her best to give Mallory every advantage in life, and the two of them had made a happy family together. But when Mallory thought of what might've been with the other half of her family, she simmered with outrage that had no outlet. Mallory had loved her mother and was trying to forgive her for the secrets she'd kept. Forgiveness was a work in progress, as was her hard-won sobriety, which had been tested in the last year.

Mallory was ashamed to admit that she'd had a few sips of beer and wine here and there while trying to fit in with her new family. Those few sips had her back to Alcoholics Anonymous meetings for the first time in many years. The tastes of alcohol she'd allowed herself during a particularly stressful time in her life hadn't derailed her recovery, but they'd scared her straight into daily meetings.

Sobriety, she'd learned, was a journey with many destinations. The drinks she'd relied upon when meeting her Gansett Island family had been the first she'd had in more than ten years. When she realized what she'd allowed to happen during a particularly stressful and emotional time, she'd been unnerved by how easily she'd put aside all her hard work with almost no thought to the consequences. That couldn't happen again.

She was beginning to get tired and thought about turning around to head back to Big Mac and Linda's house when a motorcycle came flying around the curve behind her, just missing her as it passed in a flash of metal, the roar of an engine and the stink of exhaust.

*Ugh.* If that idiot only knew the injuries she'd seen thanks to motorcycles, he'd never go near one again.

Mallory had turned toward home when a sickening sound of metal scratching against pavement had her reversing course and heading in the direction the sound had come from. Though her legs were tired, she sprinted with everything she had toward the man she saw sprawled in the street, his bike on its side about ten feet from him.

From the other direction, another jogger came toward them, arriving a second after Mallory squatted next to the man on the road to assess his injuries. Blood poured from an abrasion on his face, and his leg rested at at an awkward angle that indicated a possible femur fracture.

"What've we got?" the other runner asked when he stopped next to her.

Mallory filled him in on what she'd seen so far. "Do you have a phone? I never bring mine when I run."

"Yeah, I'll call it in." He withdrew a cell phone from the pocket of his running pants and made the call. "I'm at the scene of a motorcycle crash with a single rider unconscious and bleeding from abrasions to the head and bleeding profusely from what appears to be a compound fracture of his femur." He recited the other details in a methodical way that indicated medical training. Bending low to the ground, he peered at the growing pools of blood under the unconscious man. "Dispatch a chopper. We're going to need it." He ended the call and then pulled his T-shirt over his head to make a tourniquet for the man's leg.

"Are you a doctor?" she asked, trying not to notice his ripped chest and abdomen or bulky arm muscles. In addition to his medical abilities, he also apparently spent a lot of time in the gym.

"Trauma surgeon. You?" Still bending at the waist, he worked the man's wallet out of the back pocket of his shorts and flipped it open.

"ER nurse."

"Despite how it seems, this might turn out to be our friend Michael's lucky day." He sighed. "Twenty-four years old. From New York."

In the pearly early morning light, they stayed by the side of their victim, watching over him until help arrived. Though she was conditioned to senseless injuries after a career as an emergency nurse, it never got any easier to see a young person's life possibly changed in a matter of seconds or to think about the frightening call an unsuspecting family was about to get.

"I'm Mallory Vaughn," she said after a long silence.

"Quinn James."

No other words were exchanged between them as they listened to the sirens get closer to their location on the island's north end. Though he was unconscious, Michael's heart continued to beat and his breathing was regular, if shallow. It remained to be seen if he had suffered life-threatening damage.

EMS arrived and took over in a whirlwind of activity and shouted orders.

Mallory recognized Gansett Island Police Chief Blaine Taylor in the crowd of first responders. Blaine was married to her sister-in-law Maddie's sister, Tiffany. He walked over to her with another man who had to be six and a half feet tall.

"Hey, Mallory," Blaine said. "Did you see what happened?"

"Hi, Blaine. He was driving like a maniac and crashed after he just missed taking me out as he went by. Dr. James and I did what we could."

"You might've saved his leg," the tall guy said. "Mason Johns, fire chief."

"Oh, hi," Mallory said, shaking his hand. "Mallory Vaughn, ER nurse." Or former ER nurse, she should say, but since she hadn't yet told her own family she'd been laid off, it probably wasn't the best idea to tell someone she'd just met.

Mallory stuck around until the Life Flight helicopter arrived and took the young man to a level-one trauma center in Providence. Dr. James offered to go with him, which Mallory thought was nice of him, but the paramedics said they had it covered. As soon as the chopper left, the doctor took off running back the way he'd come, still shirtless after donating his to the cause. Mallory watched him go, noticing a slight hitch in his gait and wondering what his story was.

"Can I give you a lift home?" Blaine asked when the police and firefighters had cleared the site of debris and gotten traffic moving again.

Her muscles were rubbery from standing around, and the sun was now shining down on them, so his offer would save her the trek home, and it would allow her to make her meeting in town. "Do you have time?"

"Sure do. Hop in."

"Good to meet you, Mallory," Mason said as she walked past with Blaine.

"You, too, Mason."


Big Mac and Linda were eating breakfast when she came in the front door.

"There you are," her father said. "We were beginning to wonder if you'd jogged off the bluffs."

"I witnessed an accident and stuck around until the Life Flight came."

"Oh, we heard that and wondered what was going on," Linda said. "Anyone we know?"

Mallory shook her head and helped herself to a glass of ice water. It'd taken a few months to make herself at home here, but they'd insisted often enough that she finally relaxed and helped herself to whatever she wanted. "Tourist from New York on a motorcycle."

"Ugh," Linda said. "I hate those things, especially the one Mac bought from Ned when he was in high school. I was so sure he'd kill himself, and now Evan's got it." She shuddered. "The best part about him being away on tour is no one riding that horrible thing."

Big Mac chuckled at her tirade. "Tell us how you really feel, dear."

"I just did."

As always, Mallory giggled at their banter. They had the kind of marriage she'd once hoped to have herself, but fate had made other plans for her.

Since she had time before her meeting, she took her ice water to the table and sat with them. It was time to tell them what'd happened at work.

Big Mac gave her a look she'd seen him use on the others, inquisitive, concerned, paternal. Now it was directed at her, and she loved that. She loved having a father, and she especially loved that *he* was her father.

"What's on your mind?" he asked.

"I've been meaning to tell you that I got laid off about ten days ago."

"*What?*" Linda said. "Are you kidding? You run that department!"

"I know, and I'm sure by now they know it, too." She told them the whole story, about being escorted from the building and how it made her feel, to the generous severance package that would buy her time to figure out her next move.

"It's an outrage," Big Mac declared. "How can they treat loyal employees that way?"

"You and I agree, but that's the way it goes. I was one of the highest-paid nurses in the building, and they're having major financial problems, so the pink slip wasn't a total surprise."

"Still," Big Mac said, "it must've been upsetting to have it go down that way."

"It was, but I'm better now. Thanks for letting me hang out here for the last few days. I'll figure out my next move and get out of your hair soon."

Linda reached over to put her hand on top of Mallory's. "You're not in our hair. We love having you, and you're welcome to stay for as long as you'd like. It's boring around here this time of year. It's nice to have the company."

"I agree," Big Mac said. "Our home is your home for as long as you want to stay."

"Thank you." Mallory swallowed hard, determined not to break down in front of them. They would never know what it meant to her to have them on her side now that her mom was gone. She'd felt so alone in the world until she came to Gansett and found Big Mac and his brood. Now a big, boisterous family surrounded her, and they would get her through this latest challenge.

# CHAPTER 2

Mallory walked into the nondenominational church and took the stairs to the basement, where the AA website had said the meeting would be held. This was her first meeting on the island, but she immediately recognized the fellowship she'd found elsewhere in the encouraging signs on the wall, the circle of chairs and the table full of refreshments.

One man approached her and introduced himself as Andy. After so many years working in the ER, she was pretty good at guessing people's ages, and she put him at mid-sixties.

"Hi, Andy, I'm Mallory."

"Nice to meet you. Is this your first time with this group?"

"It is."

"A nice bunch."

"That's good to know."

"Are you a year-rounder? Don't think I've seen you in town."

"My father is. I've been visiting him."

"Ah, I see. We don't get many tourists this time of year. Another couple months, and it'll be crazy."

"I was here last summer and saw that for myself."

"I like to enjoy the quiet while it lasts. What do you do for work?"

"I'm a nurse. You?"

"Retired engineer. My missus and I always said we were going to move out here when we retired, and we did it two years ago."

"Any regrets?"

"Not a one. Wish the grandkids were a little closer, but we see plenty of them. Their folks like to visit."

Others wandered in and joined their conversation, and Mallory was immediately at ease with these people. That was the beauty of AA. No matter where you went in the world, you could always find your tribe at meetings. In her time away, she'd forgotten how comforting the fellowship could be.

The facilitator, Nina, came in a few minutes before the start time, apologizing for running late.

"When are you not running late, Nina?" Andy asked in a teasing tone.

"I know, I know," she said with a good-natured grin that put Mallory immediately at ease.

"She runs the Summer House hotel," Andy told Mallory. "She's always crazy busy."

Mallory remembered what it was like to be crazy busy. Now she was trying to get used to a slower pace and the lack of a schedule.

Nina asked everyone to take seats, and Mallory ended up sitting next to Andy with her back to the door. They were reciting the Serenity Prayer when she saw Mason Johns come in and take a seat across the circle from her.

Interesting.

Each meeting was similar, but every group had its own quirks. This one did a round of introductions before they began.

"Hi, I'm Mallory. I live in Providence, but I'm here visiting. I'd been sober for more than ten years until a few slipups recently. Thank you for letting me be part of your group."

"Welcome, Mallory," the others said.

The thing she'd always loved best about the meetings was the lack of judgment. Everyone here was wrestling his or her own demons. They offered the kind of unconditional support that put lives back on track. They'd done it once for her, and she'd paid it forward for many others over the years.

Her life wasn't off track, per se, not like it had been when she first came to AA. But she was unnerved by how easily she'd fallen back into casually drinking, as if she hadn't waged war and won a hard-fought battle.

"I'm Mason. I've been sober twelve years." As he said the words, he looked at her across the circle.

Mallory wasn't concerned about him telling anyone he'd seen her there. The word anonymous was in the name for a reason, but it was odd to see someone she knew, even if she'd only met him that morning, in a place where she knew so few people other than those she was related to and their friends.

Not that she cared about her family knowing about her alcoholism, but she'd like to be the one to tell them when the time was right.

During the next hour, several people shared their stories. One woman talked about her husband leaving her because he couldn't handle her drinking anymore. Her pain was so palpable, it brought tears to Mallory's eyes. A young man told of nearly losing a close friend in an alcohol-fueled prank gone wrong and how it had sobered him up to the realities of his addiction.

Each of them had been through hell before seeking out the help they'd found at the meetings, and Mallory was no different. Her hell had been years ago, and her mistake had been thinking she'd succeeded in putting it far enough behind her that she could occasionally indulge again. She knew better, and she'd learned that in times of stress she needed to be extra vigilant about her sobriety.

The meeting ended, and when she stood and turned to leave, she was surprised to see Quinn James sitting behind her. He nodded to her as she went by.

Very interesting.

"Hey, Mallory," Mason called to her.

She stopped to wait for him.

"You want to grab a coffee?"

"Sure, that'd be nice."

As they walked to the South Harbor Diner, the chill of the March air off the water had Mallory zipping her jacket all the way up to cover her neck. Even at five-foot-nine inches, she was dwarfed by the strapping fire chief, who had to be at least six and a half feet tall. With broad shoulders and light brown hair, he was handsome in a rugged, muscular way.

"I'm ready for spring any time now," Mason said.

"Me, too."

He held the door for her at the diner and followed her inside to a booth that overlooked the ferry landing. A waitress brought them coffee and menus.

"Are you hungry?" he asked.

"I might have an English muffin."

When the waitress returned, she ordered her English muffin, and he got a corn muffin.

"That seemed like a nice group at the meeting," she said as she stirred cream into her coffee.

"It is. I've been part of that meeting for years, and they're all good people. Like everything around here, attendance swells in the summer."

"I'm sure the alcohol-related incidents do, too."

He rolled his eyes. "You have *no* idea."

"So do you like the summer or dread it?"

"A little of both. I love the warmer weather, but I'm not so fond of the shenanigans that go on around here in the summer. At least once or twice a week, we have to Life Flight someone with alcohol poisoning off the island. It gets old after a while."

"I'm sure it does, especially when you know where they're probably headed."

"Exactly. That's how it started for me. Binge drinking in college that I didn't grow out of once I graduated. Then I wanted to stop and couldn't seem to do it on my own. Thankfully, I got help before it ruined my life."

"Same here. I suffered a painful loss when I was twenty-six and found solace in vodka. Turns out the vodka made it worse, not better."

He nodded in understanding. "I'm sorry for your loss."

"Thanks. It was a long time ago." *Some days it still feels like yesterday.* "I was ten years sober when I lost my mom. She left me a letter that finally told me who my father is, and when I came out here to find him, that's when I slipped up and had some wine and beer to be social. When I thought about it after the fact, it terrified me and brought me back to meetings for the first time in years."

"You're in the right place to get back on track."

"The crazy part was I didn't even give it a thought before I did it."

"Stress does funny things to people. I imagine it was a big deal to meet your dad for the first time, not to mention the rest of the family."

She liked how he didn't pretend not to know who her father was. The whole island probably knew their story by now. "It was so overwhelming, but wonderful, too. I'd wondered about him my whole life, and to get someone like him… Well, lucky doesn't begin to describe how I feel."

"You definitely hit the jackpot with him and the entire family."

She gave him a warm smile. "I couldn't agree more."

"So you're here for a visit?"

Was it her imagination, or was he fishing for info? "An extended visit. I was laid off ten days ago after twelve years on the job."

"Ouch," he said, wincing. "That sucks. I'm sorry."

"It was a bummer, but I'm trying to see the positives. It's a chance to try something new and shake things up a bit."

"I couldn't help but notice this morning that you seem to have medical skills."

"I was the director of emergency nursing at the hospital where I worked in Providence."

"Wow, that's impressive. You wouldn't be interested… Nah, that's ridiculous. You could do much better."

"You have to finish that thought. I'll die of curiosity if you don't."

Smiling, he said, "We're hiring people to work the rig this summer. Technically, we'd like our EMTs to be paramedics, but your training far exceeds paramedic level."

"I'm actually a certified paramedic as part of a program I instituted for my nurses to make them more aware of what goes on in the field before the patients reach us."

"Am I drooling?" He stuck out his chin dramatically. "Tell me the truth."

Mallory laughed at the silly expression on his handsome face. "No sign of drool."

"Maybe so, but I *am* drooling. Figuratively speaking."

"Of course," she said, laughing.

"Would you have any interest at all in spending the summer making very little money while treating drunks and disorderlies, accident victims and sick tourists?"

"Why, Chief Johns, you make it sound so appealing. How can I ever resist such an amazing offer?"

"You should probably resist it with every fiber of your being, but I'm hoping you won't. I'm dead serious, Mallory. The job is yours if you're looking to try something different for a few months. Unfortunately, I can only offer you a summer gig, beginning right after Memorial Day Weekend, ending Labor Day. I don't have the budget to take you on year-round."

"You may be surprised to hear that it sounds like just what I need to allow me to be here for the summer with my family while I figure out what's next."

His brown eyes lit up with pleasure. "Really? You mean it?"

"Sure, why not?" Mallory's mind raced with details she'd need to see to, loose ends to tie up, such as figuring out what to do with her house in Providence and finding a place to live on the island. But she had a couple of months to deal with all that before Memorial Day.

"You have no idea how totally you've made my day."

"Likewise. My summer just got much more interesting."

"We'll see if you're still saying that on Labor Day."

Mallory's laugh got stuck in her throat when Quinn James came into the diner, nodded to her and continued to the counter, where he purchased a coffee.

"What's his deal?" Mallory asked Mason, who turned to see who she meant.

"Not sure. He hasn't been here long. His brother, Jared, and his wife, Lizzie, hired Quinn to run the new healthcare facility they're opening in the former school."

"He said he's a trauma surgeon."

"I heard he was in Afghanistan, but I don't know anything else about him."

"Well, we know one thing," she said meaningfully.

"True. He comes to the meetings but doesn't say anything. He never misses a day."

"He'll talk when he's ready to." She hoped she'd get to hear his story.

The door opened again to admit Mallory's brother Mac and his best friend and brother-in-law, Joe Cantrell. Even after all these months, it still felt strange to realize she had five siblings, not to mention in-laws, nephews, a niece, uncles and cousins.

Mac's face lit up with pleasure at the sight of her. He and Joe walked over to the table she shared with Mason.

"Move over." That was the only warning she got before he nearly landed on her.

"Sorry about him," Joe said when he slid in next to Mason. "We're still working on his manners."

"Manners are overrated," Mac muttered.

"Work in progress," Joe whispered loudly, making Mallory laugh. "Hope we're not interrupting anything."

"*Now* you ask." Mallory had learned to jump into the scrum or get left behind in this crowd. "We're just having coffee. What're you guys up to?"

"Same thing as you," Mac said as he perused the menu. "What's Rebecca cooking up this morning?"

"Didn't you already eat?" Joe asked.

"Is there a law that says a man can only have one breakfast per day?"

"Not that I'm aware of," Joe said, shaking his head. "Mason, you got any info on this so-called law?"

"I'm all for as many meals as I can get. Go for it, Mac."

"I will, thank you," Mac said with a smug grin for Joe.

When Rebecca came to the table, Mac and Joe both ordered coffee, and Mac added an omelet with bacon, home fries and wheat toast.

Mac sat back to enjoy his coffee. "So what's going on with you guys?"

"So far today," Mason said, "your sister helped to save a guy's life, and she agreed to come work for me this summer."

Mac stared at her. "Say *what?*"

# CHAPTER 3

"Oh crap," Mason said. "I'm sorry. Did I spill the beans?"

"No worries," Mallory said, touched by his concern. "I haven't gotten the chance to tell these guys that I was laid off ten days ago."

"You were?" Mac asked, his eyes wide.

"That's too bad," Joe said. "I'm sorry to hear it."

Mallory shrugged. "I'm feeling better about it than I was, especially now that I have a summer job lined up with Mason." She smiled at him to let him know she really wasn't upset.

"You haven't said anything," Mac said. "Are you okay?"

"It was sort of traumatic being escorted from the building like a criminal after twelve years there, but I'm trying to move on."

Outrage rippled off her brother in palpable waves. "*That's* how they did it?"

"They have to do it that way or run the risk of fired employees damaging systems or property on the way out, not to mention some might get violent."

"That's so awful," Joe said. "I really feel for you."

"Who can we beat up for you?" Mac asked with a small smile that told her he was teasing. But could he ever know what it meant to her to have a brother who wanted to make things right for her?

"While I appreciate the sentiment, they're not worth it, and I'm fairly certain they're suffering without me."

"Good," Mac said. "That's the least of what they deserve."

His food was delivered, and he dove in like he hadn't eaten in a month. Over the last nine months, she'd loved learning little things about each of her siblings, such as Mac's voracious appetite for food, laughs, practical jokes, his wife and children and the rest of their family. He did everything in a big way, including love, and she adored him.

Grant, who followed Mac, was more cerebral, quieter, more likely to take it all in than lead the charge the way Mac did. Not that Grant couldn't more than keep up with Mac in the practical-joke department. He was usually subtler in his approach, however.

Adam was the family's tech wizard. To hear the rest of the family tell it, he could put a man on the moon with nothing more than a laptop and a smartphone. After he saved her phone from near disaster last summer when it got wet at the beach, Mallory was a believer.

Evan, who was currently on tour with country music superstar Buddy Longstreet, was the family musician. For Mallory, who had zero musical ability, Evan's talent was beyond impressive. Not only did he have an amazing singing voice, he played guitar, piano, the banjo, the harmonica and numerous other instruments. He had a vicious ragweed allergy that made his eyes swell up for several days in the summer and fall. Those were the kinds of details she'd glommed on to as she'd gotten to know her brothers.

And then there was Janey, the ultimate little sister, and she played the part to the hilt, driving her older brothers crazy with her teasing. Until she'd told them she was pregnant again and learned how crazy they were *about her*. They had good reason to be concerned after nearly losing Janey the day she delivered her first child, PJ.

Nearly a year after meeting them, Mallory was still finding out new things about her siblings, still hearing new stories about events that'd happened when they were growing up, and still absorbing each and every detail about them like a nosy voyeur who'd infiltrated their family. Fortunately, they seemed to understand her desire to know them and were equally curious about her, even if her upbringing had been far less eventful than theirs.

There it was again, the pang of anger that they'd been kept from her for so long, and as always, the anger was directed at her late mother, which made her feel like crap.

"Who can I see about a summer rental?" she asked during a lull in the conversation.

All three men answered at once. "Ned."

"*Ned Saunders?* Big Mac's friend? *That* Ned?"

"Yep," Mac said with a laugh. "The one and only. Our resident hobo cab driver is actually a multimillionaire land baron. He owns a big chunk of the real estate on this island. Sold my house to me."

"Mine, too," Joe said.

"Wow." The hobo cab driver description was far more fitting for Ned than land baron would ever be.

"Don't feel bad," Mac said. "We didn't know that either until a few years ago when I was looking to buy a place and Dad let the cat out of the bag."

"If Adam and Abby find a place to buy, Janey's house might be coming available," Joe said.

"You'd like that house," Mac said. "It's cozy and within walking distance of town."

"Sounds perfect."

"Adam and Abby are actively looking at houses," Joe said, "so that might happen sooner rather than later. I'll tell Janey you might be interested, if that's okay."

"Of course. Please do. Thanks."

"No problem."

"This having-a-family thing sure does come in handy," Mallory said.

Mason smiled at her across the table. "You can't be better connected around here than the McCarthys."

"I'm finding that out."

Mac's phone rang, and he took the call from his wife. "Oh wow, really? What're they saying?" After a pause, he added, "Are they going to the mainland?" He listened for a minute, his expression becoming more serious than Mallory had ever seen it. "Okay, let me know. Love you, too."

"What's going on?" Joe asked when Mac ended the call.

"Laura is in labor."

"Everything okay?" Joe asked.

"She's a month early, and apparently it's moving fast—too fast to get her to the mainland to deliver as planned."

Right before her eyes, Joe's face seemed to drain of all color.

"Joe," she said. "Are you all right?"

"Yeah… Just… Brings back memories I'd rather forget."

Mallory didn't think before she reached across the table to cover his hand with hers. "We won't let that happen again."

He forced a smile and nodded. Blowing out a deep breath, he said, "It hits me hard every time I hear someone we love is having a baby on this island, let alone two of them."

Mallory squeezed his hand before she released him. "I could take a walk over to the clinic to see if they need help."

Mac visibly brightened. "Maddie said Katie is off-island today," he said of their cousin Shane's fiancée, who was a nurse, "so David and Victoria are shorthanded at the clinic."

"I'll go see if I can help." Mallory reached for her wallet.

"I've got it," Mason said. "Go on ahead."

"Thank you."

"Any time," he said with a warm smile that made her wonder if he was interested in more than just coffee, AA meetings and paramedic service from her.

Mac got up to let her out, giving her a quick hug that warmed her heart. "Thanks, Mal."

"No problem." His affection and the use of a nickname put a lump in her throat. Before he let her go, Mac said, "Laura's going to be all right, isn't she?"

"Of course she is. I heard she did great when Holden was born. She'll be fine."

"Thanks for the reassurance. We're a little skittish when it comes to having babies."

"With good reason." Mallory had also heard the story of Mac's daughter Hailey's dramatic arrival during the tropical storm that shared her name. "I'll check in later."

Mallory ducked out of the diner and headed for the clinic, hoping there was something she could do to help her cousin bring her long-awaited twins into the world.

Laura tried to remain calm while her husband, Owen Lawry, melted down over the news that she was too far along to risk a trip to the mainland to deliver.

"That can't be right," Owen said. "Her water broke an hour ago. She's only just started having contractions. It's a month early!"

They'd been due to go to the mainland tomorrow and stay at her father's home in Providence so she could deliver in an actual hospital when the time came. Apparently, that wasn't going to happen now, and Laura focused on breathing through the pain as her husband became more agitated. Not that she blamed him. After what Janey and Maddie had been through, they both had good reason to freak out about an island delivery. It was, in reality, their worst-case scenario.

"I'm really sorry, Owen," Dr. David Lawrence said after examining her. "But I don't recommend you go anywhere, or you'll run the risk of having the babies on the ferry or by the side of a road. They're eager to make their debut. Laura is fully dilated and completely effaced."

"That can't be!"

"O." Laura extended a hand to him. "Come here."

He stopped pacing and came to her side, taking her hand.

"Calm down," she said. "I feel fine. I feel ready. David and Victoria are completely qualified to deliver these babies. Please take a deep breath and help me."

He swallowed hard and made a visible effort to relax. "Okay. I'm here. What can I do?"

"Call my dad and my aunt Linda. Ask them to come, and your mom will be waiting to hear what's going on."

"I'll take care of it. Will you be okay for a few minutes?"

She smiled up at him. "I promise."

He leaned over the bed to kiss her and then left the room.

"Vic," Laura said through gritted teeth. "I already feel like I need to push."

"Let's take a look." Victoria raised the sheet covering Laura's lap. "Oh damn, you're crowning." Over her shoulder, Victoria called for David.

He came running with Owen right behind him.

"We've got babies who want out right now."

"*Now?*" Owen cried.

Laura wanted to comfort him, but she was gripped by another fierce contraction that required her full attention.

Everything moved fast after that. The table was adjusted for delivery, her legs positioned, and Owen directed to get behind her to support her while she pushed. David prepared bassinettes for the babies.

"Okay, Laura," Victoria said, "on the next contraction, let's push."

Laura took hold of Owen's hands. "Help me, O."

He squeezed her hands. "Anything you need."

She could hear the tears and the fear in his voice. This wasn't what they'd planned, but it was happening, and the only thing they could do was roll with it. Their babies already had minds of their own.

Victoria consulted the monitor that kept track of her contractions. "Here we go."

All-consuming pain and the need to push overwhelmed Laura. The next thirty minutes were a blur of pain and pressure and tears.

Owen wiped away her tears and whispered sweet words of love and encouragement while holding her up from behind as she pushed.

"I can't," she said, gasping after a particularly strong contraction. "I can't do it."

"Yes, you can." Owen used a cool cloth that Victoria gave him to wipe the sweat from her forehead. "You've got this. You're the strongest person I've ever met. There's nothing you can't do."

Mallory appeared at the doorway. "I heard you were shorthanded today and might need some help."

Victoria looked to Laura who nodded, relieved to see her cousin and to have another medical professional to help.

"Come in," Vic said. "Happy to have you."

Mallory washed her hands and donned gloves before she came over to the bed. She placed her hand on Laura's shoulder. "How're you doing?"

"Hurts."

"No epidural?" Mallory asked Victoria.

"It was too late by the time she got here. She was ready to deliver." Victoria eyed the monitor. "Here we go, Laura."

The pain and pressure overwhelmed her once again, dragging her under to a place of intense concentration. Behind her, Owen provided unwavering support, holding her up when she lacked the energy to do it herself. He talked her through it, telling her how much he loved her, how he couldn't wait to meet their babies, how proud he was of her, how strong she was.

She focused on his voice and pushed as hard as she could until she finally found some relief.

"It's a girl!" Victoria said, holding up the baby so her parents could see her.

"Oh my God," Owen said. "We have a *daughter*!"

"Is she okay?" Laura asked.

"She's beautiful," Mallory said.

"Ten fingers and ten toes," David added as he took the baby to be evaluated.

"Why is she so quiet?" Laura asked, her heart racing with fear and anxiety as another contraction started, reminding her she was only half done. "David! What's wrong with her?"

His silence was almost as loud as the baby's until a loud cry from the newborn echoed through the room.

"That's what we wanted to hear," David said.

Laura could hear the relief in his voice.

Owen hugged her a little tighter and kissed her neck.

She could feel the dampness of tears on his face.

"Here we go again, Laura," Victoria said in an endlessly upbeat tone of voice.

The contractions were harder, sharper, more painful the second time around. They were also coming closer together, giving her little time to rest in between.

"Almost there, sweetheart," Owen said. "You've got this." He wiped her face with another cool cloth that Mallory handed him.

"You're doing great, Laura," Mallory said.

"One more big push," Victoria said.

Laura began to cry. She was so tired and in so much pain that she couldn't focus on anything else. "I can't."

"Yes, you can," Owen said. "We'll do it together." He gathered her into his arms and held her up as she screamed her way through another mighty push that finally yielded relief from the relentless pressure.

"You have a baby boy!" Victoria announced as the baby let out a lusty wail.

Laura sagged into Owen's embrace.

"You did it," he said wiping her tears and then his own.

"*We* did it."

His smile lit up his entire face. "One of each!"

"I'm so glad we waited to find out what we were having."

"Me, too."

David brought their baby girl to them, wrapped in a receiving blanket. She looked up at them with an expression that seemed both wise and stunned.

"Oh my God," Owen whispered. "Look at her."

Laura's heart melted at the reverence she heard in his voice. "Hi, baby girl," she said, nearly blinded by tears that just kept coming. Unlike the tears from earlier, though, these were tears of joy. The babies were here, they were safe, and they hadn't had to leave their beloved island to have them.

"Are we set on Joanna Sarah for her?" Owen asked.

They'd agreed to name a daughter, if they had one, after her late mother, JoAnn, and his mother, Sarah.

"I think she looks like a Joanna Sarah, don't you?"

"Absolutely. We'll call her Jo and Joey."

"I like that."

David handed their son to Owen.

"Oh damn, look at you." Owen used his free hand to rub his chest. "Is it normal to feel like you're having a heart attack after your wife gives birth?"

"That's just your heart expanding to make room for two more people to love," Mallory said.

"I love that," Laura said, smiling at her cousin.

"What's his name going to be?" Mallory asked. "I can't stand the suspense."

Laura and Owen exchanged glances, and then he spoke for both of them. "We wanted them to have the same first initial so his name is Jonathan Russell. His middle name is for my grandfather."

"Jo and Jon," Mallory said. "I love it."

Victoria, who'd stepped out for a minute, returned with Laura's dad, Frank, her brother, Shane, and her aunt Linda.

"That was quick!" Linda said when she saw the babies.

Frank came over to get a closer look at his new grandchildren, who were sleeping in their parents' arms.

"Meet Joanna Sarah and Jonathan Russell Lawry," Laura said.

"Oh wow," Frank said on a long exhale. "One of each. How perfect. And named for your mother." His voice thickened with emotion. "I love that, Princess. She'd be so honored."

Laura squeezed his hand. "I hope so."

"Katie will be so bummed she missed this," Shane said of his fiancée, who was also Owen's sister. "What a day to have professional training on the mainland."

"Take some pictures for her," Owen said.

After they posed for photos, Laura said, "You know what the best part of this day is?"

"I bet I know," Owen said.

"I bet you don't. It's that I'll never, ever, *ever* have to be pregnant again."

"But how will I recognize you, my love?" Owen asked. "You've been pregnant the whole time I've known you."

"Very funny. Wait till you find out what I really look like. You might not want me anymore."

Leaning in close to her, he gazed into her eyes as he kissed her. "Not a chance of that."

# CHAPTER 4

Later that evening, Mallory hitched a ride home with Linda. The entire family had been into the clinic to visit Laura, Owen and the babies. David had determined that both she and the twins were in great shape, and thus there was no need to transport them to the mainland for further medical attention. They'd be spending at least two nights at the clinic, where David and Victoria would keep a close eye on all three of them before allowing them to go home.

"What a day," Linda said, choking back a yawn. She'd been unflagging in her support of Laura and Owen since her arrival at the clinic hours ago.

"She appreciated you being there."

"She's another daughter to me. Her mom died so young. It was such a tragedy. Frank raised those kids all by himself."

"From what I've heard, he did it with considerable help from you guys."

"We did what we could, but we were out here and they were in Providence. Laura and Shane came out to spend the summers with us, and Frank came on weekends. We muddled through."

"Laura told me once that those summers were the highlight of her childhood."

"Did she?" Linda smiled. "That's awfully nice to hear."

"I wish I could've done what they did."

"Spend summers here?"

Mallory nodded. "I got to go to camp while my mom worked. I would've rather been here."

"I'm sure she did the best she could."

"Did she?" Mallory wanted to blame her testy tone on the long day, but that wasn't it.

"You want to talk about it?"

Mallory desperately wanted to talk about it. "I'm so angry with her, which makes me feel terrible because she's gone and can't defend herself. But I can't help it. Look what she kept me from for almost forty years! My father, my brothers, my sister, cousins, uncles, you. I'm so damned mad that some days I don't know how I'll ever get past it."

"It's understandable that you'd be upset."

"I went past upset months ago. Now I'm just downright furious. All those years, I thought I was just missing a father, but I also had five siblings and four cousins. We could've grown up together, but she chose to keep me all to herself. Her family had nothing to do with us. Do you know how lonely it is to have exactly one other person as your family?"

Linda pulled her yellow bug into the driveway at the White House, as the locals referred to their home, and cut the engine.

"You know what the worst part is?"

"What's that?"

"After all this time, I don't even know what I'm supposed to call him. Big Mac? Dad? What do I *call* him?"

"He'd want you to call him anything that feels comfortable to you. If you want to call him Dad, call him Dad."

"Will the others care if I call him that?"

"Why would they? He's your father, Mallory. You should call him Dad."

All of a sudden, Mallory realized she'd gone off on a rant and sagged against the seat. "I'm sorry. I don't mean to dump my crap in your lap."

"My lap is more than happy to accommodate your crap," Linda said.

Mallory laughed at her choice of words.

"I'm a professional mom. It's what I do best. No one can replace your mother, but I'm here if you need an ear or a shoulder."

When her eyes burned with tears, Mallory used her fingers to hold them in. "I don't want to be angry with her, but I can't help it."

"You have a right to your feelings. We all do."

"Why couldn't she have told me about him sooner? What did she think would happen if she did?"

"I don't know, but she must've been afraid of something."

"*What?* She *knew* him. She had to know he'd never try to take me from her."

"She probably never expected her parents to turn their backs on her. People do unexpected things all the time. Perhaps she felt it wasn't worth the risk to tell him about you."

"Maybe," Mallory conceded.

"You may never fully understand the why of it, Mallory, but in time, you'll make peace with it. She left you a priceless gift by giving you your father's name."

"I know, and I try to tell myself it's enough."

"But you still feel cheated."

"Yeah."

"You should talk to your uncle Kevin. He's an excellent therapist. He might be able to help you deal with those feelings."

"That's not a bad idea, especially since I'm going to be spending more time here."

"You are?"

Mallory nodded. "Mason offered me a job working on the rescue this summer, and I decided to take it. It'll buy me some time to figure out what's next."

"That's wonderful news! Your dad will be so thrilled. You're more than welcome to stay with us. We have plenty of room, as you know."

"That's very sweet of you, but you guys need your privacy. I heard Janey's house in town might be available to rent after Adam and Abby buy a house."

"That'd be ideal for you."

"I agree. I love that house."

"It sounds to me like you had a very productive day. You helped to save a life, you landed a new job, found a new home and helped deliver your cousin's babies."

"And to reward myself for that great day, I indulged in a pity party."

"Give yourself a break. In the last year, you've lost your mother, found your father and his family, and got laid off from the job that was at the center of your life. I'm surprised you're not in the fetal position after all that."

"I resort to the fetal position every now and then."

Linda chuckled. "You're going to get through this latest challenge. I have no doubt about that. You may even look back to realize getting laid off was the best thing to ever happen to you. If nothing else, it'll force you to take a look at what else is out there, waiting to be discovered."

"Right now it just feels like a mountain to be climbed."

"Shaking up your life is overwhelming, for sure. I have a good feeling about you moving out here. This place has magical restorative powers. Ask anyone. They'll tell you. I think this is going to turn out to be a whole new beginning for you, the Summer of Mallory."

"I like that. The Summer of Mallory."

"Here's to new beginnings."

While new beginnings were great, moving was not. Mallory had lived in the same house for twelve years and had accumulated way too much stuff, much of which she donated or sold at a yard sale. She spent entire nights sifting through her belongings, paring down to the necessities she would need on the island.

The rest would go into storage while the house was rented. Movers would arrive in an hour to take her bed, sofa and other furniture and household items to Gansett, while she packed her car with clothes and personal items. Both vehicles were scheduled on the three-o'clock ferry to the island, thanks to her brother-in-law, Joe. Being related to the owner of the ferry company had its perks.

She carried the last of the boxes to her car, these containing items that she'd never part with or allow out of her possession. Priceless memories she carried with her to her new life on Gansett Island.

Her realtor, Judy, dropped by to pick up the keys for the tenants who would move in on the first of June.

"I'm so jealous that you're moving to Gansett," Judy said. "I'd kill to live out there."

"I'm excited," Mallory said, and she was now that the sifting, sorting and packing portion of the move was finished. "We'll see if I'm excited when winter rolls around." Would she still be there then? Who knew? But that was part of the fun of her new adventure. Anything was possible.

"Well, good luck. I'll keep an eye on the tenants and make sure they take good care of the place. If you decide to sell at some point, you know where I am."

"Yes, I do. Thanks again for everything."

After Judy left, Mallory took one last walk through the house, spending a few moments in each empty room before she locked up and jumped in her car for the trip to Point Judith to catch the ferry. As Mallory drove away from the house she'd called home for a dozen years, she never looked back.

Three hours later, Mallory led the moving truck to her new home in Janey's tiny but cozy house and found a crowd waiting to greet her. They'd put balloons on the mailbox and strung a Welcome Home banner across the front porch.

She was moved to tears as she took it all in—her dad and Linda, Mac and Maddie, Joe and Janey, Adam and Abby, Ned and Francine, Tiffany and Blaine, Shane and Katie, Riley and Finn, Uncle Frank and Betsy and Uncle Kevin and Chelsea. The only ones missing were Evan and Grace and Grant and Stephanie, all of whom were due home soon.

As Mac and Maddie's son, Thomas, and Tiffany's daughter, Ashleigh, ran around the small front yard, shrieking with excitement, Big Mac approached the car and opened the door for her.

Mallory wiped away tears and greeted him with a big smile. After having known him for almost a year, she could no longer imagine life without him. She took the hand he offered and let him help her out of the car.

He hugged her tightly. "So glad to have you here to stay, honey."

She wanted to swoon with happiness every time he called her that. It didn't matter that he called all the girls "honey" or "sweetheart." Mallory couldn't get enough of it. "I can't believe you're all here."

"Of course we're here," he said as if it was no big deal when it was the biggest of deals to her. "You need help getting settled." Keeping an arm around her, Big Mac bellowed to the others, "Let's get that truck unloaded, boys!"

While the men helped the movers carry in her bedroom and living room furniture, the women got busy unloading boxes in the kitchen. What she'd expected to spend three days doing, they had finished in three hours. Big Mac even hung pictures on the wall and put up the curtain rods she'd bought for the living room.

"It looks like I've lived here for a year," Mallory said when the last of the boxes had been unpacked and her clothes hung in the closet. "This family doesn't mess around."

"Next is the housewarming party," Big Mac declared, pulling out his wallet. "Mac, you get the beer. Joe, you're in charge of pizza." He handed cash to each of them. "What else do we need, Lin?"

"That about covers it."

"Go to it, boys."

"Why do we gotta be the hunter-gatherers?" Mac grumbled. "That's why we have wives."

"*Seriously?*" Maddie asked. "You're actually going there?"

"I don't think she's worshipping at the altar of Mac McCarthy anymore," Shane said, referring to Mac's famous comment at Evan's wedding last winter.

"*Shit,*" Mac said, with a dirty grin. "She worships at the Mac McCarthy altar *every day.*"

"Mac McCarthy is going to be at the altar in a pine box if he doesn't shut his mouth and do what he's told," Maddie said as the others roared with laughter.

"Yes, dear," he replied with a dopey grin. "Let's get going, Joe. The natives are getting nasty."

Though endlessly amused by Mac, Mallory's stomach had dropped at the mention of beer. Hopefully, no one would notice if she didn't indulge.

"Mommy," Thomas said, "is Daddy in trouble again?"

"Daddy is always in trouble," Maddie said to her son.

"Maybe he needs a time-out."

"I think that's a wonderful idea, honey."

"Mallory, come see the pictures from our trip," Big Mac said of the fortieth-anniversary trip he and Linda had taken to Paris and England last month.

She joined her dad in the kitchen with a growing feeling of happiness and contentment. She was going to love living here.

The next morning, she attended a meeting at the church and ran into Quinn James at the coffee table.

"How's it going?" she asked. He made her nervous, which was odd because men, in general, didn't rattle her. So why did this one?

"Good. Haven't seen you here in a while."

"I was in Providence packing up my house."

He stirred cream and sugar into his coffee. "Where you headed?"

"Here for at least the summer. After that, we'll see." She glanced up at him, noting the golden stubble on his jaw and the dark circles under his brown eyes that made him look haunted. "What about you?"

"I live here now. My brother and sister-in-law are opening a healthcare facility on the island. I'm their medical director."

"I heard about that. What a great idea."

"We'll see," he said with the faintest hint of a smile.

Mallory suspected he didn't smile very often. "It's an ambitious undertaking. Congrats on the new job."

"Thanks. I'm in way over my head, but don't tell my brother or his wife. They think I'm overqualified."

"Your secret is safe with me."

"You ought to come and check it out. Your brother is the contractor."

So he knew who she was in relation to the McCarthys. Interesting. Did that mean he'd asked about her? "I'll do that."

Mason appeared a few minutes later and joined them at the coffee table, his face lighting up with pleasure at the sight of her. "You're back! And just in time for the mayhem of Race Week. Is it Memorial Day yet?"

Amused by his enthusiasm, Mallory said, "Not yet."

"I'll see you next Tuesday at seven at the barn. That's what we call the firehouse."

"You're working on the rescue?" Quinn asked.

"Yep. Got myself a summer job."

"I thought you were an ER nurse?"

"I was laid off in early March."

"Oh damn. Sorry."

Mallory shrugged. "It hasn't been so bad. They gave me a year's pay, and now I've got a fun summer job lined up to keep me busy."

"We'll keep you busy, all right," Mason said. "So busy you won't have a second to be bored."

"He keeps trying to scare me off," Mallory said to Quinn. "After twelve years in the ER, not much fazes me."

"We'll see if summer on Gansett Island can top the ER in Providence," Mason said. "If nothing else, it'll give Providence a run for its money."

"I'm looking forward to it."

"She says that now," Mason said to Quinn, who laughed, and oh damn, was he handsome when he laughed.

Nina came rushing through the door, uttering her usual apologies for running late.

"If you want to come out to the site after the meeting, I'd be happy to show you around," Quinn said.

"Um, sure, that sounds good. Thanks."

Nodding, he went to find a seat. As he walked away, Mallory again noted he had a slight limp and wondered if he'd injured himself while running or when he was in Afghanistan. She'd really like to know.

"I guess I need to get here earlier if I want to ask you out for coffee after," Mason said as he followed her to the circle of chairs.

Mallory turned to find him smiling down at her. "Sorry. Rain check?"

"Sure. Any time."

As Mallory took her seat, she again wondered if he was interested in more than a professional relationship with her. That might get awkward with him as her boss for the summer.

Nina began the meeting by leading the Serenity Prayer and welcoming new members. "Mallory, it's nice to have you back with us."

"Thank you. I'm here for the summer, so you'll be seeing more of me."

"We're happy to have you. Who would like to begin?"

Andy, the man who'd befriended her the first time she attended, talked about some recent challenges he'd encountered at social events. Nancy, a waitress at Stephanie's Bistro, talked about working in a place where serving alcohol was part of her job, and Russ, a deckhand on the ferries, discussed his struggles with the drunks on the boats after a long day on the island.

"I ask myself all the time, is that what I was like?" Russ said. "If so, I'm doubly glad I don't drink anymore."

If Mallory was going to make this her home meeting while she was on the island, at some point she had to contribute. No time like the present, she decided, signaling to Nina that she had something to say.

# CHAPTER 5

Nina nodded to her, and Mallory felt the eyes of thirty people turn to her. In the past, that would've intimidated her, but after years in the program, she had certainly done this before.

"I'd been sober more than ten years when my mother died last year." She paused when the others offered condolences. "Thank you. It was a tough loss. For my entire life, it'd been just her and me. She got pregnant when she was really young, and her parents disowned her. My father was never in the picture. I had asked about him many times, but her answers were always vague. As I got older, I wondered if maybe she didn't know who he was."

Mallory took a moment to get her emotions under control. "I found a letter in her things about a week after she died. In it, she finally gave me my father's name, and as soon as I could, I came to Gansett to find him. I thought maybe I'd just say hello and let him know he had a daughter he'd never known about. But that's not what happened. My father is an amazing person with an equally amazing family. I found out I have a stepmother, four brothers, a sister, two nephews, a niece, four cousins and two uncles, not to mention sisters-in-law and a brother-in-law.

"To say it's been overwhelming to have them in my life is putting it mildly. I thought I'd come so far from when I'd used alcohol to cope with an earlier devastating loss. It'd been years since I'd been tempted to take a drink. Until I was faced with meeting my father and his entire family, and I forgot all about ten years of sobriety in my desire to fit in and go with the flow and not have to explain that, no, I can't have that glass of wine or a beer because I'm an alcoholic. I've never been afraid to tell people that, but for some reason, I couldn't bring myself to tell *these* people."

"Do you believe they'd think less of you if you told them?" Nina asked.

"No, not at all. It's just that my relationships with them still feel so new and fragile."

"Perhaps you begin with your dad, and go from there," Mason suggested.

Mallory noticed that Quinn nodded in agreement.

"That's a good idea," she said to Mason.

"No one says you have to tell anyone," Quinn said. "My family has no idea I'm an alcoholic. They know I don't drink, but they think it's because I'm a fitness freak."

The insight from a man of so few words surprised her. "You make a good point," Mallory said. "It's not like I owe anyone the information."

"You owe it to yourself to make your life here on the island manageable, though," Andy said. "If anyone asks, and I doubt they will because people tend not to notice what's so obvious to us, just tell them you're dieting or alcohol gives you a headache. There's always something you can say to take the attention off the fact that you don't drink."

"Thank you all. This is very helpful." And it was all stuff she'd heard before, but it helped to talk about it in relation to her new family.

The meeting ended a short time later, and Mallory told Mason she'd see him at the barn next Tuesday.

"See you then," he said with a wave as he headed for the door.

Mallory waited for Quinn, who was talking to Nina. While feigning interest in her phone, she took advantage of the opportunity to take a closer look at him. Standing maybe six foot two or three, he had a muscular build and close-cropped dark blond hair. He wore faded denim jeans and a navy blue Henley. Long sleeves were pulled up to reveal strong forearms. As he listened intently to Nina, he gave her his undivided attention.

Mallory wondered what it would be like to be on the receiving end of Dr. Quinn James's full attention. A shiver went through her, making her tremble and feel ridiculous at the same time. Sure, he was a good-looking guy, but that didn't mean she had to get silly over him.

Then he was walking toward her, and Mallory shook off her inappropriate thoughts.

"Ready?" he asked.

"Whenever you are." *Duh. Of course he's ready, or he wouldn't be asking if you are.*

"How'd you get here?" he asked.

"Rode my bike."

"We can toss it in the back of my truck if you want."

"Sure, that works."

He didn't say anything else as he held the door to let Mallory go out ahead of him. She'd worn jeans and a lightweight sweater in deference to the chilly spring air and hoped her jeans looked as good on her as his did on him. More silliness. *Knock it off, Mallory. He's taking you on a tour of a building, not his bedroom.*

It had been a long time since she'd found any guy particularly attractive, so her thoughts were surprising, to say the least. She'd been frantically busy with work for so many years that things like men and dating and sex had fallen pretty far down on her list of priorities, well behind the sleep she craved after long weeks at work.

Months after her layoff, she was well-rested and more relaxed than she'd been in years. Even moving couldn't compare to the stress of a regular week at work.

She wheeled her bike over to his big silver pickup and watched the play of his muscles as he lifted the bike into the bed of the truck. Then he held the passenger door for her and waited for her to get settled before he closed it and went around to the driver's side. *Sexy, smart, mysterious* and *a gentleman—what a potent combination.*

They drove slowly through the congested downtown area. "What is all this?" Mallory asked, taking in the crowds of people and cars that clogged the streets. It was too early in the season for this many tourists.

"The start of Race Week. Races that last all day and parties that last all night. From what I'm told, it gets pretty crazy."

"I guess so."

Once they were through the downtown area, the traffic let up, and they made quick time driving to the island's north end.

Mallory tried to tell herself that the silence between them wasn't awkward, but it did make her feel uncertain. Should she say something to cut through the silence or stay quiet? Was he always this reticent, or did he talk more around people he knew well?

"How long have you been here?" she asked when the silence had stretched long enough for her.

"I got here two months before we met up at the accident site."

"What do you think so far?"

"I like it more than I expected to. My brother and sister-in-law and their friends keep me busy, and so far, the remoteness hasn't made me too crazy."

"Your brother has made quite a name for himself," Mallory said. Who hadn't heard of the young billionaire who'd walked away from Wall Street to move to Gansett Island?

"I still find it funny that everyone knows him. To me, he's still my annoying little brother."

"What's it like to have a brother who's been so successful?"

"I'm happy for him. He was always a go-getter—from the time he was the littlest kid. He was mowing the neighbors' lawns by the time he was twelve and incorporated his first business at eighteen."

"Wow, that's impressive. Do you guys have other siblings?"

"We have two sisters and another brother."

"I'm still getting used to having siblings. Finding out you have five of them when you're thirty-nine takes some getting used to."

"You're thirty-nine? You sure don't look it."

"Thanks. I'll be forty in August. That's hard to believe."

"I turn forty in August also."

"What day?"

"The ninth."

For a second, Mallory was too stunned to speak. "No way," she said after a long pause. "You were born on *August ninth* forty years ago?"

"Yep."

"Me, too."

He looked over at her, seeming as shocked as she felt. "We were born on the same day. What're the freaking odds of that?"

"Astronomical." She was about to remind him he was driving and should look at the road rather than at her when he finally shifted his gaze.

"That's crazy," he said.

"We should form a turning-forty support group."

He made a sound that might've been a laugh. "It's just a number."

"Are you where you thought you'd be at forty?" The question was probably too deep to ask someone she'd just met, but she'd been asking herself the same thing in recent weeks as she prepared to start over once again.

"Hell no. Are you?"

"Nope. Not even kinda."

"Where'd you think you'd be?"

"Married with teenagers and a mortgage and two dogs and a job I loved to hate. What about you?"

"Same thing, I guess. I certainly never expected to be starting over on a middle-of-nowhere island. That's for sure."

"We have far more than our birthdays in common. Until my mom told me where to find my dad, I'd never even been here, despite growing up in Providence."

"I'd never been here either until I came to visit Jared and Lizzie over the holidays, and she talked me into being the medical director at their new facility."

"Did she have to twist your arm?"

"Not too hard. I was looking for a change and didn't have anything better to do. I figured what's the harm in giving it a year or two? I could get the place up and running and then turn it over to someone else if I hate living here."

"Where did you live before?"

"Around. I was in the army for twenty-one years. I was living in New York City before I came here. I got out at the end of last year."

"Thank you for your service."

He glanced over at her. "You're welcome."

"Could I ask you something that's none of my business?"

"I guess…"

"Did you hurt yourself?"

"When?"

"Recently. I noticed your limp the first time we met, and wondered if you'd hurt yourself running or something."

"Once a nurse, always a nurse?"

"Something like that."

"I've got a bum knee that got me medically retired about three years ahead of schedule."

"Oh. I'm sorry. That's too bad."

"Is what it is." He took a left onto a dirt road that led to a construction site. "Here we are."

Mallory followed him inside where her brother Mac was working along with their cousins Shane, Riley and Finn as well as Mac's business partner, Luke Harris.

"Hey, Mallory," Mac said when he saw her come in with Quinn. "What brings you to our home away from home for the last few months?"

"Dr. James wanted to show me the facility."

"We'll stay out of your way," Quinn said.

"No problem, Doc," Mac replied. "We're working in the kitchen today, so you've got the run of the rest." To Mallory, he added, "We're in the home stretch, so feel free to notice what a fantastic job we've done."

"Nothing wrong with his ego," Mallory said.

"I've noticed that," Quinn said.

They left Mac and the others laughing as Quinn gestured for Mallory to go ahead of him into a hallway. "These are all offices." He pointed to several new wood doors. "Mine, the administrator and the nursing director."

"Nice that the nursing director gets the same treatment as the medical director. You don't see that everywhere."

"I made sure of that. The nursing staff will be the backbone of this place."

He took her through a large community lounge and a dining room that would allow residents to eat together. "They'll also have the option of having meals in their rooms, if that's what they prefer."

Mallory took it all in. The individual patient rooms were big, spacious and well lit, many with views of the water. "Will it cost more to live on the water side of the building?"

"A little more. Most of those rooms are already spoken for."

"This is amazing. I can't believe something like this is happening on such a small island."

"You can thank my sister-in-law Lizzie for making it a reality. She was so moved by the plight of Alex and Paul Martinez. They had to move their mom, who has dementia, to the mainland when they could no longer care for her at home. They own Martinez Lawn and Garden, so they're tied to the island and couldn't go with her. Lizzie said no family should have to face that kind of decision. Within a couple of days, she'd bought the old school and hired Mac to do the renovations. He and his team have been here all winter."

"She gets things done, huh?"

"Sometimes I think my brother has no idea what hit him when he married her, but he's so crazy about her that he'd give her anything she wants, including an old school that's about to be a long-term healthcare facility."

"That's true love."

"Yep."

"When do you plan to begin recruiting for staff?"

"I hired an agency to handle that for me. I'm meeting with the recruiter at the end of the week."

Mallory nodded in agreement. That was what she would've done, too.

"Our new administrator is starting next week. She's responsible for hiring the support staff. My brother and Lizzie have given me complete autonomy over the medical side of the house, including hiring the nursing director."

"That's great. That's how it should be."

He smiled then, and Mallory was struck dumb. His smile revealed deep grooves in his cheeks that couldn't really be called dimples but were sexy as hell nonetheless. Not to mention the way the smile lit up his golden-brown eyes. "Earth to Mallory?"

She realized she was staring at him and flushed with embarrassment. "Sorry. What did you say?"

"Do you know anyone who might be interested in a management-level nursing position, overseeing a staff of about twenty nurses?"

"I, um… After running an ER with ninety nurses and other support staff, I could do that job with one hand tied behind my back and my eyes closed."

"Or maybe you could do it with both hands and your eyes open?"

A joke. He'd made a joke. She laughed. "I could do that, too."

"So you want the job?"

"You know nothing about me! You haven't checked my references or my experience or… anything!"

"I saw you in action that day on the road. I already know you've got the chops, and you ran an ER at a top hospital in Providence."

"A job I recently lost."

"Not because you weren't good at it, but because they couldn't afford you anymore. Right?"

"Right."

He shrugged. "I'd consider myself fortunate to have a nurse with your experience on our team if you're interested in the job."

Mallory took a deep breath. Her head was spinning. A job offer had been the last thing she'd expected when she came with him to see the facility. "I… Um… I'm committed to work for Mason on the rescue for the summer."

Quinn opened the door to his office, which already looked fairly lived-in, with piles of folders and papers on the desk. He reached for a piece of paper on the desktop and handed it to her. "That's fine. We're not due to open until October. If you'd be willing to consult on the hiring of the nursing team over the summer, you could officially start after Labor Day."

Mallory perused the job description and the salary range, which was close to what she'd been making in Providence. "Would you mind if I took a little time to think about it? My plan was to spend the summer here and reevaluate in the fall."

"Of course. Take a few days, but if you're interested, I'd like to have you at the meeting with the recruiter, if at all possible."

"How about I commit to the meeting for now, and let you know about the job itself later?"

"I can live with that. If you give me your number, I'll let you know when the meeting is."

Mallory recited her phone number and watched as he punched it into his phone.

"I sent you a text so you'll have mine."

Her phone buzzed in her pocket.

He gave her a questioning look. "I feel like I've shocked you speechless with my offer."

"A little," she said with a laugh. "And that's not easy to do. It's more that I wasn't expecting it than anything else. Did you plan this whole thing? To lure me out here and wow me with the awesomeness of the place and then offer me a job you hoped I couldn't refuse?"

"That would be awfully premeditated on my part."

*Oh my God*, she thought. *He is adorable when he pours on the charm.* "Ah-ha! I knew it. And I walked right into your trap."

His face lifted in a half smile that was no less dazzling than the full one. "Hopefully, you'll decide my trap is actually a good career move."

"I'm honored that you offered it to me. Please don't think I'm not. It's just that I'm in this weird transition right now, and I want to be sure I'm making the right decision, not the most convenient one."

"Fair enough." He stared at her with an intense gaze that made her feel like he could see right through her. "Could I ask you something else?"

"Sure."

"Will you have dinner with me later?"

For a second, Mallory's brain went completely blank. He was asking her out? After offering her a job? "I…"

"It's a simple yes or no question."

Mallory studied him for a second, but his expression gave nothing away. "Is it? Is it simple?"

"Maybe. Maybe not. I guess we'll find out."

"You offered me a job."

"So I did."

"And now you're asking me out?"

"It seems that I am. Yes."

"I'm confused."

"Which part is confusing?"

"You asking me out after offering me a job in which you would be my boss if I were to accept the position."

"I'd prefer to think we'd be colleagues rather than boss-employee. Besides, I'm not proposing marriage here. Just dinner. For now."

"Why?"

His brows furrowed. "Now I'm confused."

"Why do you want to have dinner with me?"

"We're both new to the island, and I thought it would be nice to get to know each other better. Also, I'm sure my brother and sister-in-law are getting tired of having me underfoot all the time. I need to make some friends of my own. Are those good reasons?"

"Those are good reasons."

"So you'll have dinner with me?"

"I'll have dinner with you."

"Excellent," he said with the half smile that did wondrous things to his face. "Seven thirty good for you?"

"That works. Where would you like to meet?"

"I'll pick you up. Where's your new place?"

She gave him the Ocean Road address of Janey's house, which she should probably think of as hers now.

"Can I give you a ride home?"

"I'll ride the bike. It's a nice day. But thanks for the offer."

"Let me help you get the bike out of the truck."

They walked together toward the main entrance, and Mallory stuck her head into the kitchen to say good-bye to her brother and cousins.

"Have a good one," Mac called.

"You, too."

"That's my brother," she said to Quinn. "And my cousins. It still feels weird to say those words. I'd never had brothers or cousins or a sister before last year."

"That has to be surreal."

"It is, but it's also amazing. That guy in there…" In a conspiratorial whisper, she said, "He's my *brother.*"

Quinn laughed. "You look like a little kid on Christmas morning when you talk about him."

"That's how I've felt since I met them all. Like every day is Christmas, and anything is possible."

"Must be nice to feel that way," he said wistfully. Reaching into the bed of his truck, he retrieved her bike.

Mallory enjoyed watching his muscles flex under the weight of the bike. "Thank you. For the tour, the job offer and the dinner invitation. This morning turned out quite differently than expected."

"When every day's like Christmas, you never know what'll happen."

"Very true. I'll see you later."

"Yes, you will."

As Mallory pedaled the bike down the dirt lane that led to the main road, she felt him watching her go. She would admit to being extremely curious about him and wondered if he'd share more about himself at dinner. Mallory couldn't wait to find out. The Summer of Mallory was already turning out to be much more interesting than expected.

# CHAPTER 6

After watching Mallory ride away, Quinn went back inside, intending to spend some time in his office attempting to get organized. He'd never been part of an endeavor like this one, launching a healthcare facility from the ground up, and was finding it a welcome challenge. Working twelve hours a day sure beat trying to figure out what to do without the discipline of army life.

He missed everything about it—the traveling, the camaraderie, the feeling of being part of something bigger than himself. His unexpected retirement from the military had left a huge, gaping hole in the middle of his life, and he was thankful to Jared and Lizzie for giving him a new sense of purpose.

Quinn fired up his computer to check his email and was replying to a message from one of the medical equipment suppliers when Mac appeared in the doorway.

"Hey," Quinn said without taking his gaze off the screen. "What's up?"

"That's what I wanted to know. What was my sister doing here?"

"She wanted to see the place."

"How do you know her?"

"We met through friends in town."

"What friends?"

"Is there a point to this inquisition, Mac?"

"I'm not sure yet."

"Okay, well, get back to me when you know."

"She's been through a rough time."

"I know. She told me." That seemed to take Mac by surprise. "You don't need to play the protective-brother role with me. I have no intention of harming your sister in any way, so you can stand down."

"You seem like a straight-up guy," Mac said. "But you keep to yourself a lot. Don't let anyone get too close."

His general contractor was an observant sort of guy, Quinn thought. "So?"

"I'm just saying…"

"What is it exactly that you're saying?"

"Nothing in particular."

"Good talk, Mac. Glad you stopped by."

"Mac!" Luke called from the kitchen. "Get your ass back here, and leave him alone."

"Be nice to my sister," Mac said over his shoulder as he returned to work.

Despite his bull-in-a-china-shop approach, it wasn't lost on Quinn that he'd been put on notice that Mac—and probably the rest of the McCarthys—would be keeping an eye on him when it came to Mallory. She'd probably be delighted to know that Mac had played the brother card with him.

The thought brought a smile to his lips, making him realize he'd smiled more today than he had in a very long time, and the day was still young.

Mallory rode her bike to the marina, coasting down the hill into the cool spring breeze off the Salt Pond. Gansett Island was one of the most beautiful places she'd ever seen. From the panoramic water views to the lush landscapes to the hidden waterways to the ancient stone walls and crushed-shell driveways, there was something to see everywhere she looked.

With the spring flowers in full bloom and Race Week about to get underway, the island's residents were preparing in earnest for the summer season. Arriving at McCarthy's Gansett Island Marina, Mallory parked the bike and walked toward the main dock that extended into the Salt Pond. Her dad was on his knees, pounding nails into one of the wide planks that made up the pier.

He'd turned sixty recently, not that he looked a day over fifty with his wiry gray hair, gleeful smile and bright blue eyes.

"Hi there," she said as she approached him, recalling the first time she'd ever seen him, right here on this pier one week after her mother died and her letter told Mallory where to find him.

He looked up from what he was doing and smiled with pleasure at the sight of her.

Mallory wondered how long it would be, if ever, before she'd become accustomed to the fact that this extraordinary man was her father.

"What a nice surprise this is. What brings you by?"

"I was hoping I might talk you into lunch."

"Sweetheart, you should know by now that I never have to be talked into lunch, or any other meal, for that matter." He wiped beads of sweat from his brow with the sleeve of the faded Gansett Island sweatshirt he wore over shorts and rugged work boots. "Let's take a walk over to the Oar Bar."

"That sounds good."

He showed her the shortcut on a path that wound from McCarthy's Marina to McCarthy's Gansett Island Hotel, which he and Linda owned, and over to the neighboring marina where the Oar was located. They walked up the back stairs to the hostess stand, where the woman working greeted him by name.

"Hi there, sweetheart," he said. "Could I get a table for me and my daughter?"

"Of course! Right this way."

He smiled down at Mallory and placed a hand on her back to encourage her to go ahead of him. Everything he did and said thrilled her. Her dad. His daughter. It never got old.

"What's good here?" she asked, taking in the thousands of painted oars that dominated the space.

"Everything, but I love the lobster roll. Comes with fries and slaw."

"That sounds good to me, too."

When the waitress came by, he ordered for both of them. "A Diet Coke?" he asked Mallory.

She loved the way he paid attention to every little thing about her. "That'll do it," she said.

"Make it two." After the waitress walked away, he said, "I'd love a beer, but it's a little too early."

He'd given her the opening she needed to bring up one of the reasons she'd invited him to lunch. Mallory marshaled her courage and took the plunge. "About that... I wanted to tell you... I should've mentioned it sooner, but things have been so busy..."

"What's on your mind, sweetheart?"

His genuine interest made it so easy to say the words. "I'm actually an alcoholic."

"Oh... Okay."

"I'm sure you're wondering how that can be when you've seen me drink."

He held up a hand. "No judgment from me. I swear."

"That's nice of you to say, but I've been doing a lot of personal judging and wondering why I so easily forgot ten years of sobriety the minute I met my dad and his big wonderful family."

"*Your* big wonderful family."

"My family," Mallory conceded.

"Why do you suppose that happened?"

"I'm chalking it up to stress and excitement and getting caught up in the moment and wanting to fit in. None of those are excuses, but they're all I've got. I'm back to daily meetings, and I haven't had a sip of alcohol since New Year's Eve."

"At Adam's wedding?"

Mallory nodded. "I kind of snapped out of it the next day and was horrified by what I'd let happen over the last few months."

"You probably ought to cut yourself a break. Those few months in question would've tested anyone's mettle."

"I know, but still… I was disappointed in myself and vowed to get back on track. I went to a meeting that day, and I haven't missed a day since."

"It's a strong person who can look at herself with that kind of scrutiny. You should be proud of yourself for being able to do that."

"Thank you. It means a lot to have your support and understanding."

"You'll always have my support—and my understanding."

She used her napkin to dab at tears that suddenly filled her eyes. "I'm still getting used to that."

"Take your time. I'm not going anywhere. You and me… We've got a lot of time to make up for." After a pause, he said, "I find myself wondering…"

"About?"

"So many things. I want to know everything. Who your friends are, who you've loved, where you've lived, the awards you won in school, the big and little things that I missed out on."

Touched by his interest, she said, "My very best friend in the whole world is Trish Bennett. We met in second grade and have been best friends ever since. She lives in Boston and is an accomplished photographer. We've been through everything together."

"I'd love to meet her sometime."

"I'll ask her to come out to visit."

"Boyfriends?" he asked with a raised brow that made her laugh. It was too late for him to intimidate her ex-boyfriends, but he let her know that he would've made for a formidable obstacle.

"My first love was Chris Bristow in sixth grade. He never knew I was alive, but I was hopelessly devoted."

"That was his loss," Big Mac said indignantly, making her laugh.

"I couldn't agree more. My first real boyfriend was Mike Smith my junior year of high school."

"Mike Smith," he said with disdain. "That sounds like a fake name. I would've had him fully investigated."

Mallory laughed again. "I can very easily picture you doing that."

"Ask Janey about my investigative skills."

"I'll do that. Anyway, Mike and I lasted two years, until we went to colleges in different states, and our young love couldn't withstand the pressure of distance and coeds."

"He cheated?"

"He met someone else." Mallory shrugged. "It happens."

"I'm sorry it happened to you."

"Thank you, but I haven't thought of him in years. The next one was more serious." Her heart still ached when she thought of the man she'd loved with all her heart. "I met Ryan Daniels in medical school at Tufts. We got married six months after we met and did our residencies together in San Francisco."

"I knew you'd been married, but you graduated from medical school?"

Nodding, she said, "Yep." Sometimes those years felt like another lifetime, a life that had been lived by someone other than her.

"What happened?"

The waitress arrived with their food, but neither of them touched it right away. "We were almost done with our first year of residency, him in surgery and me in pediatrics. We were at work one day, and he collapsed in the operating room. By the time someone came to find me, he was gone. He was twenty-seven years old."

"Oh my God, Mallory. I'm so sorry. Did they ever find out what happened?"

"The autopsy revealed an undiagnosed heart condition." Mallory took a sip from her drink. "That was the start of a multiyear downward spiral for me. Ryan had life insurance that paid off our student loans and took care of the essentials, but that was bad in a way, because I had no real reason to go back to work. I had the money to wallow and to buy a lot of vodka." She forced a smile for his sake. "After a few years of that nonsense, my mom and Trish intervened and got me into rehab. Once I got my shit together, I discovered I'd lost my desire to be a doctor, but I couldn't let all that education go to waste. I did an accelerated program to get my nursing degree and truly found my calling as a nurse and later as a nurse manager. My career worked out for the better, but my personal life has been a little less successful. During the drinking years, I married another guy. That lasted a month before I kicked him to the curb."

"I couldn't be sorrier that you had to go through so much."

"It was a very long time ago now. Ryan will be gone thirteen years this August." And that was so hard to believe. Sometimes, it felt like just yesterday they'd been living together in their tiny apartment in San Francisco. She'd never been happier in her life than she was during the blissful but busy years with Ryan.

"There are some things the heart never recovers from."

He couldn't have said anything more perfect.

Mallory looked down at her plate. "Our lunch is getting cold."

"You want to take it to go?" he asked.

"No, I'm okay. Go ahead and eat."

He squirted ketchup on his french fries and then handed the bottle to her before reaching for the vinegar and passing that on to her as well.

Mallory loved that at some point he'd noticed she liked ketchup and vinegar on her fries as much as he did. She also took her coffee the same way he and Mac did—a dash of cream and two sugars—and adored spicy food, which Linda had told her came right from her father. Every little discovery was like another piece in the puzzle that made up the missing half of her identity.

They ate quietly, which was rare for him. He always had something to say.

"Has there been anyone else?" he asked after a long silence.

"A few, here and there. One who was more important than the others, but it didn't stick. I'm lucky to have found true love once. I'm under no illusions that I'll get lucky twice."

"Never say never. That's one of my many mottos."

"Don't worry. I haven't given up quite yet. In fact, I got asked out earlier today."

He froze with a fry halfway to his mouth. "By who?"

"Dr. Quinn James."

"He's the one running that new facility out at the old school, right?"

Nodding, she said, "Do you know him?"

"I know his brother. Seems like a good enough fellow. Richer than Croesus, or so I've heard."

"Yes, he is. Quinn also offered me a job as the director of nursing at the new facility."

Big Mac's face lit up with pleasure. "Is that right? You'd be perfect for it."

"I think you might be biased," she said, amused by his certainty.

"I'm not at all biased. You're probably overqualified for that position after all the experience you've had running the nursing staff at a big-city ER."

"Maybe so."

"Are you interested in the job?"

"I'm not sure. I need to hear more about it and get to know Dr. James a little better before I decide anything. I had a great rapport with the doctor who ran the emergency department at the hospital, which is critical. We'll see. I'm committed to Mason and the rescue for the summer, so I have some time to think about it."

"I'll confess to being totally biased in hoping you'll decide to stay after the summer."

"It's very nice to feel wanted."

"You are. I hope you know that."

"I do. You've all been very welcoming. I couldn't believe everyone was there when I arrived at the house yesterday."

"You're part of a family now, Mallory. That's what family does."

"It's all new to me, so you'll have to pardon my amazement."

"You'll get used to us. Eventually."

Mallory laughed. "I'm not sure I'll ever get used to the McCarthys."

"Sure you will." He popped another fry into his mouth. "Tell me some good stories about the crazy crap you've seen in the ER."

"If I do, you'll lose your appetite."

"Nothing can make me lose my appetite, sweetheart."

Mallory took him at his word and regaled him with stories about objects in every orifice, injuries, gunshot wounds, stabbings and the wide variety of non-emergency complaints that made every shift different from the last. He laughed until he cried at some of the crazier stories.

"What I really want to know," he said, "is what happens to guys who get those four-hour boners."

"You don't really want to know that."

"Yes, I do!"

"Suffice to say, there're needles involved."

Big Mac winced, and his complexion went pale.

Mallory howled with laughter. "I told you!"

He insisted on paying for lunch, and as they walked back to the marina, he put his arm around her shoulders. "This was nice."

"Yes, it was."

"Thank you for telling me the things you did."

"I'm glad you know. And it's okay for you to tell Linda any of it, since you will anyway."

"I love how you already know me so well," he said with a chuckle.

She leaned her head against his shoulder, because he was her dad and she could. "I have to tell you something else."

"What's that?"

"I spent my whole life wondering about my father. When I was little, I made up a man in my mind and gave him all sorts of wonderful qualities. But in my wildest dreams, I never imagined he'd be as perfect as you are."

He tightened his arm around her and kissed the top of her head. "Awww, honey. You're gonna make me bawl like a baby."

"It's true."

"Thank you. I wish I'd known about you sooner. I'm sorry that you had to grow up without me. If I'd known, that never would've happened. Not in a million years."

"I know that, and I'm still trying to make peace with the fact that my mother kept us from each other for nearly forty years. I have a lot of unresolved feelings about that."

"I'm sure you do."

"When I was here in March, Linda suggested I talk to Kevin about it. You wouldn't care if I did that, would you?"

"Hell no. He's the best. I'm sure he'd be happy to help you."

"There's no undoing the past, but it would be nice to be able to think of the mother who did everything for me without feeling bitter about what she kept from me."

"I agree. You've had a lot of upheaval in the last year. Take your time and figure out your next move, and if that move keeps you right here with us, well, that would make your dear old dad very happy indeed."

"My dear old dad," she said with a smile. "I've been working up the nerve to call you that."

Outside the main building at the marina, he dropped his arm from around her shoulders and turned to face her. "Give it a whirl. Let's see how it sounds."

She looked up at him, feeling shy all of a sudden. "Dad."

"Do it again."

"Dad," she said, smiling.

"One more time to make sure you've really got it down."

"*Dad.*"

"See? Was that so hard?"

Mallory stepped into his outstretched arms and sighed as he wrapped those strong arms around her. "Thank you so much for being you and for making this so much easier than it probably should've been."

"A year ago, I thought my family was complete, and then you came strolling down my dock and knocked the legs right out from under me. It was the best kind of shock to find out I had another daughter. I'm only sorry I didn't know sooner."

"Me, too."

"Love you, kid."

"Love you, too, *Dad.*" She looked up at him. "Thanks for lunch."

"It was entirely my pleasure."

# CHAPTER 7

Mallory took her time getting ready for the first date she'd been on since she'd ended a brief relationship last year. The man she'd been seeing had been frustrated by her lack of time for him while her mother was sick and later dying. Anyone who couldn't show some compassion during a time like that wasn't the man for her. But she'd known from the beginning that he wasn't the one for her. They'd had some fun together, and their relationship had been a nice diversion. But after having known true love with Ryan, she refused to settle for anything less. Mallory would rather be alone than be with the wrong guy.

That made it easy to prepare herself for the evening with Quinn. Whenever she went out with someone new, she kept her expectations low so there'd be no chance of disappointment.

That was her usual routine anyway. Tonight, for some strange reason, she was nervous. After spending a couple of hours in his presence, Mallory already sensed that Quinn might be different from the other men she'd dated since Ryan died. The man was sexy as hell, and she suspected his war wounds ran deeper than he'd let on earlier. She wanted to know more about him, and that already gave him an advantage over most of the men she'd dated in recent years.

So many of them overshared to the point of verbal diarrhea. She'd heard it all—from horrifying ex-wife stories to tales of their sexual conquests. No detail was off-limits in the TMI generation. It was refreshing to look forward to an evening with a man who hadn't shared his life story in the first two minutes after they met. She was curious about his life story, though, and hoped he'd open up to her on their date.

After blow-drying her hair and applying enough makeup to be presentable, Mallory went into her bedroom and stood in front of the closet for a good five minutes before she settled on dark jeans with a plum-colored sweater that did great things for her breasts. She finished off the outfit with high-heeled black boots. With the addition of a diamond necklace that had been her mother's, silver bangle bracelets, dangly earrings and a spritz of her favorite perfume, she declared herself ready to go.

Sitting on the bed, she reached for one of the few unpacked boxes that remained in her bedroom and opened it, looking for the silver framed photograph that had sat on her bedside table for the last thirteen years. Retrieving the photo, she looked down at herself and Ryan on their wedding day, all smiles after a simple courthouse ceremony followed by dinner with her mom, his parents and their closest friends. It had been the most perfect day of her life. She traced her fingertip over Ryan's handsome face, frozen forever at twenty-seven.

It felt surreal now, after so many years, as if maybe it had never happened. Despite the passage of time, she remembered so many things about him, especially the way she'd felt whenever he walked into a room and looked at her like she was his whole world. He'd left big shoes to fill, and so far, no one else had come close to making her feel the way he had. Sometimes she felt sorry for the guys she dated, because they had no idea what they were up against.

"You set the bar pretty high, my love," she said to the photo. "Wherever you are, I hope you know I've never forgotten you." Placing the photo on the bedside table, she angled it toward her bed so she would be able to see it better. Now that Ryan was here, too, her new home felt complete.

Minutes before Quinn was due to arrive, Mallory's cell phone rang, and she recognized a local Gansett Island phone number. "Hello?"

"Mallory, hi, it's Mason. Hope I'm not getting you at a bad time."

"I'm on my way out, but what's up?"

"Oh, well, I was going to ask if you might want to grab a pizza at Mario's and chat about the rescue routine. But it sounds like you have other plans."

"I do. I'm sorry."

"No need to apologize. We'll do it some other time. See you at the meeting?"

"I'll be there."

"Great. Have a good night."

"You, too."

Yikes, had he been asking her out, too? The Summer of Mallory was off to an interesting start. She no sooner had that thought than Quinn arrived with a soft knock on her front door. Mallory took a deep breath, ran her sweaty palms over her jeans and went to answer the door.

Wearing a button-down shirt that he'd obviously ironed for the occasion and khaki pants, he stood with his hands on either side of the door. "Hey," he said, his gaze traveling from her face to her feet and back up again. "You look nice."

"So do you," she said, unnerved and oddly aroused by the way he looked at her.

"Ready to go?"

"Let me grab my purse."

He waited while she locked the front door and gestured for her to go ahead of him down the stairs to the driveway, where his truck was parked.

"Let me get that for you," he said of the passenger door.

As she put on her seat belt, Mallory gave him an A-plus for manners.

"I hope you like seafood," he said when he was settled in the driver's seat. "I never thought to ask before I made a reservation at the Lobster House."

"Seafood is fine with me."

"Oh good. Tables are hard to get this week."

"My sister-in-law Stephanie just got back from the winter in California, and she's booked solid all week at her restaurant."

"Which one of your brothers is she married to?"

"Grant. He's the screenwriter. They went to LA so he could work for a few months and came back to open the restaurant for Race Week."

"I heard this week would be busy, but you have to see it to believe it."

"This time last year, Grant, Mac and Evan were in an accident when the boat they were sailing on was hit by a freighter in the fog."

"Jesus."

"From what I heard, the family had a really long, scary day waiting to hear they were all safe. Their friend Dan Torrington was with them and got hurt pretty badly. The captain of the boat was killed. His mother, Betsy, is now my uncle Frank's girlfriend. They met after the accident."

"Wow."

"The family is anticipating a less dramatic Race Week this year."

"I'm sure they are."

"So how was the off-season on the island?"

"Not as bad as I expected. It was actually kind of relaxing. I did a lot of reading and watched a ton of movies. Hung out with my brother and Lizzie and their friends. There's always something going on."

"That's what I've heard."

"If you're looking to party, it's not the place to be in the winter."

Mallory laughed. "I can't remember the last time I had the urge to party."

"It's better for us to avoid that scene, anyway."

"Yes, it is." She glanced over at him. "How long have you been sober?"

"Two years."

"Congratulations. That's a big accomplishment." She had questions she'd like to ask but didn't want to pry. After so much time in the program, she'd learned that some people liked to talk about their journey while others preferred to keep the details private. If she had to bet, she'd guess he was in the latter category.

When they arrived at the Lobster House, he held the door for her and helped with her coat. They followed the maître d' to the table, and Quinn held her chair.

Mallory looked up at him. "Thank you."

"No problem."

The waiter came to give them a list of specials that included far more detail than any average diner needed about how the food was prepared. "I'll give you a few minutes with the menu," he said after the lengthy recitation. "In the meantime, may I interest you in a cocktail?"

"I'll have a ginger ale," Quinn said.

"Make it two," Mallory said.

The waiter's face visibly fell with disappointment when he realized they wouldn't be drinking. "I'll be right back."

"He needs to work on his stage face," Quinn said.

"I know! We ruined his night."

"It is kind of a relief to be out with someone who gets it. I get tired of explaining that I don't drink. People are always curious about why."

"I know what you mean. For so many people, socializing of any kind means drinking. It did for me until it became a problem."

"You said you've been sober ten years?"

Mallory nodded. "Other than a brief slipup last year after I lost my mother and met my father for the first time along with the rest of my family."

"Those are big things to deal with all at once."

"It was a rough time in more ways than one. The thing that really freaked me out was that I never even gave ten years of sobriety a thought when I drank wine with my dad and beer with my brother and champagne at my other brother's wedding. It wasn't much, but I certainly knew better."

"You were focused on fitting into your new family and took your eye off the ball with your sobriety."

"Which we both know is something that can't happen."

"Well, now you're aware that it's possible to lose your focus, so next time you're in a situation where it would be convenient to drink, you won't."

"I certainly hope not. Have you had any tests over the last two years?"

"Every day is a test. Every day is a decision to stick with it, to not go back to the dark place."

Mallory nodded in agreement, wishing he would elaborate but refusing to push for details. If and when he wanted to say more, he would. Or he wouldn't. Either way had to be fine with her.

They took a few minutes to examine the menu and to compare notes on what looked good. When the waiter returned, she ordered a shrimp dish and he went with the swordfish.

"I'm allergic to tree nuts," Quinn told the waiter. "Anything to worry about with the swordfish?"

"No, sir," the waiter replied, "but I'll let the chef know just the same."

"Thank you."

"Tree nuts, huh?" Mallory asked when they were alone. "Have you ever had a severe reaction?"

"Just once when I was a kid, which is how we found out I'm allergic."

"Where's your EpiPen?"

Smiling, he said, "Always the ER nurse. It's in my back pocket."

"Good to know." Then she remembered what she'd ordered for dinner. "You're not allergic to shellfish or anything else, are you?"

"Nope, just the nuts."

"It's been a shellfish kind of day for me," Mallory said. "I had a lobster roll for lunch with my dad." After a pause, she added, "I really love saying that out loud. My *dad*."

"It must've been weird to meet him for the first time."

"Actually, it wasn't. Mostly because he's incredible. He was totally shocked, don't get me wrong, but he said and did all the right things—much more than I expected, in fact."

"What did you expect?"

"Nothing, really. I remember being on the ferry that morning and feeling sick with nerves. It had been exactly a week since I'd found the letter my mother left me that told me where I could find him. Part of me was incredibly excited just to see him and to fill in that blank, you know? The other half was terrified that he'd say there was no way he could be my father."

"I'm trying to see it from his point of view. A gorgeous woman shows up and says she's his daughter. What that must be like."

Mallory was stuck on his description of her as "gorgeous." Certain her face must be bright red, she cleared her throat and gave thanks for the low lighting. "After he read the letter, he was stunned speechless for a minute, and I've since discovered that's a rare thing."

"I haven't met him, but I've heard great things. Everyone likes him."

"It's impossible not to like him."

"So what did he say when you told him?"

"He said I look just like his mother." Mallory could still remember the wallop of that revelation. "I look nothing at all like my mother, so I've always wondered where my looks came from. Later, my dad showed me a picture of my grandmother as a young woman, and the resemblance is uncanny. That and the letter my mother had given me were why he never questioned my claim."

"That's so cool."

"I know. I was overwhelmed by that. That picture of our grandmother made things easier with my siblings, too."

"Were you afraid they wouldn't believe you?"

"I wouldn't have blamed them. My father and his wife, Linda, have been very successful. Here I am out of the blue claiming to be the daughter he never knew he had. They were pretty cool about it, mostly because he asked them to be. It was hardest on Janey. She was used to being his only daughter."

"Something like this brings out the best and worst in people."

"I've seen only the best of my family. I got very, very lucky. When I arrived the other day, they were waiting to help me unpack and move into my new place. What I thought would take three days took three hours thanks to their help. Of course, my dad was right in the middle of it, bossing everyone around."

"And you loved it."

"I did. I can't deny it. I've never had a tribe to rely upon. It's taken some getting used to."

"You're used to flying solo, and now that's not possible."

She appreciated that he understood. "It was my choice to move out here and live in the middle of the scrum."

"True."

"I'm dominating the conversation. Tell me about you."

"Your story is far more interesting than mine."

"Let me be the judge of that."

"Let's see. We grew up in Paramus, New Jersey, which is just outside of New York City."

"Who is we? You and Jared and who else?"

"Two older sisters, Katherine and Melissa. They're both married with five kids between them. Kath is a lawyer and Mel works for Jared's company. We also have a younger brother, Cooper. He's in grad school in Boston."

"What number are you?"

"Three out of five. Middle child and first son, who was given our mother's maiden name for a first name."

"I like it. It's not a name you hear every day."

"I like it now, but not so much when I was a kid and wished I had a name like Tom or Mike."

Smiling, Mallory said, "Isn't the middle child the one who causes all the trouble?"

"That's me. I'm the reason we had rules, or so the others say."

Mallory laughed at the face he made. "So you're the black sheep?"

"I guess so, although I never set out to be the rebel. Just sort of worked out that way."

"How so?"

"I got into a lot of trouble when I was a kid. Drinking, smoking pot, running with the wrong crowd. You know the drill. The day I turned eighteen, my dad took me to an army recruiter and told me to sign on the dotted line."

"Whoa. That's pretty hard-core."

"Though I wanted to kill him at the time, he saved my life. I was going nowhere fast until the army got ahold of me and showed me there's more to life than me, myself and I. At first, I railed against the structure, the authority figures, the *rules*. The dreaded rules. There were so many of them." He took a sip of his ginger ale. "But they wore me down over time. They forced me to grow up and get my head out of my ass. I had this drill sergeant... You've seen *An Officer and a Gentleman*, right?"

"Only a hundred times. Hello, Richard Gere in uniform."

The comment earned her one of his rare laughs, and oh, what laughter did to his handsome face. *Dear God...*

"My guy made Louis Gossett Junior's character look like a pussycat. He worked me hard. Made me hate him. Later he said it was because he saw potential in me, but you couldn't tell me that at the time. I thought he *hated* me."

"When did you find out he didn't?"

"Years after boot camp. I was a lieutenant colonel when I ran into him at a retirement party for a mutual friend. He told me then that he'd always known I would go the distance."

"That must've felt good."

"It did. We became friends after that, and we're still in close touch to this day. He's someone I truly admire."

"That's a great story. Your dad must be proud of your career, too."

"He is. Of course, he also likes to pat himself on the back for dragging me to the recruiter."

Mallory laughed. "Likes to say 'I told you so,' huh?"

"Loves it."

"So how'd you go from enlisted to trauma surgeon officer?"

"That's a whole other story."

# CHAPTER 8

While they ate, Quinn told her about starting out as a medic and applying to a program that put soldiers through college and medical school in exchange for army service afterward.

"To me it was a no-brainer. I got a free education and only owed them eight years after medical school. I'd planned to be a GP, but surgery really called to me and that's where I ended up. The years I owed the army coincided with a pretty intense period of conflict, so I rotated between tours in Iraq and Afghanistan doing front-line combat surgery and stints stateside at Walter Reed, tending to the wounded. Then I got hurt, and that was that."

Though he struck a matter-of-fact tone, she could see that he was anything but. "That must've been tough."

"More than two years later, it still is."

"What've you been up to for the last couple of years?"

"Rehabbing my leg and figuring out what's next."

"And is this it? The new facility, the new job?"

"I guess we'll see. The jury is still out."

"Funny how we're both in this odd state of flux as we stare down forty. It's not what I expected, that's for sure."

"What did you expect?"

Mallory thought about that for a minute. "I thought I'd be thinking about sending kids off to college by now. Instead, I'm contemplating a career change as well as an address change."

"You thought you'd be a young mom?"

Mallory nodded and decided to be honest with him. "I was married at twenty-two and planned to have kids as soon as my husband and I finished our residencies."

"What happened?"

"My twenty-seven-year-old husband dropped dead in the OR from hypertrophic cardiomyopathy."

"Oh God. I'm so sorry."

"Thank you. All my plans changed after that."

"I'm sure. I don't know what to say."

"It was a long time ago, and while I'll never forget him, I have figured out how to live without him. That took a while." Mallory put down her fork and blotted her lips with the cloth napkin. "I haven't talked about him in a long time, and I've told two people about him today."

"You told your dad."

Mallory nodded. "I wanted him to know."

"I'm honored that you told me."

"You should be," she said with a teasing smile. "I don't tell my sad story to just anyone. I haven't even told my siblings about him."

"I'm sure you will. When the time is right."

"Probably."

"So you were a doctor."

"I wondered if you'd picked up on that part."

"It caught my attention."

"After Ryan died, I walked away from the residency and just about everything else, for that matter. By the time I emerged from the fog of grief and alcoholism, I barely recognized myself, let alone my so-called career. I had no desire to pick up where I left off."

"That's understandable."

"My mom didn't understand at all how I could 'throw away' all that time and education and money, and after a while I began to agree with her. I got my nursing degree, and I've never looked back."

"No regrets?"

"None. I made a much better nurse than doctor. I liked being on the front lines with the patients and their families. By the time I was promoted into management, I was ready for a change and embraced that challenge. It all worked out the way it was meant to, I suppose."

"You never got married again?"

"Once, very briefly, but it didn't last a month. That was a huge mistake that occurred during the drinking years. What about you?"

"Never came close. Girlfriends here and there, but army life makes for complicated relationships, especially when you're deployed more than you're home."

"That has to be hard."

"It's all complicated. Civilian life has its own challenges."

The waiter came by to clear their plates and offer dessert.

"Split something?" Mallory asked.

"Sure. You choose."

After studying the dessert menu, she settled on flourless chocolate cake that was served with vanilla ice cream.

Quinn also ordered coffee.

"If I drank coffee at this hour, I'd be up until tomorrow afternoon."

"Since I quit drinking, I sleep like a dead man. Coffee or not."

"I have a complicated relationship with sleep." She tapped on her temple. "That's when my brain decides to thoroughly rehash every difficult thing I've ever been through."

"My sister Kath is like that. She swears by melatonin."

"That worked for me for a while but not anymore. I've been sleeping better since I got laid off. I'm sure that's not a coincidence."

"You miss the job?"

"Not even kinda, which is surprising. I thought I would, but I don't. I miss the people I worked with, but they keep in touch. I do miss having somewhere to be every day, but that's about to change when I start back to work part time for Mason."

"Have you done that before?"

She nodded. "I made paramedic training and regular shifts on the rescue mandatory for my senior nurses in the ER. I was one of six who decided to get fully certified. Who knew that would come in handy someday?"

"You're way overqualified to work on the rescue. For that matter, you're over-qualified to work with me."

"Are you rescinding your offer, Dr. James?"

"Hell no. I need you." His gaze met hers, intense and sexy. "After that first morning we met, I'd planned to ask around about you before you showed up at my meeting."

"Because you wanted me to work for you?"

"Among other reasons."

"What other reasons?"

"You're very pretty, but of course that's not news to you."

Mallory laughed at his certainty. "It's news to me that you think so."

"I do. I thought so the first time I laid eyes on you."

"When I was sweaty and winded?"

"Uh-huh." He rubbed at the stubble on his jaw. "And then when I saw you were also very capable and calm under pressure, you became even more attractive. I wondered where you'd disappeared to when you stopped coming to meetings. Mason said you were back home in Providence getting ready to move out for the summer, which was very good news."

"You… you asked Mason about me?"

Nodding, he said, "After I saw you having coffee with him at the diner, I figured he might know your deal."

"And the reason you offered me a job—"

"Was because I think you'd be great at it. Not for any other reason."

"You're making this complicated," she said softly.

"I don't mean to. I'd like very much to work with you in a professional capacity, and I'm enjoying—also very much—getting to know you personally."

"Other than Ryan, who I was married to before we began our residencies, I've never dated anyone I work with."

"Okay."

"That's it? Just 'okay'?"

"Good to know." He took a bite of the cake that she had thus far managed to ignore. Watching him was far more interesting than dessert. "Second time for everything?"

"I haven't decided anything yet," she said, putting extra emphasis on the word anything.

"Fair enough."

Because he'd opened the "this could be more than just friends having a casual dinner" door, she found the courage to press for details. "What've you been doing since you left the army?"

He sighed and then looked her square in the eye. "Fighting a losing battle to save the lower half of my leg and then learning to walk again."

"You... You're..."

"An amputee. Yes."

"Oh."

"You're the first person, other than my medical team, to know that."

Mallory failed to hide her shock at that revelation. "You haven't told *anyone*? Not even your family?"

"Nope."

"Why?"

Quinn shrugged and pushed a chunk of cake around on the plate with his fork. "It wasn't intentional. At first, I was so out of it that I couldn't have called them if I wanted to."

"How did it happen?"

"The base where I worked was hit with shell fire. I took shrapnel to the leg, the worst of it hitting my knee, which was completely shattered. I don't remember much about the first forty-eight hours, but apparently I ordered them not to contact my family."

"How come?"

"There was nothing they could do. I was being taken to Germany, and I didn't want my parents flying over there or worrying needlessly."

"So they still don't know you were injured?"

"They know and that it was bad enough to end my career, but they haven't pressed me for details. My brother Coop started a rumor that I'd had my dick blown off, thus the secrecy."

Mallory coughed on a mouthful of water. "He did not!"

"Yes, he did," Quinn said, his eyes dancing with amusement. "I assured him my dick is just fine."

Hearing him say that made her feel warm all over. "That's really funny."

"It was pretty funny. I finally told them I'd hurt my knee and was in rehab, which shut my brother up." He took another bite of the cake. "I was in the hospital for two months in Germany, arguing with the doctors, who said my leg couldn't be saved."

"What changed your mind?"

"A staph infection. Then it became a choice of my leg or my life." He shrugged as if that decision had been no big deal. "And that was that."

Though he tried to be nonchalant about it, she saw right through to the pain he carried with him to this day. "That must've been…"

"It was pretty fucking awful, but at least I know I did everything I could."

"Why haven't you told your family or anyone else?"

"I don't know. I guess I don't want anyone to see me as weak or less than or… It's stupid. I get that, but it's been almost three years. At this point, what does it matter?"

It pained her to know he'd chosen to go through such a terrible ordeal completely alone.

"It's your business to share with whomever you choose to share it with. I'm honored you shared it with me."

"Thanks for listening." He signaled for the check and had his credit card out before she could offer to chip in.

"Thank you for dinner."

"My pleasure."

On the way out, Mallory hit the ladies' room to give herself a minute alone to process everything he'd told her. He'd been unexpectedly forthcoming, but then, she had, too. She rarely told dates about Ryan or what she'd been through. But something about Quinn made her want to tell him, and apparently, he'd felt the same way. What did it all mean?

Her phone chimed with a text from Janey. *Everyone's at Steph's. Owen is playing. Come on over if you're around.*

Mallory washed her hands and dried them. She glanced at the mirror and noted her complexion was unusually flushed and chalked it up to the interesting turn this evening had taken. She took a deep breath and released it. For the first time since Ryan died, she'd met someone who had the potential to turn her life upside down. Did she want that? She didn't know anything for sure, and that was fine during the Summer of Mallory.

Taking her uncertainty with her, she joined him in the vestibule. He helped her on with her coat and held the door for her.

"My sister texted to tell me everyone is at Stephanie's Bistro. My cousin Laura's husband, Owen, is playing."

"You want to check it out?"

"Only if you do."

"Sure, it sounds fun. But here's the thing… I haven't lived here long, but I already know that news travels fast on this island. If, for any reason, you don't want the whole town knowing you went out with me…"

Mallory smiled up at him. "My family is pretty much the whole town for me, and I don't mind if they know. What about you? Any reason to keep this a secret?"

"Nope. It's not far. You want to walk?"

She hesitated only for a second, but long enough that he picked up on it.

"I can run on the prosthetic—finally—so a short walk is no big deal, but thanks for the concern."

"Sorry, of course you know your own capabilities."

"I'm pretty much back to where I was before, other than a slight limp I can't seem to shake."

"I could tell you'd been injured from the limp, but I wouldn't have known you were an amputee if you hadn't told me."

"That's good to know. Took a long-ass time to get there."

With a cool wind whipping in off the water, Mallory zipped up her coat and put her hands in her pockets. "When is it going to warm up and start to feel like spring around here?"

"Another couple of weeks, or so I'm told."

"I can't wait that long."

He surprised the hell out of her when he put his arm around her and drew her in close to him. "I'll keep you warm."

"Oh. Okay."

"Is it?"

Touched that he'd ask, she looked up at him and said, "Yes, it is."

He squeezed her shoulder. "Good."

They walked the rest of the way through the crowded town in silence, dodging rowdy Race Week participants along the way to the Sand & Surf Hotel and Stephanie's Bistro.

At the front door to the hotel, Quinn dropped the arm he'd had around her so he could open the door.

Mallory went in ahead of him, and the first people she saw in the lobby were Laura and her mother-in-law, Sarah Lawry, both of whom had babies strapped to their chests.

"Hey, Mallory," Laura said, her gaze shifting to Quinn and then back to Mallory with a raised brow.

"Hi there. Laura and Sarah, this is Quinn James. Quinn, my cousin Laura Lawry and her mother-in-law, Sarah."

Quinn shook hands with both ladies. "Pleasure to meet you."

"Likewise," Laura said. "Where're you guys coming from?"

"Dinner at the Lobster House," Mallory said. "Janey texted to let me know the whole crew is here and that Owen is playing, so we decided to come by."

"His first gig since the babies were born."

"Quinn, meet Joanna and Jonathan," Mallory said, leaning in for a closer look at the sleeping babies. "How're they doing?"

"They're starting to sleep on the same schedule, so that's huge progress," Laura said.

"How's their big brother adjusting?"

"Holden is crazy about them."

"Sometimes a little *too* crazy," Sarah said. "We've had to teach him about gentle hugs."

Mallory smiled. "That's so cute. You're feeling well?"

"I am, and I'm *thrilled* not to be pregnant anymore. Three kids in two years is my limit."

"That's superhuman," Quinn said.

"It's okay to use the word insane," Laura told him. "We do."

"Nothing insane about three perfect kids," he said.

"When we're not totally sleep-deprived, we do count our blessings. Go on in with the others. Tell Charlie that we'll be in to collect Holden in a minute."

"Will do."

"Nice to meet you both," Quinn said.

"Likewise," Laura replied.

As they walked to the back half of the hotel, Mallory pointed to the gift shop. "My sister-in-law Abby owns that. She's married to my brother Adam."

"A true family operation."

"That it is. Get this, though… Abby dated my brother Grant for years, and now she's married to Adam and working two feet from Grant's wife, Stephanie."

"I think my head just exploded."

Mallory laughed. "Don't feel bad. It took a while for me to get caught up on the McCarthy family story, too." They stepped into Stephanie's Bistro and immediately saw—and heard—the long table full of her family members.

"Damn, that's a big family," Quinn said.

"How do you think I felt meeting them all for the first time?"

"Probably as intimidated as I feel now."

"Don't worry. They'll like you."

# CHAPTER 9

Taking in the sight of the unruly crew, Mallory still wanted to pinch herself to believe that she was actually one of them. She had a *family*—a big, boisterous, hilarious, loving family. She greeted her siblings and cousins, who made room for them at the table. "This is Quinn James," she said. "Quinn, you know Mac. This is his wife, Maddie, my brother Adam and his wife, Abby, and my brother Grant."

"My wife is the Stephanie in Stephanie's Bistro," Grant said. "She's running around here somewhere."

"That's my cousin Finn," Mallory continued, "my sister, Janey, and her husband, Joe, my cousins Riley and Shane and Shane's fiancée, Katie. Shane is Laura's brother."

"And I'm Owen's sister," Katie added.

Quinn's brows furrowed. "Wait…"

"It sounds illegal," Adam said, "but they tell us it's not."

"A brother and sister marrying a brother and sister," Janey said. "Perfectly legal."

"If you say so," Quinn said with a grin.

"You're Jared's brother, right?" Maddie asked.

"I am."

"We love him around here," Maddie said. "He's doing some great things for our community."

"How do you like it here so far, Quinn?" Abby asked.

"So far so good. The winter didn't kill me or my dog, Brutus."

"You have a dog?" Mallory asked.

"I told you that."

"No, you didn't."

"I can't believe I haven't mentioned him. Jared says I'm way over the top about him."

"Pictures," Mallory said. "I need pictures."

Like a proud papa, Quinn pulled out his phone and shared a series of photos with Mallory that everyone else then wanted to see, too.

"He is so cute!" Mallory said. "I want to meet him."

That earned her a warm smile from Quinn that engaged his eyes. The effect made her feel light-headed and overheated. She started to take off her coat, and Quinn helped her. "Thanks."

A waitress came by for their drink order, and they both asked for water.

Mallory noticed the odd look Mac gave her, but was thankful he didn't ask why she wasn't drinking.

"So who's missing from this crowd?" Quinn asked.

"My brother Evan and his wife, Grace. He's a singer, songwriter and musician. They're on their way home from his tour with Buddy Longstreet. They'll be home for the summer tomorrow."

"I love Buddy's music. I'll have to check out your brother."

"He's so talented. He plays every instrument, or so it seems, and his voice is incredible."

"You sound like a proud sister."

"Oh, I am! He got me backstage passes when they played in Boston in April. I got to meet Buddy and his wife, Taylor. It was so cool."

"That sounds fun."

"It was a great night. Evan plays a lot with Owen when he's home. They're fantastic together."

"He's really good," Quinn said of Owen, who was playing "Brown-Eyed Girl" for the enthusiastic crowd.

An older man with a buzz cut and bright blue eyes came over to their table, holding a squirming, dark-haired toddler on his shoulders.

"Hey, Charlie," Mallory said. "Quinn, this is Sarah's fiancé, Charlie Grandchamp, and Laura's son Holden. Charlie, this is Quinn James."

Keeping one hand on the child, Charlie shook Quinn's hand. "Good to meet you."

"You, too."

"Sarah wanted us to tell you it's time for Holden to go to bed," Mallory said.

"Awww, Mommy and Grandma are no fun."

"Someone's gotta be the bad guy," Mallory said.

"I suppose so. All right, then, buddy, let's get you upstairs before Mommy comes looking for us."

After Charlie walked away, Quinn said, "Nice guy."

"Very nice. He's Stephanie's stepfather. He spent fourteen years in prison wrongly accused of abusing her, when it was actually her mother who abused her. Steph worked tirelessly to get him out. Grant and his friend Dan Torrington got involved, and they finally got him out last year."

"Holy shit," Quinn said under his breath.

"I know."

"I've read about Torrington and his innocence project."

"He lives here on the island now."

"He does? Really?"

"Yep. He and his fiancée, Kara, spent the winter in LA, but they're back now, too. Hey, Grant, where're Dan and Kara tonight?"

"Tonight's her birthday, so they're off being romantical somewhere."

"Listen to that disdain," Finn said, scoffing. "As if you didn't spend the whole winter in hibernation with your wife on the West Coast."

"Who invited the baby cousins?" Grant asked. "Are they even old enough to drink?"

While Finn laughed and flipped Grant the bird, his brother Riley said, "Don't lump me in with him. I'm a whole year older than him."

"I *love* the baby cousins," Janey said. "Especially when they bust my brothers' balls. Takes some of the heat off me."

"Don't talk about your brothers' balls, dear," Joe said. "It's unseemly."

"You love it when I'm unseemly," Janey retorted.

"Ewwwww," Mac, Adam and Grant said in unison.

"Gross," Mac added.

Mallory rocked with helpless laughter. She loved when her siblings got going. It was always so entertaining.

"Nothing gross about it," Joe said, earning scowls and balled-up cocktail napkins lobbed at his head by his brothers-in-law. He batted them away without losing his big smile.

"You guys are so ridiculous," Maddie said. "She's pregnant for the second time. News flash, your baby sister has sex."

"*Lots* of sex," Janey added while Joe nodded enthusiastically.

"Mac, do something about your wife," Grant said. "She's out of control."

"Oh, umm, well," Mac said.

"Do finish that sentence," Maddie said, propping her chin on her upturned fist. "I can't wait to hear how it ends."

"I have nothing to say, dear."

"Pussy-whipped," Adam said behind his hand, earning him an elbow to the ribs from his wife.

"Shut your mouth," Abby said, "or you'll be pussy-deprived."

"Oh shit," Adam said. "My heartfelt apologies, love."

"This, right here, is why I'm never getting married," Riley said, rubbing the stubble on his jaw. Like his brother, and his cousins, he had thick dark hair and the shockingly blue McCarthy eyes that Big Mac and his brother Kevin shared.

"Oh, whatever," Janey said. "My brothers used to say the same thing, and look at them now, a bunch of domesticated house pets."

"Hey," Grant said. "I'd resent that if it wasn't so true."

The others snorted with laughter.

"Is it me, or has Mac been on his best behavior since our trip to Anguilla this winter?" Shane asked.

"It's not just you," Grant said. "Everyone is concerned that he's been declawed."

"Perhaps it was because he organized a boy posse to steal our clothes when we went skinny-dipping," Abby said.

"Or that he told the guys that Maddie worships at the altar of Mac McCarthy," Katie added.

"You all can shut right up any time now," Mac said.

"Why?" Shane asked. "We're just expressing our concern about your newfound good behavior."

"Has it occurred to you fools that maybe I've decided it's time to grow up?" Mac asked, drawing shocked silence from the others.

"No way," Grant said, starting a new wave of laughter. "No fucking way."

"I'm about to be a father of three," Mac said. "No time like the present to start behaving like an adult."

"I'm so proud of my little boy," Maddie said, running her fingers through his hair. "He's coming along so nicely."

Mac purred as he leaned into her caress, his expression blissful and placid.

"Dear God," Janey said. "This might require a full-blown intervention."

"Don't you dare," Maddie said with a sinister glare for her sister-in-law.

"Yeah, brat," Mac said, "the only thing getting fully blown around here is me, so shut it."

Janey cringed. "So disgusting."

"Ain't nothing disgusting about it," Mac replied with a wink for his sister, who pretended to puke.

Mallory was weak from laughter. Their good-natured bickering, joking and pranks—some of which had been epic—were endlessly entertaining to the woman who'd grown up so alone.

"Tell Quinn about the time you girls convinced the guys that you'd hired strippers for Jenny's bachelorette party," Mallory said.

The women proceeded to relay the story of their greatest victory to date, when they'd had the guys foaming at the mouth with outrage for a full week ahead of Jenny Martinez's bachelorette party.

"Of course, my husband was the first one through the door at Syd's house that night," Maddie said. "Cost me a couple hundred bucks, but that's what I get for betting on him."

"You guys *bet* on which of the guys would be the first to show up?" Quinn asked, sounding astounded.

"Of course we did," Abby said matter-of-factly. "We all knew it would be Mac. Well, everyone but Maddie, that is."

"The vows said I'm supposed to be loyal to him," Maddie said. "Even when he gives me reason not to be."

"That is *so* awesome," Quinn said, rocking with laughter.

"You should've seen Blaine, Tiffany's husband, who is the chief of police," Mac said of his brother-in-law. "If you think I was out of my mind, he put me to shame."

"No one puts you to shame," Maddie said, "which is why you're working on being better behaved."

"It's so *boring* being good," Mac said glumly.

"Can we take bets on how long this new stage of Mac's is going to last?" Janey asked. She pulled her phone from her purse. "Place your bets. Ten bucks apiece, winner takes all."

"I call one more week," Grant said, tossing a ten her way.

"Put me down for two weeks," Joe said.

Everyone else called out their bets while Mac sat back and watched the money fly at Janey.

"I'll take one more month," Maddie said.

"You took vows!" Mac said. "You can't bet against me!"

"Sorry, love, but I don't see this new leaf of yours as sustainable long-term, and I need to make back what I lost on the strippers."

Mac only glared at her while everyone else lost it laughing.


"And that," Mallory said two hours later as they walked back to the Lobster House parking lot, "is my family."

"What a great time," Quinn said. "I haven't laughed that much in years."

"They're so fun. Sometimes I still can't believe I get to keep them. I'm glad you enjoyed meeting them."

"Every one of them is funnier than the last one."

"I know! I can't keep up with them when they start going at it."

"They've had years of experience goading each other. You'll catch up."

"Even if I never do, I get to be entertained by them on a regular basis."

"It's nice to see that truly functional families still exist."

"I agree. Yours isn't like that?"

"Not like they are. When the James siblings go at it, usually people cry rather than laugh."

"Ouch."

"Exactly. Not so much anymore, but when we were younger, it was pretty brutal. My parents used to wonder if we'd speak to each other as adults. And then when Jared struck it rich, he shared the wealth with the rest of us, which brought out the best in some and the worst in others."

"Money does strange things to people."

"Yes, it does."

"Did it do strange things to you?"

"Nah. I invested it and forgot about it while I was in the military."

"Which means you've probably made a killing on it."

"It's done all right. Jared keeps an eye on it for me, and he's a wizard. But it's never felt like *my* money, you know?"

"I can understand that, but it was nice of him to make his family comfortable when he hit it big."

"Yes, it was. He was extremely generous with all of us. The best part was that my dad, who drove a New Jersey transit bus his entire adult life, was able to retire, and my parents spend six months a year in Florida. Now he plays golf seven days a week and is tanned year-round."

"That's wonderful." Mallory paused and then glanced over at him. "That's why you didn't tell them about your leg, right? Because they were enjoying their retirement so much."

"Yeah. They'd worked so hard to support us. My mom worked in a high school cafeteria. Money was always in short supply when we were kids. They need to relax and enjoy themselves now. They've certainly earned it."

Once again, it pained her to think of him enduring such a difficult ordeal completely alone, but it told her a lot about who he really was that he'd put his parents and their best interests ahead of his own.

They arrived at his truck, and he held the door for her. Mallory's heart began to beat a little faster the closer they got to her house and the end of their evening. Usually by this point in a date, she was working out a strategy to get rid of the guy as fast as she could. But tonight… Tonight she wanted him to stay awhile longer but had no idea what he was thinking.

He pulled into her driveway, killed the engine and turned to face her, his arm propped on the back of the seat. "Thank you for a great night."

"Thank *you* for dinner and for putting up with my family."

"It was fun."

"Yes, it was."

He raised his hand ever so slightly to touch her hair.

Mallory held her breath, waiting to see what would happen next. At that moment, she wasn't thinking about the job he'd offered her or the possibility that he could be her boss. No, she was too focused on his lips and the possibility that he might kiss her.

He didn't disappoint. Leaning in, he whispered, "You're going to have to meet me halfway."

"I can do that." Mallory moved closer to meet him and noted the slight curve in his lips right before they connected with hers. And *holy wow*, the man could kiss. She edged ever closer to him, and he drew her in with his fingers buried in her hair for one hell of a kiss—tender and sweet, but also hot and needy at the same time.

When he ran his tongue over her bottom lip, Mallory gasped from the sensations that spiraled through her. It had been, she realized, a very long time since she'd experienced true desire.

He withdrew from her slowly but kept his firm grip on her hair so she couldn't get away. "*Whoa*," he whispered as his lips slid over hers.

"What you said."

She felt him smile against her lips. "You want to come in?"

"Uh-huh."

"You have to let me go so we can get out of the car."

"In a minute."

# CHAPTER 10

Quinn kissed her again, much more passionately this time, with his tongue rubbing up against hers in a sensuous dance that had her gripping a handful of his coat to keep him from retreating too soon.

By the time they came up for air, the windows were fogged and both of them were breathing hard.

He reached down to release her seat belt and then unfastened his own.

They got out of the truck and met at the front. She noticed that he looked as bewildered as she felt from the heat of their kisses as he put his hand on her lower back to guide her up the stairs to the small front porch.

Mallory used her key in the door. Even though her family told her no one locked their doors on Gansett Island, she was too much of a city girl to ever break that habit entirely.

The fragrance from a cinnamon-scented candle greeted them, giving the tiny cottage a warm, welcoming feeling. She turned on a light that bathed the living room in a cozy glow. It had taken years for her place in the city to feel like home to her, but already, this house owned by her sister spoke to her in a way the city place never had.

Quinn unzipped his coat and helped her remove hers.

"Can I get you anything to drink?" she asked.

He shook his head and raised his hands to frame her face, tipping it up to receive another kiss.

Mallory rested her hands on his hips and tilted her head to improve the angle.

Before she knew it, his arms were wrapped around her as he devoured her with his lips and tongue.

This was… unexpected. Yes, she found him attractive and interesting and slightly mysterious. She'd enjoyed the time they'd spent together, but she hadn't pictured the night ending on such a hot-and-bothered note. And where exactly was this headed from here?

The press of his arousal against her belly made it rather obvious what he wanted, but was she prepared to go *there* right now? No. Not quite yet.

"What's wrong?" he asked, shifting his focus to her neck, which made her legs go weak under her.

"I was thinking we should save something for next time."

He continued to kiss and nibble on her neck until Mallory was on the verge of saying to hell with next time.

"I have to tell you," he said gruffly, his breath warm against her tingling skin, "this was the best night I've had in a really, really long time."

Moved by his sweet words, she wrapped her arms around his waist and held on tight. "Me, too."

"Tell me we can do it again very soon. Like tomorrow night. Or is it tonight? What the hell time is it anyway?"

Mallory laughed at the way he asked that question, as if he'd lost all concept of time while they were together. "Almost midnight."

"Tonight, then. Yes?" He looked down at her, his expression fierce and tender at the same time.

"Yes."

"Good answer." He touched his lips to hers again. "I'll call you."

"Okay."

She watched him put his coat back on and walked him to the door. "Quinn." He turned to face her.

"I didn't really *want* to put a stop to that just now."

Gazing into her eyes, he stole another kiss. "That's good to know. Sleep tight."

She closed the door behind him and locked it, but waited until he'd pulled out of the driveway to turn off the outside lights. For a long time after he left, she leaned her head against the wood door and relived the delightful evening that had ended with the kind of passion she'd experienced only one other time in her life.

Her reaction to Quinn had taken her by surprise. She'd become accustomed to dates that ended with a pleasant kiss or two, occasionally some nice, sweet sex that rarely led to anything more substantial. But this... This had the potential to be more than substantial. It could be life-changing.

Did she want that at a time when so many other things in her life were changing? She had no idea, but that was the beauty of the Summer of Mallory. Anything was possible.

She turned off the rest of the lights and went into her bedroom to change into pajama pants and a T-shirt. In the bathroom, she washed her face and brushed her teeth and took a close look at her face in the mirror, noticing a hint of razor burn on her jaw as well as swollen, well-kissed lips.

Releasing a deep breath, she headed for bed, where she lay awake for a long time, reliving the best date she'd been on in years and wondering what would happen next.

She couldn't wait to find out.

After leaving Mallory's house, Quinn drove toward New Harbor and found a parking place along the seawall that led to McCarthy's Marina. He locked his truck and went down to the town dock, where he'd left his dinghy earlier.

When Quinn accepted the job at the healthcare facility, Jared had offered him the caretaker's suite at the Chesterfield, another property his brother and Lizzie owned on the island. The suite had worked out well for the winter and early spring months, but he'd wanted something different for the summer.

He'd perused for-sale ads for months before finding a thirty-six-foot sailboat for sale that met all his requirements. Not only was it in great condition, but the interior made for a comfortable place to call home for the summer.

He started the outboard motor and directed the rubber boat toward the mooring field where his boat was located. He'd been lucky to secure a mooring for the summer and loved living on the boat. It took about ten minutes to motor from the shore to the boat. Taking the bowline with him, he climbed aboard the sailboat and secured the dinghy with a loose knot.

Onboard, he unlocked the padlock on the cabin door, and Brutus came barreling out to meet him, licking his face with unbridled love and enthusiasm. Getting the dog was the best thing he'd done for himself since he got hurt. The "puppy" was now fifty pounds of true love, and Quinn adored him. "Let's go for a walk, bud."

Used to their routine by now, Brutus leaped into the dinghy and waited for Quinn to join him. Getting into the smaller boat could still be a challenge for him with the prosthetic, so he moved cautiously, aware that if he had any sort of accident out here in the dark, he'd be in a world of trouble by himself.

Once settled in the boat with Brutus propped up on the bow like a hood ornament, Quinn restarted the engine and motored back to the shore, where he and Brutus took a short walk so the dog could take care of business. He loved that Brutus stayed right with him and didn't have to be on a leash for these outings. Quinn picked up the poop and dropped it in a trashcan at the beach before they set off to return to the boat.

When they arrived, Brutus scampered off the dinghy back onto the bigger boat like he'd been doing it for years rather than weeks. Quinn was relieved that Brutus had taken to life on the boat so effortlessly. He went below to grab a bottle of water that he brought back onto the deck with him, stretching out on one of the padded seats to look up at the stars. In all his life, he'd never seen stars quite like those that appeared each night over Gansett's remote Salt Pond.

Brutus stretched out next to him on the deck, close enough that Quinn could scratch behind his ears while he looked at the stars.

He wondered if Mallory liked to sail and what she'd think of the boat he called home or whether she'd like to see his view of the stars. He'd meant what he told her about this being one of the best nights he'd had in longer than he could remember.

Even though he'd fully expected to enjoy himself, he hadn't anticipated the sort of connection he'd had with her. He hadn't told anyone about losing his leg, but somehow the story had spilled out to her without any hesitation whatsoever. He knew instinctively that he could trust her to keep his secrets private, especially because she too was a trained medical professional accustomed to maintaining patient privacy. Similarly, he suspected she didn't easily share the story of how she'd lost her husband so tragically, yet she'd told him.

And when he'd kissed her... He'd been attracted to her intelligence and competence the first time they met at the accident scene. He'd been impressed by her compassion toward other members at their AA meetings, and he thought she was flat-out gorgeous. In fact, he'd had to remind himself more than once that it was creepy to stare when he sat across from her at meetings.

Now that he knew what it was like to kiss her, he couldn't wait to do it again.

Neither of them were kids. They'd both taken their share of knocks in life and were a long way from wide-eyed innocence. Yet the time he'd spent with her filled him with the kind of optimism he hadn't felt since long before he was injured. Back then, he'd been invincible. Nothing could touch him. He could handle anything that came his way and had saved countless lives under terrible conditions.

Everything changed for him in a single second. A flash of light, a blast of heat and pain so unbearable he'd lost consciousness. When he came to and discovered the extent of his injury, he knew right then and there that nothing would ever be the same. He'd been knocked off his king-of-the-world throne and had descended into depths of despair he'd never known possible as he fought to save what was left of his leg.

The infection had won the war, forcing him to decide between his leg and his life. In a way, it had worked out for the best, because he never would've conceded to amputation if it hadn't come down to such a dire choice. His stubbornness would've led to permanent disability rather than the slight limp he lived with now that he had the prosthetic.

After the surgery, the worst part of the recovery had been the phantom pain he'd experienced in the missing limb. When patients had complained of that in the past, he'd wondered if it was psychosomatic, but now he knew better. He was a better doctor for having survived his ordeal, but he'd lost his taste for trauma surgery and the never-ending life-and-death battles that went along with it.

Jared and Lizzie's offer had come at the right time, two years after his own surgery and grueling rehab in which he'd learned how to walk with the prosthetic. He'd begun to think about his next move when Jared called with Lizzie's big idea for him to run their healthcare facility on Gansett Island.

He couldn't say yet if this was a permanent move or even a "career" he wished to pursue long-term. For now, he'd committed to staying long enough to get the facility up and running. He'd wanted to keep his options open, and Lizzie had wanted him badly enough for the job that she'd been willing to agree to conditional employment.

So for now, he was happily settled on his spacious, comfortable boat with his beloved dog, the incredible views of the pond and the stars and the bustling activity on the waterfront. The day he met Mallory had been one of his first attempts at running on the prosthetic, and he'd since become much more comfortable and was adding to his mileage with each passing week. He was giving himself another month or so before he started taking Brutus with him.

His life was back under control, for the most part, which made tonight's events that much more intriguing. Now that he had the rest of his crap sorted, for the time being anyway, perhaps there was room for something more. With he and

Mallory both in this weird state of transition, maybe this was the worst possible time to be thinking such thoughts. But after the delightful evening they'd spent together, she seemed to be all he could think about.

"I don't know about that guy," Mac said to Maddie as he pulled his shirt over his head and tossed it toward the hamper, missing by a foot.

She bent to retrieve it and threw it back to him. "Try again, Ace."

Mac balled up the shirt and made a perfect shot. "Swish."

"What guy are you talking about?"

"The one Mallory was with."

"Quinn James?"

"Yeah, him. What do we know about him anyway?"

"We know he's Jared's brother, and that Jared is a good guy who's done a lot for our community since he moved here."

"That doesn't mean his brother is a good guy."

"He's a veteran."

"And I appreciate his service, but even that doesn't mean he's good for my sister."

"You've worked with him for months. You know him by now."

"That's the thing. I don't feel like I know him any better now than I did at the beginning."

"Mallory seems to like him. That ought to count for something."

"Yeah, I guess."

Maddie washed the makeup off her face and put toothpaste on her toothbrush. "Mac... What're you not saying?"

"Nothing." He couldn't say why, exactly, he wasn't sure about Mallory seeing Quinn, but he vowed to keep a closer eye on the guy now that he knew his sister was interested. "I'm going to check on the kids."

"Do not, under any circumstances, do anything to wake them up, or I will kill you, and I'll make it hurt."

"Yes, dear," he said with a chuckle. God, he loved her even when she was threatening to kill him. After even a couple of hours away from them, he needed to lay eyes on his babies, even though Maddie had already checked on them.

He went first into Thomas's room where his soon-to-be-five-year-old son was sleeping with his arms thrown over his head and his covers kicked off. Mac covered him and kissed his forehead. "Love you, buddy," he whispered. The sleeping child never stirred.

In Hailey's room, he found his daughter sleeping with her bum in the air, per usual, and fixed the blanket that had become tangled around her tiny body. He kissed his fingertips and reached over the crib rails to sweep sweaty blonde hair off her forehead.

As his fingers coasted over her skin, her eyes popped open.

Mac bit his lip to keep from gasping and stayed perfectly still, hoping she didn't see him there. If she did, she'd want to get up to play with Dada, and Maddie would, in fact, kill him.

Thankfully, she let out a deep sigh, and her eyes closed once again.

Mac crept from the room, thanking his lucky stars that she hadn't woken up. When he returned to their room, Maddie was already in bed and rubbing lotion into her arms. Something about that nightly ritual was so incredibly sexy to him. "Everyone is good."

"Which I already knew and so did you, because I checked on them and told you they were fine."

"I can't help that I need to see them with my own eyes."

"You're a very good daddy." She held out a hand to him. "Now come over here and give Mommy some love."

Mac didn't have to be told twice. He crawled up the bed and came down right next to her. "How's my other baby?" he asked, placing his hand over the prominent bump in her abdomen.

"Jumping around like a fool. I fear this one is going to take after his daddy."

"He should be so lucky."

Mac pushed up her nightgown to kiss the baby bump and was rewarded with a solid kick to the face that made them laugh.

"See what I mean? He's going to be a holy terror like you."

"Aww, I love when you're so sweet to me."

Smiling, she combed her fingers through his hair as he continued to kiss her belly.

"He's so strong," Mac said, marveling at the waves of movement under her skin. "Hailey wasn't this active."

She met his gaze, her golden eyes conveying the depth of her love for him. "He's very strong, but I'm still scared."

"I know. I am, too. I won't feel like we're out of the woods until he's actually here. I think about Connor all the time and what he'd be doing by now and which one of us he'd look like." Mac knew that the baby they'd lost last year was never far from her mind either.

"Remember what your dad told you when we lost him?"

"He told me a lot of things."

"When the same thing happened to them, they grieved so deeply, but then they had you and realized that if the first baby had lived, they never would've had you, and they couldn't imagine life without you."

"Yeah, he did say that."

"The same will be true for us." She rested her hand on the baby bump. "Whoever this person is will soon be one of the three most important people in the world to us. He won't make us miss Connor any less than we do, but maybe it won't hurt quite so much once he's here."

"Maybe so. Are we in agreement on his name?"

"We don't even know for sure that *he* is a he."

"I don't know why that I'm so sure he's a boy."

"Will you be disappointed if he's a she?" Maddie asked.

"Hell no. Another Hailey to worship at the altar of Daddy when no one else will? I'd be totally fine with that."

"You're pathetic. You realize that, right?"

"You tell me that so often, how could I not know?"

Maddie laughed at the face he made at her. "Good thing I love you no matter how pathetic you are."

He urged her to come closer to him, arranging her so they faced each other. "That's a very good thing, seeing as how I couldn't live without you." Running his fingers through her hair, he gazed at her adorable face. "Now what am I going to do about my sister and this doctor guy no one knows anything about?"

"Nothing. You're going to do absolutely nothing. Your sister is thirty-nine years old and certainly knows how to take care of herself by now."

"That doesn't mean she should have to. She has a family now. Brothers who want to look out for her."

Maddie raised a brow that signaled her intention to call him on his bullshit. "*Brothers?* Plural? Or just one?"

"I'm sure Grant and Adam felt the same way I did tonight, and Evan would have if he'd been there."

"You're sure about this, are you?"

"Pretty sure."

"Mac, you really can't go there. Please tell me you know this."

He diverted his gaze. "If you say so."

"Mac..."

"I hear you."

"I know you care about her, and I love you for that. I'm sure she would, too. But trust me when I tell you she would not welcome your interference in her personal life. I hate to say this, but she's not Janey. She didn't grow up having to put up with you and your brothers. You're all still new to her."

"There's something about that guy. I can't put my finger on it, but there's something. He's so secretive."

"There's a difference between being secretive and being private. Not everyone feels the need to share their every thought the way you do."

"I don't do that."

Her damned brow challenged that statement, too. "If there's something to be concerned about, she'll figure that out on her own. Tell me you know that."

"Yes, I get it. I hear you. I'll behave."

She gave him her wary look that let him know she didn't entirely believe him. "Tread carefully, Mac. She's still figuring out her place in this family, and she seemed really happy tonight."

"I know. I saw that, too."

"Do I need to come up with other ways to keep you occupied so you resist the urge to meddle in your sister's life?"

"What other ways do you have in mind?"

Rising to one elbow, she leaned in to kiss him. "Something like that. And maybe some of this." She ran her tongue over his bottom lip.

"I like this topic so much better than the last one."

Maddie laughed, as he'd known she would. He loved to hear her laugh and to make her laugh. "I figured you would."

"But I hate that all we can do is kiss." Out of an abundance of caution, they'd agreed to forgo having sex until after the baby arrived. Victoria had told them it was perfectly safe, but they were taking absolutely no chances.

"Only a few more months. We can do it."

"I may expire from wanting you too much."

"Please don't do that. I need you to help me raise these three children of ours."

"I'm not going anywhere except wherever you are, but I'm not going to forget that you bet against me tonight."

As Maddie laughed, he worked his leg between hers and kissed her again, letting every other thought and worry fade away as he lost himself in her.

# CHAPTER 11

Mallory told herself that the timing of her run the next morning had nothing at all to do with the time she'd previously met up with Quinn on a run. As she pounded the pavement on the way toward the island's northernmost point, she tried to pretend she wasn't looking for him around every bend in the road.

The gorgeous late-spring day was the sort that gave Rhode Islanders hope that summer might actually show up after weeks of teasing. Everything was in bloom. The warm sun beat down upon her from a cloudless sky, and the breeze off the water was warm rather than chilly for the first time.

Sunday was the only day their AA group didn't meet, because Nina went to the mainland to see her grandchildren. Group members were encouraged to reach out to each other if needed. It was nice to have a full day free from any commitments. Mallory knew those days would be few and far between once she started working for Mason and the summer season kicked into high gear on the island.

Her efforts were rewarded ten minutes later when she saw Quinn coming from the opposite direction. She noticed the slight limp and marveled that he could run as well and as fast as he did with a prosthesis.

He slowed to a stop, a smile unfolding across his face.

Mallory had to remind herself to breathe. She'd been attracted to good-looking men before. Hell, she'd been married to one, but never before had the sight of a man made her go stupid in the head like she did around Quinn.

"Fancy meeting you all the way out here."

She knew she was required to say something, but she was still working on that breathing thing, so she nodded.

"Winded?"

"Little bit."

"Mind if I join you?"

"I was just about to head back."

"That's fine with me."

"Okay, then."

They set off toward town at a slower pace than they'd been keeping on their own.

"Tell me the truth," he said after a long silence. "Did you run out there hoping to see me?"

"*No*," she said, snorting with indignation.

"That's too bad, because I ran that way hoping to find you."

"Now I feel like an ass, because that's exactly why I went that way."

Her comment was rewarded with a true, genuine laugh that made every part of her tingle with awareness of him.

"I knew it," he said.

"Don't get too full of yourself."

"Too late for that."

Mallory loved that he admitted to looking for her, that he'd hoped to see her again, and that he'd laughed, something she already knew he didn't do very often.

"What're you up to today?" he asked.

"Nothing much until later. We're having a welcome-home party for Evan and Grace."

"That sounds fun."

"After being here for six weeks last summer, I already know there's always something going on in my family. It keeps things interesting, that's for sure."

"What were you doing here last summer?"

"I took some vacation time to assist in caring for a terminally ill island resident. Shane's fiancée, Katie, was involved, and when she told me about the young single mom with lung cancer, I knew I had to help if I could. Plus, it gave me a chance to get to know my new family a little better."

"Wow, that's so nice of you to put your own life on hold for someone you didn't even know."

"I came to know her quite well. I was awed by her courage. We all were."

"What happened to her kids?"

"They've been taken in by Seamus and Carolina O'Grady. Carolina is my brother-in-law Joe's mom, and her husband, Seamus, helps Joe run the ferry company."

"And they're doing okay?"

"From what I've heard, they're all adjusting. The boys are really young, so there's a blessing in that, but it's sad that they won't remember much about their mom."

"That's so sad."

"It is, but kids are resilient, and they've got great champions in Seamus and Carolina. They'll be okay. Eventually."

They ran in companionable silence for a while, the steady rhythm of their feet on the pavement the only sound other than seagulls squawking overhead.

"How do you feel about sailing?" Quinn asked as they got closer to town.

"In general or as something I might want to do?"

"Both."

"In general, it looks like fun, but I've never actually done it."

He stopped running so suddenly, they nearly collided. "You've never sailed? As in *never*?"

"As in never."

"Well, that won't do. We need to fix that. I'm taking you sailing. Today." He glanced at her. "Unless you have other plans."

"I don't have other plans until later."

"So we'll go sailing, then?"

"We'll go sailing."

"Excellent," he said with one of his rare full smiles that were becoming less rare the more time they spent together.

"What can I bring?"

"Just a sweatshirt. It can get chilly out there this time of year. Leave everything else to me."

"Where're we getting the boat for this excursion?"

"I live on my boat."

This time, Mallory stopped short. "You *live* on a boat?"

"Uh-huh."

"Where is it?"

"On a mooring in the Salt Pond."

"What did you do in the winter?"

"Stayed in a suite at the Chesterfield that my brother and Lizzie made available to me. That was nice, but I like the boat better."

With each new discovery, Mallory's perception of him evolved. War veteran, trauma surgeon, amputee, middle child, dog owner, boat dweller, sexy devil. The combination of all these qualities made for an interesting man to spend time with.

They took the final turn before Mallory's house and jogged up to the gate in the white picket fence that surrounded the small yard. Janey had told her she put in the fence to protect her menagerie of special-needs pets.

"Do you mind if I bring Brutus?"

"Doesn't he live with you?"

"Yeah, but I can take him to Jared's for the day if overly enthusiastic puppies who don't realize they're too heavy to sit in your lap at fifty pounds aren't your thing."

Mallory laughed at his description of the dog. "He sounds charming."

"I think he is, but I kind of have to. I'm under no illusions that everyone will find my baby charming."

That he referred to Brutus as his "baby" was swoon-worthy and made him even more attractive than he already was to her. "I'm looking forward to meeting him, and I'm fine with having him on the boat."

"Great," he said. "I'll pick you up in an hour." He turned and jogged off toward the Salt Pond he called home.

Mallory rushed through a shower, shaved her legs and dried her hair before putting it up in a ponytail. She debated shorts or jeans, settling on the jeans and throwing a pair of shorts in her bag in case it was too warm for the jeans later. Wanting to contribute something to their day, she packed up a bunch of grapes along with sliced cheddar and crackers.

With ten minutes until Quinn was due to arrive, she went back to her room for a sweatshirt, sunscreen and a Red Sox ball cap to protect her face from the sun.

Then she began to feel insecure about bringing too much stuff.

"Stop," she told herself. "You're only taking things you might need, and he won't care." Her gaze landed on the photo of her and Ryan from the wedding. She picked up the frame and took a good look at the man who'd been her husband. The more time that passed, the harder it was to remember the little details that had made up their life together. Like the sound of his voice, for example. About five years ago, she realized she couldn't remember what he sounded like and had only their wedding video to refresh her memory. That had scared the hell out of her. How could she *forget* such an important thing?

She'd realized then that she was going to live without him far longer than she'd lived with him, and there was no possible way she could hang on to every little thing that had made them who they were as a couple. That had been like losing him all over again and had gotten her started on a regular habit of writing down important things that she never wanted to forget. She now had notebooks full of remembrances of Ryan and her mother, who'd been the two most important people in her life until a year ago when she met her father and the rest of her family.

Now her circle was so much larger, and there were so many more memories created on a regular basis that warranted remembering. Such as when her nephew

Thomas and his cousin Ashleigh had run bare-ass naked through the Christmas gathering at Big Mac and Linda's, playing "naked boy-naked girl." Not that she feared ever forgetting that gem, but she wrote it down just the same, along with Mac's prank gone wrong in Anguilla when the guys stole the women's clothes while they were skinny-dipping.

The McCarthy family was always up to something, and Mallory never wanted to forget anything from her time with them.

Quinn's knock on the door had her returning the photo to its place of honor on her bedside table. She picked up her bag off the bed and headed toward the door, where he waited for her wearing jeans and a white polo shirt. His hair was still damp from the shower, and he smelled good enough to eat. *Dear God, where did that thought come from?*

She hoped her face wasn't bright red as she accompanied him to the driveway where he held the passenger door to his truck for her.

"You clean up well," he said when they were on their way toward her father's marina.

"Funny, I was just thinking the same thing about you."

He glanced over at her, and they shared a smile.

Her heart beat fast and her hands were sweaty. She couldn't remember reacting this way to a man—or a boy—since she was in high school and dating her first boyfriend. Then she'd been nervous about what he might expect from her, with good reason as it turned out. Now, she was undone by the first real connection she'd felt with a man since she lost Ryan.

Her relationship with him, at least at the beginning, had been more about surviving medical school than fast-beating hearts or sweaty palms. Sure, the attraction had been off the charts, but they were so consumed by school that the attraction often took a backseat to the rest of the demands on them.

It was funny, at her age, to feel giddy about a guy. She wouldn't have thought that was still possible, but Quinn had proven otherwise.

Near the marina, they parked along the seawall, and he led her toward the dock where he'd left his dinghy.

Of course it was too much to hope for that they would escape without running into her dad on the dock.

When he saw her, he stopped what he was doing and came right over, giving her a kiss on the cheek that made her heart sing. She would never get used to the easy way he doled out his boundless affection. "This is a nice surprise. What brings you by?"

"This is my friend Quinn. Quinn, my dad, Mac McCarthy. Everyone calls him Big Mac, though."

"Nice to meet you, sir," Quinn said, shaking Big Mac's hand.

"You, too." Big Mac sized up Quinn with obvious paternal interest that had Mallory hoping he wasn't about to embarrass her too badly.

"I had the pleasure of meeting most of your other kids last night," Quinn said. "An entertaining group."

Big Mac's face lit up with pleasure, and Mallory gave Quinn points for saying the perfect thing to her dad, who took such pride in his family. "That they are. Where're you two off to on this fine day?"

"Quinn is taking me sailing."

Her dad's smile faded noticeably, making her want to ask if it was okay if she went, which was silly. She didn't need his permission, but damn if she didn't want his approval. So she went ahead and asked the question. "Is that okay?"

"You know what you're doing out there?" he asked Quinn.

"Yes, sir. I've been sailing all my life."

"What will you do if you see even the slightest sign of fog rolling in?"

"We'll head back in. I'm no fan of fog, believe me."

Big Mac seemed to breathe a sigh of relief. "Okay, then. Sorry for the inquisition, but I nearly lost three of my boys in a crash in the fog last Race Week. Fog and I aren't friends anymore."

"I understand completely, and you have my word that Mallory will be very safe with me."

Mallory got the feeling that Quinn was talking about much more than sailing at this point.

After a long pause in which he never blinked, Big Mac said, "Good enough." Shifting his gaze to Mallory, he said, "Let me know when you're back on dry land."

"I will." And for the first time since she found out that he was her father, she spontaneously went up on tiptoes to kiss his cheek. "Don't worry."

"Might as well tell me not to breathe."

She patted his chest. "I'll check in when we get back."

"You do that. Have a good time."

"We will."

Quinn gestured for her to go ahead of him down the ramp that led to the floating dock where his dinghy was tied. "Did I just pass a major test there?"

"I think so."

"Are you... Are those..."

Mallory dabbed at her eyes. "I'm sorry. It's so silly, but that was the first time I've ever introduced a man to my dad and watched him go into protector mode. You'll have to excuse me for acting like a ninny over it."

"You're not acting like a ninny. You're acting like someone who finally has the daddy she always wished for."

His kind assessment had the tears flowing fast and furious, much to her dismay. She wiped them away with the sleeve of her shirt.

Then he was there with his arms around her, holding her while she took a moment. She breathed in the incredibly appealing scent of soap and citrus that, when combined, made for a rather potent formula. "I'm okay now." She took a deep breath. "I'm sorry. Didn't mean to put a damper on the day."

"You didn't."

"I'm still getting used to it all, you know?"

"I totally get it, and no apology needed."

Mallory took advantage of the ride to the boat to get herself together. As they passed the far end of the McCarthy Marina pier, her dad waved to her.

Mallory returned his wave, noting that his usual big smile was missing from his face. After what happened last year, he was more worried than he would've been about one of his kids going out on the water.

One of his kids… *I'm one of his kids.* A wave of regret and sadness for everything she'd missed with him and her siblings had her weeping again the way she had after she first met them and came to understand exactly what her mother had kept her from by refusing to reveal her father's identity. She hated herself for having a meltdown in front of Quinn, but she couldn't seem to help it.

He tied up to a bigger than expected sailboat and helped her onboard, passing her bag to her, all of it done without acknowledgment of her blubbering-mess status.

She noted that he moved more carefully than usual as he transferred from the dinghy to the boat.

Brutus barked a greeting from the cabin.

"Before I let him out, you want to talk about it?"

"You can let him out. He wants to see you, and it's probably hot in there."

"The hatches and windows are open for him. I'll try not to let him jump on you, but he's enthusiastic when meeting new people."

"I'm ready."

# CHAPTER 12

Quinn unlocked the cabin and ordered Brutus to be nice as he introduced the adorable dog to Mallory. In the scope of two seconds, Brutus managed to lick most of her face and make her laugh so hard, she nearly forgot she'd been crying two minutes earlier.

"Brutus! Stop it. Sit down and be a good boy."

Brutus's rump dropped to the deck, and his tail thump, thump, thumped with excitement. A mixed breed of multiple colors, he had floppy ears and big paws. Mallory immediately thought he was adorable.

"What a good boy you are," Mallory said, framing his face with her hands and scratching his ears.

"He loves that."

"I can tell," she said, laughing when Brutus's eyes seemed to roll back in his head from pleasure.

"You've made a friend for life."

The comment touched her and made her wonder if he was talking about the dog or him.

"Keep an eye on him while I get the boat ready?"

"Yep."

Quinn went up to the front of the boat to do something with the sails, and by the time he returned to the cockpit, Brutus was practically in Mallory's lap.

"Push him away if he gets to be too much."

"He's a love."

"He does good snuggle."

"He certainly does."

Quinn pulled the navy cover off the sails, cranked on something and tugged on some ropes, the combined effect raising a huge sail that flapped in the wind.

Brutus barked at the sail.

"Hush," Quinn said. "You know what that is." He went back up to the front of the boat to cast off the mooring, setting them free.

Mallory noticed that he was careful in the way he moved about the boat, as if he didn't entirely trust the prosthetic. She wanted to ask him about that but wasn't sure if the question would be welcome. Instead, she contented herself with petting Brutus and watching Quinn assess the wind and the sails as he took the big silver wheel to steer the boat. Ropes were adjusted until he was satisfied.

Then he sat on the other side of the cockpit, propping one leg on her bench and keeping one hand on the wheel. "Now you can say you've been sailing."

"I love it." She found the entire experience exhilarating, from the salty sea air to the glide of the boat through the blue water to the heat of the sun on her face and her handsome companion. "Thanks for taking me."

"Happy to have you." He glanced up at the sails, made an adjustment on the wheel and then turned his formidable gaze on her. "You doing okay?"

She nodded. "Sorry about that before. Sometimes… It's just hard to be reminded of what I was denied my entire life by my mother. My feelings toward her are very complicated these days, and of course, that makes me feel bad after everything she did and sacrificed for me. And it's compounded by the fact that she's not here anymore and can't defend herself."

"You can still appreciate the things she did for you while being angry about what she kept from you."

She smiled at him. "I can? Really?"

"Yes, I give you permission to do both at the same time."

"She was afraid he'd try to take me away from her."

"Did she have reason to fear that?"

"Not because of him. I think it was more because her parents disowned her when she got pregnant out of wedlock. That was a big deal back then. She probably panicked at the thought of ending up all alone."

"I've known him all of five minutes, and I can already say he doesn't seem the type to take a baby from its mother."

"I knew that right away, too, but she was young and alone and afraid. That's all I've got when it comes to defending what she did." She looked down at Brutus, who was now sleeping with his head on her chest and his body between her legs. "I keep thinking I've gotten over the anger, and then something will happen, like just now, to remind me of what I missed."

"And then you're mad all over again."

"With a dead woman who can't defend herself and who did everything for me."

"You should cut yourself a break, Mallory. What she did, for whatever reason she did it, was unfair to you and your father. Admitting that doesn't take anything away from what a good mother she was to you. If you can, try to separate them in your mind."

"You're absolutely right, and that's what I'm trying to do, but every so often, it gets muddied. I have a whole lot of emotions where she's concerned. Mostly I miss her and wish we'd had more time together. I don't know what I would've done without her when Ryan died so suddenly. She came out to San Francisco the day he died and stayed for a month."

"Maybe if you think about that stuff when the anger hits, you'll be able to reconcile it a little better."

"Maybe so."

"After I got back to the boat last night, I was thinking about you losing your husband the way you did and how awful that must've been."

"It's the worst thing that's ever happened to me, by far."

"I was wondering—and don't tell me if it's too hard to talk about—but how did you hear about it when it happened?"

Touched by his interest in knowing the details, Mallory shifted her gaze to the water rushing by the boat as she thought back to that long-ago day that had changed everything. "I was in the NICU with a set of micro-preemie twins, thinking the very worst thing that could happen to me that day would be losing one of them. It was a really complicated case, and my attending had put me in charge of their care, and nothing else, for my entire shift. I'll never forget what he said when he left me to do rounds. 'Don't take your eyes off them for a second, not even to pee or eat or anything until I get back.'"

"Sounds like a real prince among doctors."

"He was actually the best. I learned so much from him, but he was exacting, to say the least, and I never wanted him to be unhappy with me. So I did exactly what he told me to and watched over them like a hawk."

She took a deep breath before she continued. "One of the NICU nurses came in to tell me I'd received an urgent call from the surgical ward, asking me to come down there immediately. I had no idea why they'd want me there. What's funny is that it never occurred to me for one second that it was something to do with Ryan. I took my eyes off my babies to look at her, and the expression on her face told me whatever was going on, it was bad. She said my attending was on his way to take over for me, which scared me even more than I already was. By then I was certain I was about to get fired, although I couldn't for the life of me figure out why. The attending came rushing in a few minutes later and told me to go. Just go, he said. The nurse was a friend, and she went with me down to the surgical ward, where I was met by what seemed like the entire medical staff. One of them, Ryan's closest friend at work, put his arm around me and took me off to the side to tell me he'd collapsed in surgery.

"At first I thought, oh, good, he only fainted. We can work with that. But then I asked which room he was in, and his friend started crying. Even then, I still wasn't prepared for him to say that Ryan had basically dropped dead."

"Who would ever be prepared for that?" Quinn said softly. He turned the boat and switched to her side of the cockpit, nudging Brutus to move to the other side so he could sit closer to her. He raised his arm, and Mallory slid closer to him, loving the way his arm felt around her shoulders.

"I don't remember much after that. I have big blank spots in my memory."

"I don't remember much of anything for two weeks after I was injured. I swear that's the brain's way of protecting you from things you're better off not knowing."

"Probably. That day marked the start of a long downward spiral for me. I went from being a married doctor to widowed and, a couple of months later, unemployed when I couldn't work up the fortitude to return to a job I'd loved. I never stepped foot in that hospital again."

"Can't say I blame you."

"I lasted about six months in San Fran before I packed up our place and went home to my mother in Providence. The drinking got pretty bad after that, until my mom got my best friend, Trish, involved, and the two of them wrestled me into rehab. They saved my life, but you couldn't tell me that then."

"It started with pain meds for me after I was injured. I know what it's like to not want help that others are forcing on you."

"Mom and Trish did the right thing, but it was a long, hard-fought battle that was finally won the second time I went to rehab."

"What did the trick that time?"

"A counselor helped me see I was using alcohol to numb the pain of my loss rather than confronting the pain head on. So I confronted the pain head on, and that was tons of fun. But I was better afterward. Something clicked that time, and when I got out, I had no desire to go back to the way I'd been living before. That's when I started taking steps to become an RN and pick up the pieces of my professional life, such as it was."

"Why'd you decide to become a nurse rather than finishing your medical training?"

"I wanted to be more involved with patient care than I'd been as a resident. I used to envy the nurses who had a real rapport with the patients that we often didn't have the time to establish."

"I can understand that. As a trauma surgeon, I had very little contact with the patients under my care. I pieced them back together and handed them off to the clinical staff. The nurses did most of the heavy lifting."

"It won't be like that here, you know. You'll be very involved with all of them—and their families."

"Believe it or not, I'm actually looking forward to that. Hey, are you hungry?"

"I could eat something. Oh, and I brought some snacks that are in my bag."

"Take the wheel and keep it right where it is."

"Wait, you want me to *drive* the boat?"

"I want you to take the helm. If you're going to be a sailor, you need to learn the lingo. Come here. I'll show you how before I leave you in charge for a minute."

Mallory stood and took a second to get her sea legs under her before she joined him at the helm.

"Put your hands right here." He maneuvered them so she stood in front of him. Reaching around her, he placed his hands on top of hers and helped her gain a feel for how the wheel controlled the boat. "See?"

"Uh-huh." She wasn't sure how she was supposed to learn anything with him wrapped around her. Then he dropped his hands from the wheel, put his arms around her and kissed her neck.

"You're doing great," he said, his breath warm against her sensitive skin.

"I'm going to crash if you keep that up."

"No, you won't. I won't let you."

Mallory wanted to lean back against him, to let him hold her up when the load became too heavy to carry on her own. For someone who prided herself on fierce independence, that thought alone should've made her think twice. But with him pressed against her, she couldn't be bothered with anything as boring as thinking.

"You got it?" he asked.

"I hope so."

"I'll be quick."

Because it felt so good to be held by him, she wanted to ask him not to let go. But she didn't say that or anything when he left her in charge of the boat and went down to the cabin. Mallory had things under control until the sail caught a gust and the boat began to list to the side. "Quinn! What's it doing?"

"Heeling. Totally normal. Steer the boat into the wind if it becomes too much for you."

She did as he directed and marveled at how that slight adjustment righted the boat, but it also made the sails flap uselessly.

"Too much," he said. "Fall off a little bit the other way."

She made that adjustment and smiled when the sails filled, propelling them forward once again.

"You're a natural," he said when he came up with a tray of sandwiches, chips, fruit, cookies and bottled water.

"Sure, I am," she said with a laugh. "What do I do when we run out of water over there?" She nodded to the beach that was getting closer by the second.

"We tack, which is the sailing term for turning. Let me show you how."

He walked her through the steps from releasing the main sheet—which he said was another word for rope—and turning the boat, and how to always watch out for her head when the boom came across the cockpit. "It's too high to hit you on this boat, but that's not the case on all boats. You haven't lived until you've taken a boom to the skull."

"Sounds pleasant."

"It's not. Trust me on that. You want me to take over?"

"Not yet. I think I might be figuring it out."

He handed her half a turkey sandwich wrapped up in a napkin.

"Thank you. You're going to spoil me if you keep feeding me."

"I can live with that."

Brutus lay with his head on his paws, staring at Quinn, begging without making a scene. Quinn rewarded the dog's patience with a big piece of sandwich and a handful of chips.

"Something tells me that dog is frightfully spoiled."

"Ridiculously so," he conceded. "And I make no apologies for it."

"Nor should you. He's a good boy."

"He really saved me when I was at my lowest point after rehab when I was trying to figure out my next move. One of the nurses at the rehab facility suggested I get a dog when I was ready to. She said having a pet would force me out of my pity party and get me out for the daily walk I refused to take on my own. She was right about both those things."

"Nurses are wise, wise people."

"You don't have to tell me that."

"I had a question after last night, too," she said tentatively.

"What's that?"

"Your family wasn't notified when you were injured?"

"They were, or I should say Jared was. He was listed as my family contact when I was on active duty. They knew I'd been injured. I just never told them the full extent of it."

"I'm still trying to understand why you'd choose to go through such an ordeal by yourself."

"I didn't intentionally choose to go through it alone. It just sort of happened that way. At first it was about trying to save my leg, and then… After…" He sighed. "I felt like such a failure."

"Why? You couldn't help that you got an infection."

"No, but I still felt a profound sense of failure afterward. All my medical training, and I couldn't save my own leg. I'm not saying it was rational. It's just how I felt, and I didn't want anyone around me then."

"You were grieving."

"I guess. I'd also been away from home a long time by then—almost twenty years. I was used to doing things for myself." He stood to take a closer look at where they were. "We're going to need to come about again. You got this, salty dog?"

"Yep." Mallory pointed to the entrance to the Salt Pond, where the Coast Guard Station was located. "Can we go out there?"

"It might be a little sporty outside the pond. You up for that?"

"Define 'sporty.'"

"Windier, rougher, a little wilder." He waggled his brows to punctuate the statement, and the double meaning wasn't lost on her. Was exiting the pond a metaphor for walking on the wild side with him, too? And what exactly would that entail?

Mallory decided she wanted to find out. "Let's do it."

He talked her through the steps of navigating the boat through the narrow channel that took them out into open ocean, where the water was, indeed, sportier than it had been in the pond. Off in the distance, they could see a huge gathering of sailboats that Quinn told her was part of Race Week.

"Let's head over that way," he said, pointing toward the northern tip of Long Island. "Out of the way of the racing."

It took all of Mallory's concentration to keep the boat on course as they coasted over two-foot "rollers," as Quinn called them. To her, they were waves. The wind and the sun and the salt air made for an exhilarating experience, not to mention the sexy man who was taking such pleasure in watching her sail the boat.

"You really are a natural," he said.

"I don't know about that, but it sure is fun."

"I've created a monster. I'll never get my helm back."

"I'm totally hogging it. You want a turn?"

"Nope. It's much more fun watching you do it."

Mallory wasn't sure what got into her when she said, "I'm not sure I'm doing it right, though. You might need to come over here and check my work." As her not so subtle message registered with him, she took great pleasure in watching his brows rise above his aviators. It was all she could do to refrain from giggling.

After standing and taking a second to make sure he was steady on his feet, he moved like a stealthy cat, circling the helm until he was behind her. Resting his chin on her shoulder, he said, "From what I can see, you're right on course."

In for a penny… "I'm not so sure. You should probably take a closer look."

"Come to think of it, you might need a few adjustments. Here, let me help." Pressing his body to the back of hers, he reached for her hands on the big chrome wheel.

"That's so much better," Mallory said.

His lips nuzzled her neck, setting off a chain reaction throughout her body. "You were doing fine by yourself, but this is definitely better."

And wasn't that the truth? Being with him made her feel lighthearted and unburdened, two emotions that had been in short supply since her mother died and her life changed in ways she couldn't have predicted. After being further upended by the loss of her job, the last thing she ought to be feeling was euphoric the way she did right now, with a hot guy wrapped around her as she steered a boat through choppy seas. She'd been doing okay on her own. But this… This was so much better.

When she turned to tell him so, he kissed her, using his hand on her face to keep her there. She opened her mouth to his tongue and completely forgot that she was supposed to be steering the boat. The sails fluttered in the breeze as the boat foundered. Mallory couldn't be bothered with righting it, and apparently, neither could he. She turned completely so she faced him, resting her hands on his hips as his arms encircled her.

The boat bouncing in the waves jolted them apart and tested their balance.

Instinctively, Mallory held on tighter to him so he wouldn't fall.

He laughed when he assessed their predicament.

"Don't quit your day job to give sailing lessons, Doc," she said, smiling up at him as he reached around her for the wheel.

"No plans for that. Don't worry."

"I was doing great until my teacher distracted me."

He kept one arm around her while he got them back on course. "In my defense, I was enticed by my sexy student."

"I have no idea what you're talking about."

"Sure, you don't. What do you say we head for calmer water and drop the anchor for a while?"

"That sounds good to me."

He took control of the wheel but kept his arms around her as they sailed to the west side of Gansett and ducked into a little cove. "Be right back," he said when he went to drop the sails and the anchor.

Knowing now what she did about his ordeal with his leg, she marveled at the way he maneuvered on the boat. He moved carefully but didn't let his disability hold him back. There was much to admire in that, she thought, watching him as he returned to the cockpit, where Brutus was still sound asleep and Mallory waited eagerly for whatever came next.

# CHAPTER 13

"How's this?" Quinn asked of the scenic little cove.

"It's beautiful." The sun was warm, and the view of the rugged Gansett coastline exceptional.

"I found this place a couple of weeks ago and have come here a couple of times."

"You do all this by yourself?"

"Brutus is with me."

"You know what I mean. Do you ever worry about being out on the boat alone?"

"No."

Mallory immediately regretted the question. "I didn't mean to offend you."

He held out his hand to encourage her to join him on the seat. "You didn't."

She took his hand and sat next to him.

"I'm quite determined to do everything I did before as well as I did it then, and I'm getting there. The one thing I refuse to do is be afraid to do things because they might be hard, you know?"

"Yeah, I do, and that's a good way to be."

"So no, I'm not afraid to be out here by myself, but it's a lot more fun with you along for the ride." He tucked a stray hair that had escaped from her ponytail behind her ear. Keeping his eyes open and his gaze fixed on her face, he leaned in slowly to kiss her again.

Mallory reached for him and ended up reclined on the seat with him warm and heavy—and hard—on top of her as he kissed her with desperate thrusts of his tongue. She responded in kind, her tongue caressing his, and buried her fingers in the fine silk of his hair.

"Is this okay?" he asked, keeping his lips on hers.

As she nodded, she knew he meant the position as much as the desperate nature of their kisses. "It's okay."

"Good answer."

He tipped his head for a better angle and went back for more.

They kissed until her lips were numb and the rest of her body on fire for him. She worked her hands under his T-shirt and explored his muscular back, making him tremble from her touch. Good God, the man could kiss, and he made excellent use of the rest of his body by moving against her suggestively.

In the back of her mind, she thought perhaps she should put a stop to this or at least slow it down, but she couldn't find one good reason to do either of those things when it felt so damned good to be held and kissed by him. She'd forgotten how fun it could be to start something new and exciting with a guy, especially one as sexy and interesting as Quinn.

He withdrew slowly, continuing to tease her with his tongue and the slick movement of his lips over hers. "What're you doing to me?"

"Same thing you're doing to me."

"You want to take this somewhere more comfortable?"

"Like where?"

"Have you ever made out in a V-berth before?" As he spoke, he covered her face and neck with kisses before returning to her lips.

"Can't say that I have."

"You've been missing out."

"So this is something you've done a lot of?"

Smiling down at her, he shook his head. "Never on this boat."

"I hate to miss out on things."

Using his arms, he pushed himself up and off of her and then extended a hand to help her up. She took note of the huge bulge in the front of his pants and licked her lips in anticipation of what might happen next.

Mallory followed him into the cabin, giving him an extra minute on the stairs. He seemed to have the most difficulty navigating stairs and big steps, such as the one from the dinghy to the boat or the dock to the dinghy. Otherwise, except for the slight limp, you'd never know he'd lost part of his leg. He'd adapted amazingly well, and his upper-body strength was obvious when he used his arms to propel himself onto the V-shaped berth that was his bed.

When he extended his hands to her, Mallory stepped forward, took hold of his hands and moved into the space between his legs.

"Hi there," he said.

"Hi."

"Welcome to my bedroom."

"It's nice." With navy accents and shiny wood on the walls, the small room had a cozy, nautical vibe that Mallory found charming.

"You should've seen it when I first bought it. I had to refinish all the woodwork and re-cover all the cushions. It was a mess."

"You did a great job."

"It was a fun project. My brother and Lizzie thought I was nuts for taking this on at the same time I was overseeing the renovations at the facility, but this helped to keep me busy in my free time."

"You like to be busy?"

He nodded. "Keeps me from thinking too much."

Mallory thought about that for a second. Was that why she'd always kept herself so frantically busy when she was working? So she wouldn't have too much time to think about the things that hurt too much? Was that why her emotions, past hurts and new ones, had been so close to the surface in the last few months? Because she didn't have the enormity of her job to occupy most of her waking thoughts?

"What're you thinking?"

She shared her thoughts with him.

"Losing your job was a big deal in more ways than one."

"Months later, I'm still figuring out all the many ways it was a big deal."

He released her hands and raised them to frame her face. "There're lots of ways we can keep you busy so you don't have too much time to think."

"Like how?"

"More of this, for one thing." He kissed her softly, gently, tentatively, as if it were their first kiss all over again, as if they hadn't just been kissing each other's faces off outside. The sweetness totally disarmed her and had her swaying precariously on her feet. "Does that take your mind off your worries?"

"That takes my mind off everything, except you."

"Perfect. Come up here with me."

Using those strong arms, he scooted backward and made room for her to join him. Mallory kicked off her flip-flops, put aside her concerns about too much too soon and reminded herself that in the Summer of Mallory, there was no such thing as too much or too soon.

His pillows smelled like him and the cologne she would forever associate with him. He lay on his side, looking at her, seeming to wait for her to make the first move. Watching him watch her, Mallory decided that while this might be the Summer of Mallory, she wasn't about to become someone totally different overnight.

"What is it, exactly, that we're doing here?" she asked.

His eyes lit up with something resembling amusement, which she supposed was better than anger or disappointment that she would ruin such a moment with probing questions.

"What do you think it is?"

"You can't answer a question with a question."

"Yes, I can. I just did."

She scowled playfully at him. "I don't know."

"Do you always need to know what something means before you try it?"

"Usually."

He curled a strand of her hair around his index finger. "What do you want it to be?"

"I don't know that either. I'm not sure I'm in a good place for it to be anything other than fun. I don't even know where I'm going to be living in a few months—here or back on the mainland or what."

"That's fair enough." To his credit, he made no mention of the job offer. She appreciated that he wasn't pushing her on that. Not yet, anyway.

"Maybe so, but that doesn't tell me what *you* want it to be," she said.

"Last night, after I got back here, I realized that was the best night I've had since before I got hurt. Being with you and your family and friends… It was good."

"It was a fun night."

"I haven't done anything like that in a long time."

"Like what?"

"A date in which I make an actual effort to get to know a woman—and her family, in this case."

"So what's your normal routine?"

"I haven't had a normal routine in a couple of years, but before that, it was sort of hit and run. I deployed a lot, and when I wasn't out of the country, I liked to party, among other things. The seeds for my addictions were sown long before I got hurt."

"What else besides booze and pain pills?"

"I liked sex a little *too* much." He looked directly into her eyes. "Is that a deal-breaker?"

"Only if you haven't dealt properly with it."

"I haven't had sex in three years, if that tells you anything."

*Three years? Holy cow.* "Ummm, it tells me a lot of things."

He laughed—hard, harder than she'd seen him laugh yet. "Like what? Do tell."

"Like you must be about to blow."

That made him laugh again. "I've learned to control myself a lot better than I used to."

"What do you suppose was at the heart of that?"

"I had a big opinion of myself. Bad-ass trauma surgeon, saving lives for a living. I deserved to blow off steam in my free time, and I never had any problem attracting women who were willing to help me out with the steam-blowing."

Mallory tightened her lips, suspecting he wouldn't appreciate her laughing at his choice of words.

"I'm kind of a hot mess, sweetheart. You might want to think twice before you cast your net with me."

"I appreciate the warning, but I don't see a hot mess when I look at you."

"Oh no? What do you see?"

"A man who has traveled a difficult road and has taken positive steps to get his life in order and his body back in working condition." She squeezed his biceps. "Did you have arms like these before you were injured?"

"Not so much. They weren't flabby or anything, but I worked out hard in rehab to build up my upper-body strength to compensate for the loss of my leg."

"That doesn't sound like a hot mess to me. You've conquered addictions and lost your leg, and yet here you are, overseeing a huge new professional endeavor in a place that's all new to you while restoring a boat in your spare time and raising a very nice puppy. I don't think you give yourself enough credit."

"I kinda like the way I look to you. It's better than my view."

"I like the way you look to me, too." She ran a finger over the light stubble on his jaw and along his bottom lip.

He surprised the hell out of her when he pounced, biting her finger lightly but hard enough to startle and arouse her.

"You're so cute when you're surprised," he said, pushing up on one arm to kiss her nose and then her lips.

"I hate to tell you, but nearly forty-year-old women are not *cute*."

"You are." All signs of humor and teasing were gone when he zeroed in on her lips. "You're also gorgeous and sexy and funny and smart."

Mallory was so incredibly drawn to him, despite his past, despite the worrisome things he'd shared with her about his sex addiction, despite everything her better judgment might be telling her. She reached for him and brought him down to her, drawing him into a sexy, tongue-twisting kiss that quickly went from just another kiss to hands moving frantically, legs intertwining and bodies pressed tightly together.

Something had been decided between them in the last few minutes. What, she wasn't entirely sure yet, but it felt like it had the potential to be monumental. She hadn't expected anything quite like that when she accepted his invitation to dinner and then sailing, but it was happening nonetheless, and she wasn't exactly trying to stop it as she sent her hands on a greedy quest under his T-shirt.

He sucked in a deep breath when her hands connected with his skin and then quickly recovered his mojo with deeper, hotter, more intense kisses. His hand coasted over her ribs to cup her breast, his thumb rubbing her already hard nipple until it ached. Right when she was about to beg him to do that under her shirt rather than on top of it, he got the message, his hand moving fast to dip under her shirt and up to caress her breast. "Ah, damn, no bra?"

"It's built into the shirt."

"Best. Shirt. *Ever.*"

Mallory's laugh quickly became a moan when his talented fingers went to work on her already rigid nipple as he pressed his erection against her belly. Was she really prepared to throw all caution to the wind and let this play out to its natural conclusion?

He squeezed her nipple.

Hell, yes, she was prepared for all sorts of natural conclusions.

Then he was lifting her shirt over her head and replacing his fingers on her nipple with his equally talented lips. She could barely breathe as he worshiped her breasts, moving from one side to the other, as if that was the destination rather than a stop off on a much more significant journey. He seemed perfectly content to stay right there, to torment her with his lips and tongue and even his teeth. *God…*

She grabbed a handful of his thick hair and held on for dear life while he kept up the sensuous torture. "Quinn," she gasped, "you're making me crazy."

"Am I?"

"You know you are."

"What could I do to make you feel better?"

Incredulous, Mallory raised a brow. "Do I really have to spell it out?"

"A little direction would be welcome."

She reached for his hand and put it between her legs.

"*Ohhh*, third base. I'm a *big* fan of third base."

Even though she was insanely aroused, she couldn't stop the laugh he drew from her. "You're funny."

"Not usually. That's your influence."

Her heart gave a little jolt, knowing he'd had little to laugh about in recent years. "I'm glad to give you a reason to laugh."

His fingers found the heart of her desire and began to caress her through her jeans. "You do. I laugh more and smile more with you than I have with anyone in far too long."

"If you keep saying things like that to me, I'm going to forget that we're supposed to be having casual fun here."

"What would happen then?"

"I might get attached to you."

"I'd be okay with that."

Mallory closed her eyes and released a deep breath. "I'm afraid of getting too involved when I don't know for sure where I'll be in a few months."

"You said this is the Summer of Mallory, right?"

"That's the plan."

"Maybe it could be the Summer of Mallory and Quinn?"

"That could get messy."

A dirty smile unfolded slowly across his handsome face.

"Stop! You know what I mean."

He tugged at the button to her jeans and drew the zipper down slowly, going for maximum effect—or that was how it seemed to her. Laying his hand flat on her abdomen, he said, "What do you say? Should our summer of fun start now?"

How was she supposed to make a decision like that when his hand was so perilously close to the place that throbbed with desire for him?

Without moving his hand, he drew her nipple into his mouth, licking and sucking on the tip until Mallory arched into him, all but begging him to make the next move. He didn't disappoint. He yanked her pants down and drove his hand inside her panties, nearly finishing her off before he ever touched her. Then he made it better by actually touching her and proving he knew what he was doing.

Mallory grasped his arm, her fingernails sinking into his skin while he kept up the suction on her nipple and coaxed her to an orgasm that had her crying out and thankful there was no one around to hear her—except him, of course. Her pleasure came to a sudden halt when Brutus landed on top of them, knocking the air from her lungs at a critical moment.

"Damn it, Brutus," Quinn said, removing his hand from between her legs to fend off the excited puppy. "Your timing sucks."

Mallory laughed even as she gasped for air. "He shouldn't be able to make that jump yet."

"There's a lot of things he shouldn't be able to do," Quinn said with a scowl for the dog, who yipped playfully at him. "Spoiled brat." Looking down at Mallory, he said, "Sorry about that."

"No apology necessary." She glanced at Brutus and then at Quinn. "Is there any chance he might take another nap?"

"Not for a while."

She could see the genuine regret in the way his mouth twisted with displeasure. Letting her gaze travel down the front of him to the bulge in his pants, she licked her lips and then looked up at him again. "I guess I'll just have to owe you one, then."

His eyes heated with desire. "I guess you will."

Mallory pulled her pants up and tried to find her shirt.

He took her by surprise when he cupped her breast and dragged his thumb over her nipple. That was all it took to restart her recently satisfied libido.

Brutus whined and then barked.

Moaning, Quinn dropped his head to Mallory's chest. "That means he has to pee."

While laughing at his distress, she caressed his hair. "Your baby needs you."

"My baby is a pain in my ass." Quinn found her shirt and handed it to her, his regret apparent. "Come on, Brutus. I'll take you to the beach." At the word "beach," Brutus leaped off the bunk and headed outside. "You want to come?"

"You guys go ahead. I'll stay here."

He gave her a quick kiss. "Be right back."

# CHAPTER 14

Mallory watched him go, noting the way his jeans molded to his sexy ass. She'd wanted a moment to herself after the earth-shattering orgasm. She hadn't experienced anything like that—with a guy, anyway—in years. It was nice to know it was still possible. The kind of craving desire she'd experienced with Quinn reminded her of being with Ryan. It had been like that between them from the start, and she'd never had that kind of physical connection with another man, until now.

That was kind of scary to acknowledge. She'd only recently met him, had spent time alone with him exactly three times, and already she recognized feelings she'd had only once before. The idea of having what she'd had with Ryan and potentially losing it again made her entire body cold with fear.

She put her clothes back to rights, sat up and smoothed her hair with trembling hands. If there was one thing she knew for certain, it was that she couldn't possibly survive that kind of disaster a second time. She'd barely survived the first time.

Being with Quinn was fun and exciting, but it was also risky, and she needed to keep her eye on the ball where he was concerned. Protecting herself and her damaged heart had to be paramount. Brutus had actually done her a favor by interrupting them before things went any further.

She needed to take a step back, to really think this through before she got any deeper into a relationship she hadn't expected to have. The Summer of Mallory was about having fun, not getting serious, and this thing with Quinn, whatever you might call it, had serious written all over it.

By the time he and Brutus returned from the beach in the dinghy, Mallory had regained her composure and her determination to consciously control whatever happened next rather than going with the flow and being sucked unwittingly into his alluring web. If she was going to end up in that web, she would do so intentionally, not because her hormones went spastic whenever he kissed her.

Brutus came bounding up to the cockpit well ahead of Quinn, who moved slower and more carefully as he went from the smaller boat to the bigger one.

Mallory put all her focus on the puppy, who licked her face with an exuberance that made her laugh. He was so damned cute.

"He's salting on my game," Quinn muttered.

"What does that mean?"

"He's getting what I want."

"Which i ?"

"More of  u." Reaching for the hem of his T-shirt, he pulled it up and over his head, reveali  a spectacular man chest, chiseled abdominal muscles and tattoos that banded  und his biceps that she hadn't noticed the first time she saw him shirtless the   y they met.

Mallory  nt stupid in the head as she took in the perfection before her and quickly forgo  er resolve to be deliberate and intentional where he was concerned.

*Screw th*

Quinn s  the way she looked at him, and it had a predictable effect on him. Goddamned  rutus. If it wasn't for him, Quinn might still have his hands and lips on her na  d body. But maybe Brutus had done him a favor interrupting them before things  ot completely out of control.

He hadr  been with a woman since he lost his leg, and he wasn't sure he was ready to   someone see his stump, to make himself that vulnerable, even if

Mallory would be the ideal person to be the first. She was a nurse. She'd seen it all. Nothing about his injury would be new or particularly revolting to her.

Even knowing all that, he wasn't sure he was ready to go there. It was ironic, really, when you considered his sex-addicted past when the notion of being afraid to have sex would've been so foreign to him as to be laughable. He used to get laid so much and so often that he'd forget who he'd slept with and who he hadn't. He certainly wasn't proud of that chapter in his life, but he'd learned through a lot of therapy to own it as part of his history.

He'd put that version of himself so far in the past that he no longer bore any resemblance, except physically, of course, to that guy. Mallory made him want to be the best version of himself, and he was determined to be that for her, which meant taking it slower than he ever had before with a woman.

He had many good reasons to take his time with her. One, she wasn't sure if she'd be staying after the summer, and he was committed to being here for at least the next couple of years. Two, he hadn't been intimate with anyone since he lost his leg. And three, he refused to fall into old habits of letting his dick do the thinking for the rest of him.

So while his dick was very, *very* interested in the amazing, sexy Mallory Vaughn, the rest of him needed to take a pause and not let things get out of control the way they had earlier, until he was sure he was ready to take the next step—and that she was, too. Underneath her enthusiastic response to him, he'd sensed her reticence, even if her actions had indicated interest.

They both had a lot on the line and carried deep scars they didn't need to make worse with a summer fling gone wrong.

He'd taken his shirt off because he was hot, but now he recognized his error in the hungry way she studied his bare chest. Her hungry stare had his dick standing up to take notice of her. *Stand down,* he ordered his wayward appendage, grimacing when said appendage told him to fuck off and surged to full mast. Naturally, she noticed that, too.

Sighing, Quinn sat next to her in the cockpit.

She drew her legs up and wrapped her arms around them, the protective pose not lost on him.

"Speak to me," he said, nudging her with his shoulder.

After a long silence, she said, "That got kind of intense before."

"Good word for it."

"I'm not sure that's the best idea."

Quinn wanted to say it had felt like a pretty damned good idea to him, but he didn't. "How come?" He had his reasons for taking a step back, but he wanted to hear hers.

"I'm in this really weird place right now with so many things up in the air, and getting serious with someone is the last thing I ought to be doing until I figure out the other stuff."

"So let's slow it down."

"Define 'slow it down.'"

"We hang out without tearing each other's clothes off every chance we get. For now, anyway."

Mallory laughed at his blunt statement. Her infectious laughter made him smile. With her face resting on her folded arms, she looked over at him. She could've passed for twenty something in that position, and in that position, and he found himself incredibly drawn to her. "And you'd be okay with that?"

"Sure, I would. I'd be okay with anything that gets me more time with you, even if it's hands-off platonic time."

"I feel like I'm being hot and cold with you, and that's not my intention."

"I know that." He reached for her hand and linked their fingers. "So what do you want to do now?"

"Can we maybe sail some more? That's really fun, especially when you help me stay on course."

Quinn smiled at her. "Sure, we can do that."

Quinn dropped her off at home around five o'clock, leaving her with a platonic kiss on the cheek and a promise to "hit her up" later. The sailing had been spectacular, as had the company. They'd settled into fun, flirty banter for the remainder of the afternoon, and Mallory had been relieved that they were on the same page with taking it slow.

She'd loved her first time on a sailboat. Quinn had been a patient teacher as he showed her the secret to keeping the boat on an even keel. If only it was as simple as a small correction here or there to keep the rest of her life on an even keel. Mallory had been "heeling" hard since her mother died, with her orderly life tipped upside down by the discovery of her father and his family. She'd only begun to right the ship when she lost her job and her footing once again.

Now that she was settled into her little cottage on the island for the summer, she could begin to make the subtle adjustments that would put things back where they belonged.

Here she was at nearly forty, trying to reinvent herself once again. The last time she'd been forced to reinvent herself and her life, she'd been shattered by grief that she'd tried to numb with alcohol. This time, she was facing reinvention stone-cold sober and eyes wide open to the many possibilities. Those possibilities certainly included Quinn, but she would proceed with caution with him.

As she showered, she thought about how easy it would be to say to hell with caution and dive headfirst into what was sure to be a thrilling... *something*... with him. An affair? A relationship? A summer sex fest? Twenty years ago, she wouldn't have had a second thought about jumping into whatever it turned out to be. Now she knew the pain of heartbreaking loss all too well and was wise enough to protect herself from ever having to feel that pain again.

Mallory dried her hair and took note of the slight windburn that colored her cheeks and nose. She dressed in jeans and a sweater and grabbed the brownies she'd baked earlier before heading out to Janey and Joe's house for the welcome-home dinner for Evan and Grace. She was also looking forward to spending more time with Grant, Stephanie, Dan and Kara, all of whom had spent the winter in Los Angeles, but were home now for the summer.

After just a couple of days here, it was already apparent that her personal life on Gansett was going to be much busier than life in Providence had ever been. Every night, or so it seemed, there was something going on in her family and their group of friends. That was fine with her. The more she got to see of her siblings, their families, her cousins, uncles and, of course, Big Mac and Linda, the happier she was.

Every time she was with them, she learned something new about her family, whether a funny old story from when her siblings were growing up, or something Big Mac and his brothers had done when they were young men. She added each new detail to her growing list of information about them. Sometimes she still felt like a voyeur who didn't actually belong among them. But that was her hang-up, not theirs. They'd never been anything other than completely welcoming to her.

On one of her earlier visits, she'd made a point of figuring out where everyone lived. Janey and Joe's house was located less than a mile from Mac and Maddie's. The Cantrells' big contemporary home was lit up with interior and exterior lights. Cars, pickup trucks and a random motorcycle that she recognized as Evan's were parked outside the house.

Mallory gathered her jacket, purse and the plate of brownies and went up the walkway to the front door. She wasn't sure if she should knock or let herself in, but after having witnessed the way the others walked right into each other's homes, she twisted the knob and stepped into chaos.

Though she was used to the McCarthy family volume by now, it still came as a surprise to someone who was raised without siblings or cousins. Life with her mom had been like being raised in a church compared to what it was like to be with the McCarthys.

"Mallory," Janey called, "you made it. Come in!"

She hung her coat and purse on one of the hooks in the entryway and headed for the kitchen, which was where all the noise was coming from. In addition to their immediate family, Ned and Francine Saunders were there, as were Luke Harris and his pregnant wife, Sydney, who was seated on a chaise in Janey's family room, and Grant's lawyer friend Dan Torrington and his fiancée, Kara Ballard. Joe's mom, Carolina, her husband, Seamus, and their boys Jackson and Kyle, came in shortly after Mallory arrived.

Big Mac intercepted Mallory after she said hello to everyone. "Good to see you back on dry land," he said with a kiss to her cheek.

"Did you get my text that we were back?"

"I got it, and thank you for that." His brows furrowed. "You were out there a long time."

"Oh, um, were you keeping tabs on me?" she asked, secretly pleased by his obvious concern.

He looked at her with an "are you crazy?" expression on his face. "Of course I was."

"Well, I'm fine, and we had a great time."

"You liked sailing, then?"

"I loved it. Quinn said I had a good feel for the boat, whatever that means."

"That's high praise from someone who knows what he's doing."

"You aren't harassing Mallory, are you, dear?" Linda asked when she joined them.

"I am not 'harassing' her," he said with a wink for Mallory. "I'm simply inquiring as to how her day on the water was."

"You had fun?" Linda asked.

"I did."

"What's going on with that doctor fellow?" Big Mac asked.

"Mac!" Linda said. "Leave her alone."

"I'm her father. I can ask her what's going on." To Mallory, he said, "Can't I?"

Hearing him say that, even after all this time, was like being a kid on Christmas. "You can certainly ask, and I can certainly decline to reply."

Linda laughed while he scowled playfully. "She's got you figured out, my love."

"What do we know about this guy anyway?" he asked, brows furrowed.

Amused by his paternal bluster and moved by his protectiveness, she said, "We know that he served his country, moving from enlisted to trauma surgeon in the army, for twenty-one years before retiring due to injury. We know he's one of five kids, his brother is the billionaire Jared James, and he's been hired to be the medical director of the new long-term healthcare facility here on the island. The next time I see him, I'd be happy to ask if I can reserve a room for you for when you need it."

"When I need it," he said with an indignant huff while Linda laughed again. "That'll be the day." He eyed her shrewdly. "He treats you nicely?"

Mallory's mind went immediately to the V-berth and the memory of his hand inside her panties. She was sure that her face had to be bright red. Thank goodness for windburn. "Yes," she said, swallowing hard, "he treats me very nicely. He's a good guy. You don't have to worry."

"Clearly she has no idea what it's like to be the father of daughters," he said to his wife.

For the second time, Mallory spontaneously kissed his cheek. "This daughter loves having a father who cares about who she's dating."

"You say that now," Janey commented when she joined them. "Wait till he crashes your date because you missed your curfew."

Mallory knew the smallest pang of regret that she would never have such an experience with him. "He did not do that."

"You know he did! It was when I first started dating David, and we were standing outside the gate at home when he came out and started talking about his gun collection—"

"He has *guns?*"

"No," Janey said, scoffing. "What he has is a big mouth and a vivid imagination."

Mallory bit her lip to keep from dissolving into laughter she knew her father wouldn't appreciate.

"First of all," Big Mac said sternly, "you were fifteen years old and thirty minutes late getting home. Second of all, you were not just standing outside the gate. You were swapping spit with that boy, and he's lucky I didn't kill him for daring to put his filthy hands on my Princess."

Janey rolled her eyes at Mallory. "You see what I had to put up with?"

"I do, and I feel your pain." She wished she could've experienced the same things Janey had with him and tried to tell herself that it was enough that he was flexing his paternal muscles now. But it would never be enough, and once again, the resentment toward her mother flared up inside her in the form of a sharp pain in her chest.

"How about a drink?" Janey said. "You probably need it after putting up with him."

"*Him* is in the room, and *he* can hear you maligning *him*, Princess."

"I'm very sorry, Daddy."

"You are not."

Linda patted his chest. "Don't pout, babe."

"What's Dad pouting about now?" Evan asked when he came over to give Mallory a hug. "Good to see you."

"You, too. Welcome home."

"He's mad because his daughters are calling him out on his BS," Linda said.

"Oh, I love when that happens," Evan said, rubbing his hands together.

"And here I actually missed you while you were gone," Big Mac said, drawing a huge smile from his youngest son.

"Good to be home?" Mallory asked her brother.

"So good. If I never see another hotel room, that'll be just fine."

"Don't listen to him," Grace said as she came over to hug Mallory. "Buddy put us up in the finest hotel rooms you've ever seen. Our little place here looks like a hovel after all that luxury."

"That hovel is our home, love," Evan reminded her as he put his arm around her.

"Until we buy that big new house you promised me from all the royalties from *my* song." The song "My Amazing Grace" that Evan had written had gone all the way to number one on the country charts, spurring Buddy's request for Evan to join him on the recently completed tour.

"Ohhh, when is that happening?" Linda asked.

"Soon," Evan said, with a smile for Grace.

"With lots of bedrooms for my future grandchildren, I hope," Big Mac said.

"You know it," Evan replied. "What've you got in inventory, Ned?"

"Whateva ya want," Ned replied. "I got something fer everyone."

"Nice to have the island's land baron in the family at times like this," Grace said.

"Anything fer you, sweetheart," Ned said.

The front door opened, and Adam came in by himself. Mallory hadn't known him long, but she could see at first glance that something was different about him. Apparently, the others saw it, too.

"Uh-oh," Evan said in a low tone. "What's up with him, and where's Abby?"

"I have no idea on either count, but you can bet I'm going to find out," Linda said.

# CHAPTER 15

The others greeted Adam, asked for Abby, who was not feeling well, and worked together to get dinner laid out for the masses.

Mallory was never quite sure how they made it look so simple to feed so many people. Everyone contributed, and they ended up with a delicious feast every time. Joe had grilled steak, and there were potatoes, salad, garlic bread, pasta salad and baked beans. The sea air had given her an appetite, and everything looked good to her.

Dan and Kara entertained them with stories about their ongoing efforts to keep her mother from taking over their wedding.

"She's furious that we're having a clam bake for the meal," Kara said.

"How come?" Maddie asked. "That sounds yummy."

"She wants filet mignon and foie gras and other stuff I can't pronounce," Kara said. "We want casual and fun and low-key. She wants highfalutin, high style and high stress. She's driving me crazy! Oh, and the kicker? She thinks it's rude that I didn't invite my sister Kelly, you know the one that stole my boyfriend who's now her husband?"

"Um, point of order, babe," Dan said. "He's your *ex*-boyfriend."

Kara laughed along with everyone else. "Make that my *ex*-boyfriend."

"Much better," Dan said, patting her leg.

"So what do you do about that?" Janey asked. "If you don't want her there, you shouldn't have to invite her."

"That's what I say," Kara replied. "But she goes on about how Kelly is my sister, and it's time for bygones, yada, yada."

"Sorry," Sydney said, "but the bitch stole your man. Er, um, your *ex*-man. She doesn't get to come to the wedding, sister or not."

Everyone agreed with Sydney.

"You see why I choose to be part of this family rather than the one I was born into?" Kara asked.

"And we're damned happy to have you," Stephanie said.

Mac ended up seated next to Mallory at the large picnic table on Janey and Joe's back deck. He had his daughter Hailey on his lap and was sharing his dinner with her.

Mallory noticed how he cut tiny bites of steak for the little girl and kept a careful watch over her to make sure she was taking one bite at a time. Hailey's wispy blonde hair fluttered in the light breeze, forming a halo around her sweet face.

"She's a hungry girl," Mallory said.

"She's growing. At least that's what Maddie says. She's hungry all the time lately." He glanced at Mallory. "Dad said you went sailing with Quinn James today."

News traveled fast on Gansett, especially within the McCarthy family. "Yep."

"How was that?"

"Fun."

"So you like him?"

"You could say that."

"Does that mean you're officially seeing him?"

"I wouldn't call it that." Not yet anyway... Mallory put down her fork and looked over at him. "What do you really want to ask me?"

"I don't know, exactly. There's something about him that makes me think he has secrets. He's closed off. Remote."

Mallory suspected she already knew most of Quinn's deep dark secrets, and since he'd been forthcoming about what he'd already told her, she had no reason to believe he wouldn't be about other stuff, too. "Just because someone isn't an open book like you are doesn't mean they're a bad person."

"I know. It's just that I've worked with him for months, and I don't feel like I know him any better than I did on day one. That gives me pause."

And it gave Mallory further insight into how someone who was usually very reserved had shared an awful lot with her on their two dates.

"Just be careful, okay?"

"Are you playing the part of the big brother, little brother?"

"Nah. Maddie told me to stay out of it, but I needed to say something to you."

"I appreciate your concern. I really do. I've never had brothers to look out for me before."

"I told my lovely wife that you'd appreciate me looking out for you."

"Look out, yes. Interfering, no."

"Gotcha." He wiped Hailey's face and helped her with a sippy cup. "I get that this family thing is all new to you, but being the little brother is all new to me. It's not just you who's had to do some adjusting."

"I know. You've all been very generous about welcoming me into the family."

"I hope you know that we're all very happy to have you. At first, it was strange and surprising and…"

"Weird?"

"Yeah, that," he said with a laugh. "But it's not weird anymore. You fit right in like you've always been here."

Oh dear sweet baby Jesus, he was going to make her cry.

"Mallory? What? What did I say?"

She shook her head and fought a valiant but ultimately unsuccessful battle to contain her tears.

"Mac!" Maddie swooped in. "What did you do to her? I told you to leave her alone about Quinn James!"

"Mallory is seeing Quinn James?" Evan asked. "Jared's brother?"

"Since when?" Grace asked. "Why doesn't anyone tell us anything?"

And then Mallory was laughing as she mopped up her tears.

"What did he say to make you cry?" Maddie asked, glaring at her husband.

"He was being sweet," Mallory said.

"I didn't mean to make you cry," Mac said.

Mallory rested her head on her brother's shoulder. "They were happy tears."

"You're almost as weird as Janey, and that's saying something."

"I heard that!" Janey called from across the deck.

"Pipe down, brat. I'm talking to my *other* sister."

"Don't listen to a word he says, Mallory," Janey said. "It's all BS."

"Not all of it," Mallory said with a warm smile for Mac.

"Where're Tiffany and Blaine tonight?" Grace asked.

"They've got the meeting with the prosecutor in Jim's case tomorrow morning," Maddie said of her sister and brother-in-law. "She wasn't in the mood for a party, but she said to send her love and to tell you welcome home."

"They'll be glad to put that behind them," Evan said.

"We all will." Dan Torrington held up the hand that had been slashed by Tiffany's knife-wielding ex when he showed up at Dan and Kara's engagement party looking for trouble. He'd found it and had been charged with multiple felonies that could see him disbarred, if not thrown in prison.

"On a happier note, you guys have to hear the stories of Evan's groupies from the road," Grace said, making her husband groan.

"Oh, do tell," Grant said. "Were there panties involved?"

"So many panties!" Grace said. "Everywhere we went, they'd leave them in envelopes at the front desk of the hotel, along with their photos and phone numbers."

"No way," Mac said. "What'd you do?"

"Mostly I had to talk my lovely wife out of committing homicide on a daily basis."

"I would've loved to have been a fly on the wall for that," Joe said.

"I admit, my jealousy wasn't pretty," Grace said to laughter.

"It's a good thing my Gracie was there to protect me," Evan said, "or it might've gotten ugly."

"When she saw online pictures of them chasing you around?" Mac asked.

"Definitely then," Evan said while the others howled with laughter.

"Some of them have zero self-respect to be chasing after a married man," Grace said indignantly.

"Look on the bright side," Evan said. "You got a whole bunch of new panties out of it."

"*Ewww*," Stephanie said. "You did *not* keep them?"

"Hardly," Grace said, rolling her eyes at her husband. "I burned them."

"Should we tell them how you set off the smoke alarm in one hotel?" Evan asked.

"We said we'd never speak of that again," Grace retorted.

They were still laughing at that when a voice Mallory couldn't immediately identify called out from inside. "Where's the prodigal son?"

Evan lit up with pleasure at whoever it was and jumped up to greet the new arrivals.

Alex Martinez came onto the deck with his pregnant wife, Jenny, in tow along with Jared and Lizzie James and… And Quinn, who looked around at the group until he found her, his gaze locking on her with an intensity he didn't try to hide from her curious family members, many of whom immediately homed in on the hungry way he stared at her.

While Alex and Jenny hugged Evan and Grace, Mallory tried to pretend like she wasn't caught in Quinn's cross hairs, and of course Mac noticed the way he was looking at her.

"So you're not officially seeing him, huh? Does he know that?"

"Shut *up*, Mac."

He busted up laughing, and Hailey, that traitor, joined in, her deep belly laugh bringing a smile to Mallory's face.

Joe got drinks for the new arrivals and then lit the fire in the big stone fireplace on the far side of the deck. Everyone pulled up chairs, and somehow, Quinn ended up next to her.

"Fancy meeting you here," he said, nudging her with his shoulder.

"At my sister's house?" she asked, raising a brow to call him out.

His low chuckle made her blood feel warm and thick as it moved through her veins. "Touché."

"So you admit that you came here to see me?"

"I came here because the people I was with wanted to see your brother and his wife."

"Ouch. That hurts."

Under the cover of darkness, he took hold of her hand. "And because I knew you'd be here, and I missed you after I left you earlier."

"Good save."

His laughter drew the attention of every set of eyes on the deck that were related to her, and a few that were related to him.

Jared stared at him, seeming astounded to hear Quinn laugh.

"Can we get the superstar to play for us, or is he all burned out?" Alex asked.

"You can't afford me anymore," Evan retorted to laughter as he reached for the guitar that had been propped in the corner.

"Ohhh, he's too good for us," Alex said.

"You know it," Evan said, tuning the guitar.

"When do you guys have to leave again?" Jenny asked.

"Not until September," Grace replied.

"Oh good." Jenny rested her hands on her rounded belly. "You'll be here when all the babies arrive."

"I thought Buddy only toured in the summer when his kids were out of school," Stephanie said.

"He used to do that, but now his kids are older, and they want to be home with their friends in the summer," Grace said. "So he and Taylor stay home with them in the summer, and she joins the tour once in a while whenever she can get away."

"That's a hard way to live," Grant said.

"They know it's only for a few more years until their youngest is through high school," Evan said. He strummed the guitar, his head tipped, and listened carefully, making sure the tuning was to his liking.

He looked up to smile at the arrival of Josh Harrelson, who'd run Evan's Island Breeze Studios in his absence, and Fiona Connolly, who had taken over Grace's pharmacy while she was away.

Evan put down the guitar to greet Josh with a bro hug while Fiona got the real thing from Grace.

"Thank God you're back," they both said at the same time.

"Does that mean you missed us?" Evan asked.

"Big-time," Fiona said. "I can't handle the summer without you, Grace."

"Well, you've got me for the summer."

"Who wants to hear some new music I wrote on the road?" Evan asked.

After a chorus of "me," he picked up the guitar again and began to strum the intro to a song that he said was called "Smells Like Nostalgia."

*We lived, in a vacation*
*But I still dreamed of Grand Central Station*
*Black-bodied angels, need to get high*
*Money's their drug, in their high-rise*

*Black cherry, taste in your mouth*
*That November we drove down South*
*I had some coffee, while you took a drag*
*We were so brilliantly, perfectly sad*

*You look like how the Fourth of July made me feel*
You're not real, you're not real
You smell like what nostalgia probably would
You're too good, you're too good

Brown leather seats in your sedan
*I can still see them, well, I think I can*
*I heard your headlights had finally burst*
*I heard it was the worst*
*Summer of your whole life*
*I guess I'm just that type*

*Wind whipping through my hair*
*I can taste freedom, every inch of the air*
*I Angela Chase all my dreams*
*But only find teenage wastelands it seems*

*You look like how the Fourth of July made me feel*
*You're not real, you're not real*
*You smell like what nostalgia probably would*
*You're too good, you're too good*

*You feel like holding my breath for too long*
*It feels wrong, it feels wrong*
*And you taste like defiance on the tip of my tongue*
*I feel young, I feel young*

*Pink sky, blue clouds*
*Where are you now? Where are you now?*

Mallory immediately loved the vibe of the song, especially the lyric, "You look like how the Fourth of July made me feel."

Everyone loved the song and applauded enthusiastically when Evan played the final notes.

"You think we can get that one recorded this summer?" he asked Josh.

"My studio is your studio."

"Did I hear a reference to Angela Chase in that song?" Mallory asked.

"You sure did," Evan replied. "That was Grace's contribution."

"'My So-Called Life' ruled my universe back in the day," Grace said.

"Mine, too!" Mallory said. "I devoured that show!"

"I've never even heard of it," Stephanie said.

"Oh my God," Grace said. "Two words: Jared. Leto."

"One more word," Mallory added. "Netflix."

"I'm on it," Stephanie said.

Evan continued to play while the others began to chat again.

Hailey toddled past Mallory, tripping on her own feet. Mallory lunged forward to save the little girl from falling and ended up with her niece cuddled up to her, thumb in her mouth, eyes heavy and sleepy.

"She's adorable," Quinn said.

"We like her."

"How old is she?"

"She'll be two in July." Mallory had long ago committed the birthdays of the little ones to memory and was working on trying to remember all the other ones, too.

"You want one of your own?"

Startled by the question, she looked over at him. "Might be too late for me."

"You and I both know it's not too late if everything still works."

"It still works, but I haven't thought about having kids of my own in years." Not since her husband died so young and so suddenly, she thought, but didn't share that with him. She didn't have to. She could see that he understood what she meant. "What about you?"

He shrugged. "Never even came close to that, but you never know what might happen. I wouldn't say no to a little cutie like Hailey."

Imagining him holding his own little girl made her heart do a funny lunging thing that left her breathless and aroused. For God's sake. How did he do that to her with words alone?

"You want to get out of here?" he asked in a low tone that only she could hear.

"No, I do not want to 'get out of' my sister's home."

His face lifted into a sexy half smile. "Poor choice of words. Let me rephrase. Would you like to go somewhere that we can be alone? Is that better?"

Mallory had to restrain the urge to squirm in her seat. Yes, she wanted to be alone with him. Very much so. But she was still concerned about too much too soon with him. "I thought we agreed to slow it down."

"We did."

"Soooo…"

"Are you planning to jump me the second we're alone?"

"No!" *Maybe.*

"All right, then. Nothing to worry about."

Despite the casual way he said that, Mallory suspected she had everything in the world to be worried about where he was concerned.

# CHAPTER 16

Needing a breather from the crowd on the deck, Adam went into the kitchen to get a beer, popped it open and drank half of it in one big gulp before catching himself. Getting wasted wouldn't fix anything, even if it would take his mind off his problems for a few hours. He was tempted until he thought of Abby at home alone, hiding out while she licked a new set of wounds. Adam had wanted to stay home with her, but she'd insisted he come to welcome Evan and Grace home.

He leaned against the counter, looking down at the floor, wishing he could wave a magic wand and make the terrible ache he and Abby were both feeling go away.

"What's wrong, Adam?" his mother asked when she came into the kitchen. He had no doubt that she'd come looking for him. "And don't say it's nothing when I can clearly see it's something."

Resigned to having to share their devastating news with his family, Adam said, "Abby and I heard from the fertility specialist who saw her last week. She basically told us it's never going to happen the old-fashioned way, even with fertility treatment."

"Oh no," Linda said on a long exhale. "I'm so sorry."

Shrugging, he said, "It is what it is, but it's a bitter pill for Abby to swallow."

"And you. It is for you, too."

"I'm far more concerned about her than I am about me. Every time we get bad news about her health, she withdraws so deep into herself that I can't reach her no matter how hard I try."

"Is that why she didn't come tonight?"

He nodded. "It's hard for her to be around the baby boom knowing it'll never happen for her."

"That's totally understandable."

"It's not that she doesn't love all the kids—the ones we already have and the ones on the way."

"I know that, Adam." She came to stand next to him, curling her hands around his arm and resting her head on his shoulder. "You don't even have to say it."

"Can I say something totally selfish, and do you promise to never repeat it?"

"Of course to both."

"I can feel this situation changing her, and I'm so afraid the changes are permanent. She's remote, as if she's sealed off her heart, and she hardly ever smiles or jokes, and she…" She recoiled from his touch, not that he could tell his mother that. "She's not herself."

"And she won't be for a while, not until she finds a way to deal with this news and to figure out a new way forward. It's a blow, Adam, especially to someone who wants children as badly as she always has."

"It makes me feel like shit that I can't give her the one thing she wants more than anything."

"It's not your fault, and it's not hers. The universe has a different plan in mind for you two."

"I hope it's okay to say I'm a little pissed off at the universe right now."

"It's okay, and this too shall pass. You two are going to be marvelous parents someday. I know that in my heart of hearts. It may not happen the way you planned, but it *will* happen."

Her certainty made him feel a tiny bit better. "I should probably get home. I don't like to leave her alone for too long when she's so down."

"Be patient with her, honey. She'll come around, and she'll remember that you didn't ask for more than she could give you at this difficult time. I'll never forget the way Dad was with me after we lost our first baby. He just held me and let me take the lead, and somehow we got through it together."

"After Mac and Maddie lost Connor, he told me about what happened to you guys. I had no idea."

"It's hard to talk about even almost forty years later. One thing I learned from that is things work out the way they're meant to. If that baby had lived, we wouldn't have had Mac."

"And that would be bad?"

She nudged his ribs. "Stop!"

Adam chuckled. "Just kidding."

"You get what I'm saying."

"Yeah, I do, and I appreciate the advice. This is a tough one."

"It's probably the toughest thing you'll deal with as a married couple, and your marriage is still very new. Be gentle with each other."

"I'm trying."

"That's all you can do. Be there for her and love her through it."

"Thanks, Mom." He finished his beer and set the bottle on the counter. "I'm going to head home."

"Drive carefully, sweetheart, and let us know if you need anything."

He hugged and kissed her. "We will, thanks." Adam went outside to say his good-byes to the others and drove home thinking about what his mother had said. He knew she was right, and eventually they'd get past the initial shock and despair, but he hoped they still had a marriage left when they got there.

Abby had turned on the outside lights for him at their new A-frame-style home on the island's west side. The small gesture filled him with an unreasonable feeling of hope that maybe the woman he loved beyond reason was still inside the quiet, remote person she'd become over the last few months. With each new piece of bad or difficult news since she'd been diagnosed with polycystic ovary syndrome, or PCOS, she'd retreated further into herself, leaving him feeling lonely for her even when she was sitting across from him at dinner or lying next to him in bed.

He went into the house through the garage and noted the flicker of the TV coming from the family room. Abby was curled up on the sofa, her eyes glued to the TV, though he doubted she had any idea what was on.

"Hey," he said.

"Oh, hi, you're home. How are Grace and Evan?"

"They're good. They said to tell you they can't wait to see you."

"That's nice. Glad they're home safe." She pulled her feet back so he could sit with her on the sofa.

"Everyone missed you."

"I'm sorry. I wasn't up for the mob scene tonight."

"I understand." He reached for her hand and was encouraged by the way she curled her fingers around his. "Let's go to bed."

"Okay," she said, but with none of the enthusiasm she'd once had for going to bed with him.

She shut off the TV, and he helped her up, leading her through the dark house to the stairs. In the daylight, they had a spectacular view of the water. At night, they could lie in bed and look at the stars through the high windows. They'd both loved the house at first glance, especially the extra bedrooms it had for the children they still hoped to have. What a difference a month could make.

They stood at side-by-side sinks in the master bathroom and brushed their teeth. Abby put on the moisturizer that she applied every night and brushed her long dark hair until it shone like spun silk.

*Fuck this shit and the polite silence. Fuck the distance and fuck the bullshit.*

The thoughts came one right after the other, and rather than take the time to think through what he should do about them, he acted, taking her into his arms and kissing the stunned expression right off her face. He kissed her until he felt her yield, until she began to kiss him back, until the desperate, grinding feeling that she was slipping away from him began to let up ever so slightly.

Without breaking the kiss, he turned her toward their room and walked her backward until the bed connected with her legs, taking her down and him with her. He kissed her like it was the first time all over again, and he so remembered their first kiss, as if it were yesterday rather than more than a year.

For the longest time, she'd been Grant's girlfriend and then his ex. It had never occurred to Adam that Abby could be the love of his life. And then he'd run into her on the ferry when both of them were at the lowest point in their lives. After that, it hadn't taken long to be unable to picture his life without her at the center of it. And damn it, that was where she still belonged.

He kissed her until he was certain she was no longer thinking about doctors or fertility or malfunctioning reproductive organs. Then he moved to her neck, kissing and nibbling on the sensitive skin there.

Her arms encircled his neck, her fingers sinking into the hair he wore a little too long because she liked it that way.

Adam began pulling at her clothes, desperate for more now that he'd had a taste of her sweetness. He could never get enough of her, especially lately when she'd been so hard to reach. No more of that. No more. He helped her out of her T-shirt and cupped her breasts. Normally, he'd want to arouse her to the point of madness before he proceeded to the main event, but tonight he needed the connection more than the madness.

He removed her panties and quickly pulled off his own clothes, the whole time waiting for her to stop him, to say not tonight or give him some other reason why they shouldn't the way she had so many times recently. Thankfully, she didn't say anything and held out her arms to welcome him into her embrace when he came down on top of her with nothing between them now but love and need.

What did it say about the state of their marriage that he couldn't remember the last time they'd made love? That was going to change, starting right now and every night going forward. Things were going to be the way they used to be, back when they were first together and couldn't keep their hands off each other, before they knew they couldn't have children, before everything had changed between them.

He took himself in hand and entered her slowly and carefully, giving her time to adjust while watching her face for any sign of distress. But he didn't see distress when he looked at her. Rather, he saw serenity and a small smile that was another thing he hadn't seen in a while.

His plan was working. Adam gathered her up into his arms and held her close to him while he made love to her.

"Missed you so much," he whispered. "I don't need anything else but for you to be happy."

She hugged him tighter, moving with him as he moved in her, and for that moment, everything that was wrong felt right once again.

"Love you, Abby. More than you'll ever possibly know."

"Love you, too. I'm sorry, Adam."

He kissed the words off her lips. "Shhh. No apologies. We're starting over right now, and it all begins right here with us." Withdrawing from her, he kissed his way down the front of her until he was settled between her legs. He made love to her with his mouth and fingers, paying attention to the subtle changes in her breathing that told him she was close to release.

"Give it to me, sweetheart." He sucked hard on her clit, keeping it up until she clamped down on his fingers and cried out from the pleasure he gave her. Moving up, he entered her again and drew in a sharp breath at the intense desire he felt every time with her.

She ran her hands down his back to slide over his ass, pulling him deeper into her.

That was all it took to let go of his self-control and give in to the overwhelming pleasure. Afterward, he came down on top of her, breathing hard and more in love with her than he'd ever been.

After a long moment of silence, he said, "That, right there, is what matters. We matter. You and me. *Us.*" He raised his head and looked down at her, brushing the hair back from her face. "I know you're heartbroken, and I get it. I really do."

"I don't think you can understand being the one who can't have children, but I know you want to."

"What I want, Abby, is for our marriage not to be ruined by disappointment. What I want is my wife, with children or without them, I want *my wife*. I want *you*." He used his thumbs to brush aside her tears. "Please don't do this to me, Abby. Don't make me have to practically force myself on you to get things back on track."

"You didn't do that."

"That's how it felt. At first."

"I made an appointment with Kevin."

Astounded, Adam stared at her. "You did?"

"Is that okay, him being your uncle and all? It's not like we have a million therapists to choose from here."

"It's fine with me. Of course it is. Whatever you need to feel better."

"I want to feel better, Adam. I know it might not seem like it, but I do. I hate feeling like this."

"How, exactly, do you feel? I'd really like to know."

"Like… Like the world has ended or something."

"It hasn't. We still have everything we had before this happened. We haven't actually lost anything until we lose us."

"Do you think that's going to happen?"

"I'll never, ever, *ever* let that happen. There is nothing you could do, nothing in this universe that could make me want to be anywhere but right here with you." He continued to brush back her hair and wipe the tears from her face. "I'll fight for you and for us with everything I have, but you have to help me, Abby. I can't do this by myself. Can you help me?"

"I couldn't do this without you. Don't let me push you away. Don't let me get away with it."

Adam smiled down at her. "I won't, baby. I promise."

"We've still got it," she said, returning his smile as she ran her hands over his back.

That got his motor running all over again. As he made love to her a second time, he vowed to keep making love to her, morning, noon and night, if that was what it took to keep disappointment from ruining their marriage.

# CHAPTER 17

After most of the crowd had departed, Mallory stayed to help Janey do the dishes and clean up the kitchen. While she washed, Janey dried. Joe was upstairs trying to get PJ settled for the night. When Mallory insisted on staying to help clean up, Quinn had told her to text him when she was heading home and had left with his brother and sister-in-law.

"Where's your menagerie tonight?" Mallory asked of Janey's special-needs pets that no one else had wanted until they'd found a loving home with her.

"In the basement where they can't get underfoot and steal all the food when no one is looking." She took a bowl from Mallory and began to dry it. "You really don't have to do this. We can finish in the morning."

"I don't mind at all, unless you want me out of here."

"Not even kinda. If you go, I'll have to help Joe. PJ will think it's playtime, and I won't get any sleep at all tonight—and sleep is all I want lately."

"You're feeling good, though, right?" Mallory had been horrified to hear of the placental abruption Janey had suffered giving birth to PJ. That she might've died before Mallory ever had a chance to meet her was an unbearable thought.

"I feel great. Just tired, but that's normal, especially the second time around when you already have a little one to take care of."

"What're your doctors saying about your risk level?"

"It's high, and I'm going to be on full bed rest at Uncle Frank's house in Providence during the last month."

"That's a good idea."

"I keep telling myself that, but the idea of a month in bed makes me crazy. I had bed rest with PJ, too, and about lost my mind."

"It'll go by fast."

"I guess, and it's comforting to know we'll be minutes from the hospital."

"Sounds like you've got it all worked out."

"Except the part where I'm scared out of my mind that something will go wrong again."

"You'll be right where you need to be. Try not to worry."

"Can I ask you something, and will you tell me the truth?"

"Of course," Mallory said. "Anything you want."

"As a nurse, do you think I'm crazy for letting this happen again after what I went through the last time?"

"No, Janey, I don't think that at all."

"Really? Because sometimes I wonder if the whole world doesn't think Joe and I are insane for having another baby."

"What happened with PJ is very, very rare. There's no reason to believe it's going to happen again, and if it does, it won't happen on a remote island without an OB and a surgical suite. I'm sure your doctor will recommend a C-section around thirty-eight weeks, just to be on the safe side."

Janey nodded. "That's what they said."

"All right, then. No chance for disaster."

"I just have to get to thirty-eight weeks without a disaster."

"Try not to think the worst. It's not good for you or the baby."

"I know. I've been meditating and breathing and doing everything I can to stay calm, but nine months is a long time to be anxious. It's taking a toll on Joe, too. He tries to hide it, but he's not sleeping well and is tightly wound."

"You two need a couple of nights away from it all. Why don't you take off and go somewhere? I'll watch PJ."

Janey stared at her as if she had three heads. "Are you for real?"

"Yes," Mallory said, laughing. "I'm sure the grandmothers would help, wouldn't they?" She did have a new job, after all, and couldn't be with the baby around the clock.

"They would and Joe gets a small break after Race Week before the season officially kicks into high gear. Are you sure?"

"Yes!" Mallory laughed. "Go for it. I gotcha covered. My offer even includes pet sitting."

Janey hugged her. "You're the best sister I've ever had."

Once again, Mallory had to blink back tears because of something one of her siblings said to her. "Same goes."

"I'll talk to Joe and see what we can work out. I know it can't be this week because Seamus and Carolina are going to the mainland to finalize their adoption of Jackson and Kyle, so Joe is on duty at work."

"That's so exciting," Mallory said. "They must be thrilled."

"They are. The boys are adapting so well, all things considered. Losing their mom at such a young age was a terrible blow, but Seamus and Caro have done what they could to fill the void. And now they're making it official. I hear there's a party to celebrate soon."

"Never a lack of parties around here."

"And people say island life is boring."

"Not in this family."

"So tell me... What's up with you and the hunky Dr. James?"

"Ummm, we're friends?"

"With or without benefits?" Janey asked.

Mallory laughed at the blunt question. "Is this what it's like to have a sister?"

Janey nudged her. "You know it. Answer the question."

"With partial benefits. For now, anyway. We have the same exact birthday. That's kind of cool, right?"

"That's very cool. You should go for it with him. He's a stud."

"Are you talking about me again, babe?" Joe asked when he came into the kitchen.

Janey rolled her eyes. "You wish."

Joe flexed his biceps. "Am I or am I not a stud?"

"I think that's my cue," Mallory said, gathering her purse and the plate she'd brought with the brownies.

"Guess what, Joseph? My lovely sister has offered to stay with PJ so we can get away by ourselves for a couple of nights. What do you say?"

"I say can we go now?"

Both women laughed at his quick reply.

"How about in a week or so when I get used to my new schedule on the rescue?" Mallory said.

"I suppose I can wait that long," Joe said. "That's nice of you, Mallory. Thank you."

"I'm looking forward to some time alone with my nephew. I've got lots of spoiling to do."

Janey groaned. "He's already spoiled rotten."

"No such thing." Mallory hugged Joe and walked with Janey to the front door. "Thanks for a fun night."

"Thanks for the cleanup help."

Mallory zipped her jacket. "No problem."

"Hey, Mallory?"

"Yeah?"

"I just wanted to say…" She paused, seeming to collect her thoughts. "When I first heard about you, I didn't react the way I should have, and I just want you to know that I'm really glad you're here and that I have a sister. I always wanted one while growing up with the four animals we call brothers, and... I'm, well, I'm glad you're my sister."

Deeply moved, Mallory hugged her. "Thank you so much for that. I couldn't have dreamed this family, but I'm so happy to be part of it and to have you as my baby sister."

"As long as you don't call me brat, we're all good."

Mallory laughed. "I'll try to refrain."

Janey pulled back, and they both dabbed at their eyes. "So is your stud doctor making a house call tonight?"

Shaking her head, Mallory said, "Good *night*, Janey."

With her heart full after the night with her family, she got into her car and debated whether or not she should text Quinn. At this hour, a text could be construed as a potential booty call, but she'd promised to let him know when she was heading home, so she went ahead and sent the text.

*On the way.*

She put the phone in her purse and concentrated on driving, resisting the temptation to see if he'd replied.

"You're so incredibly tense," Dan said to Kara as he massaged her shoulders. He'd brought her home right after dinner at Janey and Joe's because he could tell she wasn't in a partying mood tonight. Now he had her positioned in front of him in bed and was trying to help her relax. "Your muscles are like rocks."

"It's wedding stress. I can't take much more of it."

"I have a suggestion that might not win me any points with my future mother-in-law but will win me all sorts of points with my future wife."

"I can't wait to hear this."

"Stop taking her calls. Stop reading her texts. Just stop everything with her."

"You want me to stop speaking to my mother a week before our wedding?"

"Well, I don't *want* that, but she's making it impossible for you to enjoy what should be the happiest time in your life, and I find that highly unacceptable."

Kara turned her head so she could see him behind her. "I love when you go all lawyerly on me."

"Then how about I file an injunction prohibiting her from contacting you until after we say 'I do'?"

"As much as I love the thought of that, I'd hate to have you stuck in her cross hairs, too. It's bad enough that I'm there."

"I'd happily take a bullet for you."

"Don't even say that. I've had enough of you being injured to last me a lifetime."

His low chuckle drew one from her, too. "That's what I want to hear. Laughter and happiness and nothing but pure joy, which is what I feel when I think about being married to you."

"I can't wait to be married to you. I just wish the wedding hadn't turned into such a circus."

"The wedding could be an actual circus with a big top, elephants and clowns, and I wouldn't give a flying fuck as long as you were there to marry me."

"You mean that, don't you?"

"I mean it."

"So you're suggesting I let the wedding turn into a circus?"

"I'm suggesting you do it exactly the way you want it and ignore anyone who tries to deter you from having what you want on *your* day. And PS, babe, we're paying for it, not them, so we get to do exactly what *we* want." He'd insisted on paying for it so she could have it her way, thus the months of back and forth with her mother, who wanted to control the whole thing.

"That's true."

"So, no more calls or texts or fights with your mother?"

"No more."

"That's my girl."

"I hope you know what a shit show you're marrying into with my family."

"I'm not marrying them. I'm marrying you, the one person in this entire world I can't live without. If that means taking on the Ballard family shit show, too, then sign me up."

"You're crazy, you know that?"

"How can I not know when you've been telling me that since the day we met?"

She rested her head on his shoulder, and he put his arms around her. "I have an awful feeling that Kelly is going to show up whether I invite her or not."

"So what? Let her see how happy you are with the rich, handsome stud you landed while she's stuck with Matt the cheater for the rest of her life."

Kara laughed so hard her body shook with it, which pleased him endlessly. "Not sure which part of that was funnier—you calling yourself a rich, handsome stud or her being stuck with Matt the cheater for the rest of her life." She wiped laughter tears from her eyes. "In case I forget to tell you this, I'm so glad you forced yourself on me until you wore me down and got me to fall in love with you."

"I'm afraid I have to object to your terminology. There was no 'force' involved. Rather, I employed a combination of devastating charm and a level of perseverance never before required with any woman to get you to fall madly in love with me. It was a tough battle at times, but well worth it in the end."

"You're too much, Torrington."

"Maybe so, but I'm just enough for you, and I can't wait to marry you."

"I can't wait either."


Seated with Jared and Lizzie on the back deck of their house, Quinn scratched Brutus behind the ears and enjoyed the fire Jared had lit. "Outdoor fireplaces are all the rage on this island, huh?"

"We love ours," Lizzie said. "After I saw Alex and Jenny's, I asked Jared to build one for us."

"And whatever my lovely wife wants, she gets," Jared said with an indulgent smile for his wife who was cuddled into his lap as usual.

"Oh hush. As if you don't get what you want, too."

Quinn put his hands over his ears. "Lalalalala. Can't hear you."

Lizzie giggled. "You're one to talk. I saw you snuggled up to Mallory tonight. What gives, big brother?"

Quinn loved his brother's wife. He truly did. She was perfect for Jared and had brought much-needed balance to his insane life. Quinn barely recognized the man that Jared was now—relaxed, decompressed and crazy in love with his adorable wife and her passionate desire to help people in need. Only because he loved her so much did he indulge her nosiness. "I was not *snuggling* with anyone."

"Semantics. What's up with her?"

"I don't know yet."

"But you admit there's *something* up?"

"Lizzie," Jared said with exasperation. "Leave him alone."

"You leave *me* alone," she retorted. "You know I need the info on everything that goes on around here."

"Sorry, bro," Jared said. "At least if she's badgering you, she's not badgering me."

"You love when I badger you."

Quinn put his hands over his ears again. "Lalalalala. Make it stop."

Lizzie giggled some more. "If you spill the beans, I won't have anything to badger you about."

"I promise," Quinn said, "that when there are beans to spill, you'll be the first to know."

"I can live with that," Lizzie said.

"Thank goodness," Jared said. "Can we talk about other stuff now?"

"Like how your parents want to come visit?" Lizzie asked.

"They do?" Quinn asked, shocked to hear that.

Jared nodded. "They said if Mohamed won't come to the mountain…"

"I assume I'm playing the role of Mohamed in this drama?" Quinn asked.

"You assume correctly," Jared said, "and PS, thank you for sucking me into your drama."

"It's not intentional. Trust me on that. When are they coming?"

"They said sometime this summer, so we have time to prepare."

Quinn had tried to be a dutiful son. He called home every Sunday without fail and sent gifts for birthdays, holidays and his parents' anniversary. But he hadn't actually seen them in far too long and had felt guilty about it for a while now.

He was saved from having to further discuss his parents' upcoming visit when David Lawrence and his fiancée, Daisy Babson, pulled into the driveway in front of their garage apartment next door and came over to say hello.

"You're back!" Lizzie said, jumping up to hug David and Daisy. "Did you have a good trip?"

"We did," Daisy said. "It was nice to be off the island for a couple of days, and we got to see Marion, too."

"When she says it was nice to be off the island, she means it was nice to have access to stores," David said. "Lots and *lots* of stores."

Daisy laughed. "It's true. I went a little wild buying stuff for our new house and the wedding."

"That sounds like fun to me," Lizzie said.

"Not me," Jared added.

"Or me," David said. "But if Daisy is happy, so am I."

"Awww," Lizzie said, "you two are so cute. Don't forget we've got your caterer coming out on Tuesday to talk wedding plans."

"How could we forget?" Daisy said. "We're so excited to finalize everything."

"When's the big day?" Quinn asked.

"September," Daisy said, "but the time is flying by. Thank goodness we're doing it at the Chesterfield, and Lizzie is taking care of everything for us."

"Almost everything," Lizzie said. "Did you get a dress?"

"I did, and I love it."

Lizzie clapped her hands. "Fantastic! I can't wait to see it."

"I can't wait to show you. I was by myself when I bought it, and no one has seen it yet."

"I offered to give an opinion," David said, "and was schooled about the superstitions surrounding these things."

"Which you should've known since this isn't your first time being engaged," Daisy said with a teasing smile for him.

"Everything about this time is different." He put his arm around Daisy and kissed her. "I had nothing to do with planning that wedding. I wasn't even here."

"Ancient history," Daisy said, smiling up at him.

"I meant to ask, how was Marion?" Lizzie said.

"Not great," Daisy replied glumly. "She's definitely declined since we last saw her. She didn't recognize me at first."

"That's so sad," Lizzie said with a sigh. "Alex and Paul are talking about moving her home once our facility is open."

"That'd be a blessing for them to have her closer," David said.

"They're so grateful for what you all are doing with the facility," Daisy added. "They can't wait to move her back to the island."

"I've been thinking we should name the facility for Marion," Lizzie said. "She's the one who inspired the idea."

"That'd be amazing," Daisy said. "Alex and Paul would be so thrilled."

"That's a great idea, hon," Jared said. "I like it."

"Then it's done," Lizzie said. "I'll let Alex and Paul know tomorrow."

Daisy hugged her. "Thank you so much for honoring Marion in this way."

Lizzie returned Daisy's embrace. "It's so nice to be able to do something with Jared's obscene fortune to make things better for people we care about."

While everyone else laughed, Jared huffed. "There is nothing *obscene* about my fortune." Though his tone was indignant, his expression was full of love for his irrepressible wife.

"We're off to bed," Daisy said. "See you all in the morning."

"Good night," Lizzie said for all of them.

# CHAPTER 18

"Tell me more about this Marion who inspired our facility," Quinn said after David and Daisy went up to their apartment over the garage. "How does Daisy factor into the story?"

"One day, Marion wandered off and ended up in town in a rocking chair on Daisy's front porch."

"She went from their place to town by herself?" Quinn asked.

"Yeah, and she was barefoot, so her feet were all cut up. That's when the guys realized it was really getting bad and they needed to make some changes. They hired Hope to be her live-in nurse."

"Home nursing didn't work out?"

"It did for a while," Lizzie said, "but the specialist recommended in-patient care, and the mainland was their only option. They're tied to the island because of their landscaping business, so it was an awful quandary for them."

"Enter my gorgeous wife with the idea for a facility out here," Jared said. "Someone mentioned the former school as a possible site, and she had me out there at seven o'clock the next morning."

"I don't believe in sitting on a good idea."

"It's a great idea," Jared said, "and it's going to immediately benefit our friends, not to mention so many others."

"Naming it for Marion is a nice touch," Quinn said.

"Thanks," Lizzie said. "I'm glad you agree."

"Just FYI," Jared said, "it wouldn't matter if you didn't agree."

Lizzie elbowed her husband in the ribs, drawing a grunt of laughter from him. "Ow."

"Be nice to me, or you'll regret it at bedtime."

"Yes, my love."

After staying with them over the holidays, Quinn knew how loud bedtime could be in this house. His phone lit up with a well-timed text from Mallory. *On the way.*

"That's our cue, Brutus," Quinn said, standing slowly and giving his leg a second to adjust.

Brutus let out an enthusiastic "woof."

"Is that code for booty call?" Lizzie asked.

"Jared, do something about her."

"Sorry, bro. I've done what I can, but she's incorrigible."

"Thanks for a fun night, you guys," Quinn said. "Talk to you tomorrow."

"Bye," they called as he walked toward the dark driveway. He was almost to his truck when he stepped into a small hole in the yard and pitched forward. It happened so fast, he didn't have time to react and hit the ground hard, his shoulder taking the brunt along with his bad leg, which wrenched within the prosthetic and slammed against the ground, making him scream from the pain.

Brutus barked and then licked his face as he whimpered in concern.

"Quinn!" Jared called out to him as he ran across the yard. "Oh my God, are you okay?"

The pain was so intense, Quinn could hardly breathe, let alone speak. He held up a hand to let Jared know he was okay.

"Lizzie, go get David!" Jared dropped to the ground next to Quinn. "Tell me what to do. I don't know what to do."

Quinn was trying not to be sick from the pain. "Give me a second."

In the background, Quinn heard footsteps pounding down the stairs that led to David's apartment.

"Give him some room," David said. "Talk to me, Quinn. What hurts?"

Everything? "I wrenched my bad leg. I'm okay."

"You're not okay," Jared said. "Let's get you inside where David can check you out."

The one thing Quinn didn't want was anyone checking out his leg. He could do that himself. But he was too shaken after the fall to get behind the wheel, so he let Jared help him up, and between him and David, they got him inside while Lizzie and Brutus followed. His prosthesis was still in place, but pain radiated from the stump for the first time in more than a year. *Fuck.*

Quinn hated having to rely on anyone for anything, especially mobility, but his leg hurt so bad that he ceded to them, letting them do the work to get him settled on the sofa.

"Your lip!" Lizzie said. "It's bleeding!"

Quinn touched his fingers to his lip and discovered she was right. He must've bitten it when he fell. "Sorry, everyone. Stepped in a hole and lost my balance. Nothing to worry about."

Despite his assurances, they hovered over him, and David asked if he could take a look. Here it was, the moment of truth he'd tried to avoid with his family. "So, um, here's the thing… I lost my right leg, just below the knee, two years ago, and I have a prosthetic that was jolted when I fell, thus the screaming. Hurt like a motherfucker."

Jared stared at him, his face devoid of expression. "You *lost* your leg?"

"Yeah."

"And you didn't think to mention that to anyone?"

"It's kind of a long story."

"We've got all night, because you're not going anywhere in this condition."

*Mallory. Damn it, he needed to text her.* "I think I dropped my phone out there. Can you grab it for me, Lizzie?"

"I'll be right back."

Quinn took advantage of the reprieve to close his eyes and focus on breathing.

"Jared," David said, "will you give us a minute alone?"

"Um, yeah," his brother said, but Quinn could hear the reluctance in Jared's voice.

"Why don't you let me take a look?" David said.

Quinn would prefer that no one ever looked at it, but he gave a brief nod to give David permission to pull up the cuff of his khaki pants to reveal the prosthetic that sat just above where his knee should be.

David made quick work of removing the prosthesis. When he gently touched the stump to examine it, Quinn sucked in a breath and broke out in a cold sweat.

"You're going to have some bruising that'll make it painful to wear the prosthesis for a couple of days. Do you have crutches?"

"I've got some in my office."

"How about I ask Jared to get them for you?"

"I think he's been drinking."

"I can drive," Jared called from just outside the room. "I quit drinking a couple of hours ago."

"So much for doctor-patient confidentiality," Quinn grumbled.

David smiled. "He's worried about you."

"I know."

Lizzie returned with the phone and brought it into the living room, stopping short at the sight of his prosthetic standing next to the sofa. Thankfully, David had covered his stump after he looked at it. Quinn watched as Lizzie tried and failed to not stare at the artificial leg.

"The phone, Lizzie?" he said.

"Oh. Right. Sorry." She handed it to him. "I'll, um, just be in the kitchen with Jared if you need us."

"Thank you." He wrote a quick text to Mallory. *Took a damned fall and hurt my bad leg. Stuck at Jared's. Sorry about tonight.*

She responded right away. *Oh my God! Are you all right?*

*I will be. Hurt my pride more than anything.*

*I'm so sorry. Let me know how you are later.*

*I will.*

"So about the crutches?" David asked.

"Yeah, I guess I need them."

"I'll send Jared after them." David got up and left the room, leaving Quinn alone to ponder the many ways this situation totally sucked.

Jared came into the room, car keys in hand. "I'll be right back."

"I'll be here."

"I can't believe you didn't tell me or any of us about this."

"Sorry."

"What did you think we would say?"

"To be honest, I wasn't thinking about anyone but myself. Maybe that makes me a selfish bastard, but that's all I was capable of at the time. Then a year went by and then another one, and there was never a time when it felt right to say, oh by the way, I lost my leg a couple of years ago, but I never told you about it."

"You've always been a lone wolf, Quinn, and I've tried to give you the space you needed, but knowing you went through something like this all alone… Well, that makes me hurt for you."

Before Quinn could reply, Jared turned and walked away. A minute later, Quinn heard the roar of Jared's Porsche starting up outside.

"Fuck," he muttered under his breath. Despite what Jared had said, Quinn could tell his brother was hurt to have been kept in the dark about the full extent of his injury.

"Do you need anything?" Lizzie asked softly.

"How about a couple of painkillers and a glass of water?"

"Of course. Coming right up." She returned a minute later with the water and pills, which he took right away. It'd been quite a while since he'd taken pain meds, and he hated that he needed them again. "Thanks."

She perched gingerly on the far end of the sofa. "Do you need anything else?"

"Just a do-over of the last half hour."

"I'm so sorry you fell. I told Jared he needed to fix that hole in the yard, and he was going to do it next week."

"Not your fault, sweetheart. Don't worry about it."

"I... I'm really sorry. About your leg and everything you went through."

"Thanks. Jared's pissed."

"He's hurt more than anything and sad to think of you enduring such an awful ordeal by yourself."

"I get that it's hard for you guys to understand, but that's how I needed it to be at the time. It wasn't my intention to leave anyone out. It was more that I wouldn't have been able to handle being invaded by my family when I had all I could do to deal with everything else that was happening. I'm not sure if that makes sense, but it's the only explanation I have."

"You don't owe us an explanation, Quinn. You did what was best for you, even if it might not have been what was best for everyone else."

"I'm glad you understand. Maybe you can help me out with Jared."

"I'll do what I can."

Someone knocked on the back door, and Brutus let out a menacing growl.

Lizzie got up to answer the door. "That might be David coming back."

Quinn couldn't believe when she returned with Mallory in tow or how upset and concerned Mallory seemed to be. "What're you doing here?"

He watched her eyes shift to the prosthetic and appreciated that she didn't linger there. Instead, she gave him her full focus. "I heard you could use a qualified nurse," she said with a small a smile.

Quinn appreciated her subtle attempt to make light of the situation. He held out his hand to her, and she came across the room to take hold of it.

She knelt next to the sofa. "Are you okay?"

He wondered if she realized that he could tell she was taking a visual assessment of him as a medical professional rather than potential lover. Once a nurse, always a nurse. However, she was here not as a nurse. She was here because of the relationship they'd been forming over the last few days, and that was what mattered to him. "I'm fine. Sorry to upset everyone."

"It wasn't your fault," Lizzie said. "We knew that hole was there, and we should've fixed it before now."

"It was no one's fault," Quinn said. "Just a stupid accident."

Lizzie's phone rang in the other room, and she ran to get it.

Quinn could hear her reminding Jared of the code to the lock at the building.

"Come home with me," Mallory whispered. "Let me take care of you."

Moved by her offer as well as the caring way in which she looked at him, Quinn nodded. "I don't need to be nursed, but I'd love to come home with you."

"Good." She leaned forward to kiss him. "Scared me to hear you were hurt."

"That's because you like me."

"I never said that."

"Yes, you did."

"When did I say that?"

"When you came rushing over here in the middle of the night to check on me."

"It's hardly the middle of the night. It's not even midnight."

"You like me," he said again with a cocky grin that had her rolling her eyes and calling to Lizzie over her shoulder. "He's fine. Don't let him tell you otherwise."

He squeezed her hand. "I'm fine now that you're here."

She let out a deep breath when she seemed to realize he was really okay. Seeing the prosthetic standing next to the sofa must have been a jarring reminder that despite the many ways he'd overcome his disability, a simple fall was anything but for him.

He relied on humor to defuse the tension, but he was sure she saw right through that to the strain that still gripped him.

She stayed right by his side until Jared returned with the crutches a few minutes later.

He came into the room, said hello to Mallory and leaned the crutches up against the sofa.

"Thank you, Jared," Quinn said. "If it's okay with you guys, I'm going home with Mallory."

"To your home or hers?"

"Hers. I can't manage the boat on crutches."

"You know you're welcome to stay here, right?"

"Yeah, I know, and I appreciate it."

Jared gave a curt nod and left the room.

"He's still pissed," Quinn said to Mallory.

"Give him a day or two to get his head around it. He'll be fine."

"I hope so," Quinn said, and he meant that. He'd greatly enjoyed the time he'd spent with Jared and Lizzie since he'd lived on the island and had felt closer to his brother than ever. He'd hate to have something like this come between them now.

Mallory helped him up and held the crutches for him while he got his bearings.

He hadn't touched the crutches in more than eighteen months, and using them now brought back memories he'd much rather forget.

Seeing him standing up, Brutus went crazy, running all around, darting between his legs and making a menace of himself.

Mallory grabbed hold of the dog's collar. "Easy, buddy. You don't want to knock Daddy down."

"Would you, um, get that, too?" He tipped his head toward the prosthetic.

"Sure, no problem."

He made his way slowly and painfully out of the living room and went toward the kitchen, where Jared and Lizzie were sitting at the table. "Sorry about all this," Quinn said.

"Please don't apologize," Lizzie said. "It's not your fault."

"On the bright side, at least we know about your leg now," Jared said with a bitter twist to his tone.

"Jared—"

"We'll talk tomorrow," Jared said. "It's late, and everyone's tired."

"Okay."

Jared walked them out, staying on his left side while Mallory took the right.

This time Quinn stuck to the sidewalk and driveway rather than the lawn, which was what he should've done the first time around. It was habit to take the quickest path, and he was still learning that the quickest path wasn't always the best one when you had a prosthetic.

Standing beside Mallory's car, he handed her the crutches and got into the passenger side. He had a sudden memory of rehab, where he'd been taught to do the most mundane things, such as shower and get into a car, with only one leg. He'd been doing pretty well pretending he still had two good legs, until one wrong step brought him right back to reality.

Brutus leaped into the backseat and made himself comfortable. Lizzie brought the bag Quinn had packed with the dog's food and toys when he brought him to their house earlier.

"I never asked you if it's okay if he comes, too."

"Of course he can come. I know you guys are a package deal."

"Thanks for having us."

"No problem."

"You say that now…"

"You don't scare me, and neither does Brutus." They waved to Jared and Lizzie as Mallory backed the car out of the driveway and headed for her place in town.

"Thanks for coming. You didn't have to do that, but I'm glad you did."

"I had to see for myself that you were okay."

"Because you like me."

She huffed out a laugh that had him smiling in the dark. Without her coming to his rescue, he wouldn't have had a single thing to smile about after his fall. But now the fall seemed almost secondary to her running to him when he got hurt, as well as offering to bring him to her house and nurse him.

"So what do these nursing services you offered include? I assume that sponge baths are a no-brainer, but what else can I expect?"

"Ice packs to help with all your swelling issues."

"Are we still talking about my leg?"

"Depends. Are you having swelling issues elsewhere?"

"I might if you own one of those naughty nurse outfits."

"No naughty nurses and no sponge baths."

"I should've stayed at Jared's."

She gave him a haughty look that he loved. "You want me to take you back?"

"No, thank you. But the sponge bath is negotiable, right?"

Thanks to the streetlights, he could see her roll her eyes. "I expect better from you than this, Doctor."

"I'm not a doctor right now." He rested his hand on her thigh. "I'm a patient, and I'm feeling very, very dirty."

# CHAPTER 19

It was one thing to know he was an amputee and another thing altogether to see stark evidence of it in the prosthesis that had sat on the floor next to the sofa, in the sag of his empty pants leg and in his need for crutches.

Overriding everything else was Mallory's concern for him. From the second she'd gotten his text, she'd known she would never sleep until she saw him and made sure he was okay. She hadn't driven there planning to ask him to come home with her. That had slipped out before she could actually think about whether it was a good idea. All she knew was that she didn't want to leave him, so it had to be a good idea to take him home.

And now, he was showing her he was totally fine in the way he flirted with her, which was a welcome relief even as his hand on her thigh caused secondary issues.

"You're a very pushy patient. Nurses have names for patients like you."

"What kind of names?"

"Perv, for one."

"Ha," he said on a bark of laughter. "If I'd had a nurse as sexy as you while I was in the hospital, I would've been called a perv for sure. Most of my nurses were guys."

"How boring for you."

"No kidding. Just my luck that all the pretty female nurses had other patients."

"Or just their luck."

"Probably more their luck."

"I'm sure they were all well aware of the sexy trauma surgeon on their ward. Nurses have been known to compare notes about their patients."

"What kind of notes?"

"Oh, things like, 'holy hell, that one is hung,' to 'poor guy, not a lot going on down there.'"

"No way."

"You don't think so?"

"I don't think so."

She started to laugh. "You'd be right. I've never had that kind of conversation, except of course when the reason they were there involved that area of their anatomy."

He shuddered. "I'd rather lose part of my leg than be in the hospital for a penis injury."

"You'd be surprised how many penis injuries we get in the ER. I'd be happy to tell you all about them if you're interested."

"I'll pass, but thanks for giving me something to think about other than my own predicament."

"Does this count as a predicament?" she asked.

"Sort of. I mean, I live on a boat, and I can't manage that on crutches. David said there's going to be bruising and swelling in the stump, which means the prosthesis won't be usable for a couple of days. So I'm effectively homeless."

"You are not. You can stay with me, and you could've stayed with Jared."

"I'd much rather stay with you, if you're offering."

"I believe I already offered."

"For tonight, not a couple of nights."

"For as long as you need."

"What if 'as long as I need' turns out to be like… forty years?"

Her heart skipped a beat at the thought of that. She'd have time later, when his hand wasn't on her thigh, to figure out why her heart went crazy at the thought of years with him. "Let's see how tonight goes and take it from there."

This guy was going to be trouble. Big, big trouble, and the more time she spent with him, the less afraid she was of his kind of trouble.

Mallory pulled into the driveway and got out to retrieve his crutches from the backseat. She had to refrain from offering help she knew he wouldn't want, and once he had the crutches in hand, she left him to go unlock the front door and turn on the outside lights.

Then she went back out to check on him, retrieve his prosthetic, Brutus and Brutus's bag from the car.

Quinn was making slow but steady progress on the crutches. "Is it pathetic that my dog has an overnight bag but I don't?"

"Hardly. I'll go out to the boat tomorrow and get you anything you need."

"I need a toothbrush."

"You're in luck. I stocked up before I moved and have an extra one."

He fumbled a bit on the three stairs that led to the porch.

Mallory stood behind him, ready to intercede if he stumbled, but he recovered his balance and made it to the door she'd left propped open for him.

"I've forgotten how tedious the crutches are," he said, his tone tight with frustration and aggravation.

"It's just for a couple of days. No big deal. Good thing you've got those powerful arms to do all the work for you."

"This is exactly why I became a gym rat after my injury. Upper-body strength is crucial."

Mallory tried—and failed—not to stare at the play of his arm muscles that were visible even under the Henley shirt he wore. Then she realized she was staring and blinked several times to clear her brain of salacious thoughts about his biceps. Had she ever had salacious thoughts about biceps before? Not that she could recall.

"Come in here and get comfortable," she said, leading the way to her bedroom on the left side of the short hallway.

"In case you were wondering, this was not the way I intended to score an invite to your bedroom."

"I wasn't wondering, but thanks for clarifying."

He made a sound that might've been laughter, but it came out more like a grunt as he negotiated the doorway. "Which side is yours?"

"Doesn't matter. You take the side closest to the bathroom, which is that way."

He sat on the left side of the bed and propped the crutches against the bedside table. "Exhausting."

Brutus curled up on the floor, but kept his gaze trained on Quinn, his concern obvious.

Mallory sat next to Quinn and took his hand. "Temporary setback. That's all this is."

"Keep telling me that, will you?"

"Any time you need to hear it."

"Thanks for reminding me this isn't the end of the world."

"No problem. How about some ice for your leg to combat the swelling?"

"That'd be good. Thanks."

"Coming right up." She kissed his cheek and went to the kitchen to fill a bag with ice that she wrapped in a towel. When she returned to the bedroom with the ice and a bottle of water for him, he was sitting against the pillows with both legs on the bed. "You want to put it over your pants or right on the leg?"

He hesitated and then glanced up at her, looking madly vulnerable. "If you see it, you won't forget that you like me, will you?"

"Of course I won't. Don't forget I've seen far worse."

"I… I haven't shown it to anyone except doctors."

"Is this why you've been celibate so long?"

Nodding, he said, "I couldn't bring myself to go there with a woman. Until now."

"I promise you there's nothing about your injury or what it looks like that could make me change my mind about whatever is happening between us. I realize it's the biggest thing to ever happen to you, but it doesn't make you any less attractive to me. As long as you're comfortable, so am I."

He took hold of her hand and brought it to his lips, wincing when his sore lip made contact with her skin. "There's nothing you could've said that would be better than that. I seem to have frequent cause to thank you for being you."

"You don't have to thank me, Quinn."

"Yeah, I really do."

"So about the ice…"

He took a deep breath, released her hand and reached for the hem of his pants, drawing the fabric up to reveal what was left of his leg.

Mallory took a quick look at the new bruising and swelling, and then applied the ice bag. "It doesn't look too terrible," she said. "A few days of ice and crutches and you should be back in business with the prosthetic."

"I hope so." He patted the spot next to him on the bed. "I need some hands-on nursing, stat."

He really was too cute and too funny for her own good.

"Allow me to slip into something more comfortable first."

"Oh, please do, by all means."

Mallory went into the bathroom and changed into pajama pants and a T-shirt. She debated whether or not to keep her bra on and decided to take it off because she hated sleeping with it on. As she brushed her hair and teeth, she gave herself a silent talking-to about keeping her head about her in the face of his considerable charm, not to mention his vulnerability, which had really gotten to her.

*You may be fighting a losing battle here*, she thought, studying her reflection in the mirror. *Why exactly are we fighting the battle anyway? This guy is the whole package—sweet, smart, sexy, handsome as sin, funny and flawed in ways I can certainly relate to. Am I so afraid of getting hurt again that I'll never take another chance? Is that how I want to live?*

Mallory shook her head. She didn't want to live fearfully. She wanted to live *fearlessly*, and there had been a time in her life, before the rug was pulled out from under her, when the idea of debating a situation like this with Quinn would've seemed ridiculous to her.

*I want to be more like that girl, unafraid and audacious, willing to take some risks and roll the dice. That girl would've dived headfirst into love with a man like Quinn, without taking even one second to weigh the potential consequences.* That's how she'd ended up married to Ryan in medical school, long before they should've taken the plunge. How glad she'd been after he was gone that they'd had a few years together. It had been better than nothing.

The same was true now. Whatever this became with Quinn would be worth the risk. She already knew that for certain. She wanted him. He seemed to want her, if the shameless way he flirted with her was any indication. So go for it, she told the girl in the mirror. It's the Summer of Mallory, after all.

Mallory left the bathroom intending to jump onboard and enjoy the sure to be wild ride with him, no matter where it might lead.

Still propped up against the pillows, Quinn was sound asleep in her bed, the water bottle still in his hand but tipped at a precarious angle.

Smiling, Mallory rescued the water, covered him with a blanket and shut off the light before getting into bed next to him. The wild ride would have to start tomorrow.

Jared was too wound up to sleep, so he returned to the deck and threw another log on the fire. He stared at the flames, processing what he'd learned about his brother tonight. He'd lost part of his leg and hadn't thought to tell his family. Who the hell did that?

Quinn did. That was how he rolled, how he'd always rolled. The lone wolf who did his own thing, especially after he joined the army and was away more than he was home.

The family had known he'd injured his leg, but that was all he'd told them other than he was fine and dealing with rehab.

Jared had known something was terribly wrong but had respected Quinn's boundaries. Had that been the wrong thing to do?

Lizzie came out to join him and curled up on his lap. "You're spinning."

"Can you blame me?"

"Not at all. It was a surprise to both of us."

"I just keep going round and round about why he would keep such a big thing from us. Did he think we wouldn't understand or want to support him or be with him?"

"Maybe he just wanted to be left alone, and this was the best way to make that happen."

"Two years ago, maybe so, but he's been here for months and had plenty of chances to say, hey, Jared, by the way, I ended up losing the bottom half of my leg. He never did that."

"We've never told him that we've been trying to get pregnant and having no success."

"Yet."

"Yet. But it's been months, the same months he's been here, and we've never told him that."

"So what's your point?"

"Some things are just private, even between siblings."

"Losing a leg is private?"

"To him, yes."

"I don't get it," Jared said with a deep sigh.

"You don't have to. It's what he wanted, and it was his business to share or not share, just like us trying to get pregnant is our business to share or not share."

"I guess."

"Sweetheart, look at me." When she had his attention, she kissed him. "I get that this was a shock. It was for me, too, but please don't let it cause a rift between you and your brother. It's not worth it. No matter what, we can't undo the past. Now you know what really happened to him. Go forward from here."

"My Elisabeth with an s is not only gorgeous, she is wise, too."

"So you agree?"

"I agree. He must've had his reasons for not telling us, and whatever they are, they're his reasons."

"Exactly. And to his credit, look how well he's recovered that we never suspected his leg had been amputated. Other than a slight limp, you'd never know he'd ever been hurt."

"That was true until tonight. I feel terrible that he fell because of the hole you told me to fix."

"What have you learned from this?"

"Fix the holes so no one gets hurt."

"No! Listen to your wife. She's always right."

He laughed. "I walked face-first into that one."

"With your eyes wide open. Can we talk about Mallory rushing over here to get him?"

"That was a bright spot in an otherwise awful hour."

"I like them together. She's good for him."

"I don't want to talk about them."

"What do you want to talk about?"

"Us. Kiss me, sweet Lizzie."

She wrapped her arms around his neck and did as he asked, leaving him dizzy with longing for her, which was nothing new. Every time she came near him, he wanted her.

Nuzzling her neck, he whispered in her ear. "Wanna fuck?"

Lizzie laughed the way she always did when he said that.

"Is that a yes?"

"When do I ever say no to you?"

"Um, other than that one time you famously said no to my proposal?"

"As we've discussed many times since then, I never actually said no."

"That's still up for debate, love." Sliding his arms under her, he scooped her up and carried her inside, stopping only to close the door with his foot while she flipped the lock and shut the lights off.

He carried her into their bedroom and put her down on their bed.

She held out her arms to him, and he gladly let her wrap him up in her love. "Are you okay?"

"I am now. Thanks for talking me down."

"Any time. That's what I'm here for."

"That's not all."

"What else?" she asked, smiling suggestively.

"To be my best friend and the love of my life."

"Jared," she whispered, placing her hands on his face. "Sometimes I still can't believe that we get to spend the whole rest of our lives together."

"Believe it, baby. You're all mine."

# CHAPTER 20

Tiffany Taylor got up before the sunrise and longed for the coffee that used to jump-start her day pre-pregnancy. Now she had to settle for non-caffeinated tea that didn't do a thing to jump-start anything. It did, however, soothe her upset stomach, so that was something.

She'd been dreading this day for weeks now. She was due to meet with the prosecutor trying the assault case against her ex-husband, Jim Sturgil, who was also her daughter Ashleigh's father.

Thankfully, Maddie had invited Ashleigh to sleep over with them last night. Tiffany didn't need to worry about her little girl as long as she was with Maddie.

She curled up on the sofa, the one Blaine had gotten for her after Jim left and took all their furniture with him. Through the big sliding doors that led to her deck, she could see the sky turning pink from the sunrise. Normally, she loved this time of day, the calm before the storm of life with a toddler.

The baby she carried moved inside her, making her belly flutter from one side to the other. Blaine loved to watch that happen. He was endlessly fascinated with their unborn child and couldn't wait to meet him or her in person. They'd decided not to find out what they were having, which was fine with her.

In an otherwise peaceful time in her life, today's visit with her past was an unwelcome intrusion. She deeply resented the actions of her ex-husband that had led to her having to testify against the father of her child. That was the last thing she wanted to do. Though Jim had brought all this on himself, would Ashleigh believe that when she was old enough to find out that her mother had helped get her father convicted of a felony, ensuring he'd be disbarred, too?

By now, Blaine was more Ashleigh's father than Jim had ever been, even before he lost his mind and left her and Ashleigh for reasons that were still unclear to Tiffany. What did it matter now anyway? She was happily remarried to Blaine, expecting his child, and Ashleigh had adjusted to their new family situation, accepting Blaine as a father figure even as she wrapped him around her tiny little finger.

Heavy footsteps on the stairs had her looking up to see her husband coming toward her, wearing only boxers. His muscular chest and arms were on full, delicious display, and his hair stood on end the way it did every morning.

Placing her empty teacup on the table, Tiffany smiled, because how could she not smile at the sight of the man who'd made everything right in her world again?

"You're up early, baby," he said as he dropped to the sofa next to her and wrapped his arms around her. "I don't like waking up alone."

"Sorry. I was awake and didn't want to bother you when you get so few opportunities to sleep in this time of year."

He kissed her neck and cheek on his way to her lips. "You know how much I love to be bothered by you."

When she returned his kiss, Tiffany tasted toothpaste and sexy man.

"Are you fretting about today?"

"A little."

"A little or a lot?"

She smiled. How well he knew her. "A lot."

"I'll be right there with you, and we'll get it over with as fast as possible."

"For now. I'll still have to testify when it goes to trial."

"Maybe he'll wise up and plead out when he realizes he's totally screwed."

"Giving up without a fight isn't his style."

Blaine ran his fingers through her hair.

Tiffany curled into him, taking the comfort he provided just by being there.

"Do you want me to make you some breakfast?"

"I don't think I could eat. My stomach is in an uproar."

He flattened his hand on the curve of her belly. "You need to feed my baby."

"I will. After."

"How about a shower?"

"That I do need."

"Come on. I'll help you."

"Is that a line?"

He chuckled as he steered her up the stairs with his hands on her hips. In the bathroom, he helped her out of her robe and nightgown and followed her into the steaming-hot shower where he gently washed her hair and every other part of her.

Tiffany wrapped her arms around him and held on tight.

"Everything's going to be fine, sweetheart. I promise."

"What will Ashleigh think of me when she finds out that I helped put her dad in jail?"

Blaine tilted her chin, forcing her gaze to meet his fierce one. "None of this is your fault. Not one tiny part of it. You're being legally compelled to meet with the prosecutor. You didn't volunteer, and you don't have a choice. When the time comes, we'll tell her that if need be, but I have a feeling she won't ask about it."

"Why do you think that?"

"Because she's going to grow up happy and well-adjusted and very well loved by both of us. There won't be anything lacking in her life."

"He's still her father, Blaine."

"I know that, and she will, too, but that'll be a minor detail to her."

"For now."

"Let's deal with today and worry about tomorrow when it gets here. Can you do that?"

"I can try."

He kissed the top of her head and held her close. "You're the strongest person I know, Tiff. I have no doubt whatsoever that you're going to get through this and every other challenge that comes your way."

"Maybe so, but I'm so glad I have you here to keep me sane. I'd be losing it if I didn't have you to tell me everything is going to be okay."

"You'd be fine. You were fine before me, and you'd be fine without me."

"But I like this so much better."

"Me, too, baby." He kissed her lips. "Let's get this over with so we can get back to being blissfully happy."

An hour later, Tiffany sat across from Sam Rhodes, the assistant attorney general, who'd taken the eight o'clock boat from the mainland to meet with her and Dan Torrington, who'd been assaulted by Jim. Their testimony would be critical to the prosecutor's case, and he'd wanted to ensure they were all on the same page before next month's trial.

Dan and his fiancée, Kara Ballard, were seated on the same side of the table as Tiffany and Blaine in the conference room at the public safety building that housed the police and fire departments.

"I want to thank you all for meeting with me today," Rhodes said. "My goal here is to make sure we're completely ready for trial. It's important that you tell me everything you remember about that day, so there can be no surprises."

"You have the police reports," Blaine said. "We were very thorough in our reporting of this incident."

"I do, and I commend your department for an excellent job, Chief, but I need to ensure that the testimony matches the reports. Mr. Torrington, I'd like to start with you."

Dan walked Rhodes through the incident, from the second Jim showed up uninvited at the engagement party at the Summer House last summer. He'd been drunk and disheveled with an ax to grind against Dan, whom he accused of ruining his law practice on the island.

"Why did he think you'd done that?"

"I came out here looking for some peace and quiet and a place to write my book, and when people heard I was here, they started coming to me for legal advice. I'd gotten my Rhode Island license when I helped to get Charlie Grandchamp out of prison, so once the word got out that I was taking a few clients, I had more than I could handle. Apparently, that was the death knell for his already struggling practice."

"Why was his practice struggling if he'd been the island's only lawyer?"

"I can answer that," Tiffany said, marshaling the courage she needed to fill in the blanks for the prosecutor so she could be done with this unsavory incident. "When Jim left me, he did so in grand style, taking every stick of furniture we owned, except my bed and our daughter's bed. He even took the dresser that held her clothes. When the word got out, people around here didn't like that he'd done that, and then, when I wanted to open my business, he made trouble for me. The island's residents went to bat for me with the town council and left him humiliated once again. His reputation took a beating during all that."

"The police report states that you attempted to confront your ex-husband at the engagement party, Mrs. Taylor," Rhodes said.

"I did."

"Why did you do that?"

Tiffany glanced at Blaine, remembering how furious and frightened he'd been by her attempt to defuse the situation. "I was trying to stop him before he made it worse. I asked him to think about our daughter and what he'd be doing to her if he hurt someone."

"And he had the knife in his hand at this point?"

Tiffany swallowed hard. "Yes, he did."

"Then he called my wife a stupid bitch, and I grabbed him around the neck," Blaine said. "He fought back, and that's when Dan got hit by the knife."

Rhodes took furious notes, nodding as they added each new detail.

"What're the chances that he's going to take a plea?" Dan asked.

"Slim," Rhodes said. "According to his attorney, he's very defiant."

"Still." Tiffany shook her head in disbelief. "After all this time, he still doesn't get that he brought this on himself."

"I'm not seeing any indication of that," Rhodes said.

"Could I talk to him?" she asked, drawing a shocked stare from her husband. "Maybe if I could remind him what's at stake for his daughter, he might be willing to see reason."

"That's not happening," Blaine said in the flat, emotionless tone that reminded her of how angry he'd been after she confronted Jim at the engagement party.

"What if it would help?" she asked him. "What if I could convince him to take the deal and spare all of us a trial that his daughter will one day have to hear about?"

"If you'd like to see him," Rhodes said, "I could make that happen."

"She's not going anywhere near him," Blaine said.

"I'll let you talk about that on your own," Rhodes said, apparently sensing a marital meltdown in the works. "In the meantime, I appreciate your help in filling in some of the blanks for me, and I'll be in touch ahead of the trial." To Dan and Kara, he said, "I understand your wedding is next weekend. Please accept my congratulations."

"Thank you," Dan said. "Are we done?"

"For now," Rhodes said.

The four of them left the conference room, and no one said a word until they were outside.

"We'll see you at the wedding?" Dan said as he shook hands with Blaine.

"Yes, you will. Looking forward to it."

"See you then." Dan put his arm around Kara and led her to the parking lot.

Tiffany looked up at Blaine, who was staring off in the distance, his handsome face devoid of expression. "Say something."

"Let's go home."

They drove in uneasy and unusual silence that fried her already rattled nerves.

At home, Blaine held the back door so she could go in ahead of him.

"Are we going to talk about this?"

"Nothing to talk about it," he said. "It's not happening."

"That's not how we operate, Blaine. You don't give me orders like I'm one of your officers."

"No, you're my wife, the most precious thing in my world, and there's no fucking way I'm letting you talk to that scumbag."

Knowing he was running on pure emotion rather than anger, she went to him, slid her arms around his waist and rested her head on his chest, hearing the strong beat of his heart against her ear. "Even if it would help to put an end to this before trial?"

"Even then."

"I think it's worth a shot. If I can convince him to take a plea, he'd do less time in jail, and none of us would have to be put through a trial that Ashleigh will surely remember, despite our efforts to shield her from the details."

"And who's going to shield you?"

Tiffany looked up at him. "You will."

"He'll never talk to you if I'm there."

"You'd go with me and wait for me outside the room and be there for me afterward, wouldn't you?"

"Yeah, of course I would—if it were happening, which it is not."

"I want to try this, Blaine, and I'm asking you to support me."

"Don't do that thing you do when you want your way and think you can bewitch me into forgetting my own name."

She blinked rapidly and smiled up at him. "Would I do that to you?"

"Yes, you absolutely would. You do it all the time."

"Only when I'm sure that what I want is the right thing for all of us."

After a long pause in which he stared down at her, his golden-brown eyes intense and tender at the same time, he said, "Are you sure about this, baby?"

Tiffany nodded.

"All right, then," he said with great reluctance that she could hear in his every word. "We'll do it your way."

# CHAPTER 21

The first thing Mallory felt when she woke up was heat, the kind that came from either a furnace or the body of a sexy man pressed up against her, a heavy arm around her waist and warm lips against her shoulder. Not a terrible way to wake up, she thought, smiling at the realization that Quinn had sought her out in his sleep.

For the longest time, she lay there enjoying the feel of his body against hers, the comfort that came from his company—even when he was asleep—and anticipation for the day ahead. She hadn't lived here long, and already she could feel her life changing in ways that she not only welcomed but embraced with open arms. More of her big boisterous family, one-on-one moments with her father, stepmother and siblings, a fun new job to keep her occupied during the summer and now this, whatever it was, with Quinn.

This was what she'd needed—a fresh new start and the time to really get to know her new family.

For the first time since she lost Ryan so many years ago, she didn't feel rootless or detached from herself as much as the people around her. She didn't feel like her wheels were spinning while she stood in place letting her life happen to her rather than the other way around.

Her young, dynamic husband would surely approve of these developments, as he'd wanted nothing more than for her to be happy and content. She let her gaze shift to the photo of him on her bedside table, drinking in the sight of his adorable face and the big smile he'd worn for their entire wedding day.

"Is that Ryan?" Quinn asked, his voice gruff with sleep.

Startled to realize he was awake, she said, "Uh-huh."

"Handsome guy."

"Yes, he was."

"Gorgeous bride."

"I clean up well."

"Yes, you do, but you don't need to clean up to be gorgeous."

"Are you always this charming first thing in the morning, Dr. James?"

"When I have the proper inspiration."

Mallory's heart fluttered in approval of his reply. Handsome, sexy and charming—a deadly combination, at least as far as she was concerned. "How's your leg?" During the night, she'd heard him get up once to use the bathroom and had forced herself to refrain from offering help. He'd gotten around okay on the crutches, and she'd breathed a sigh of relief when he got back in bed.

"Hurts like a motherfucker."

"Let me get you some pain meds."

"In a minute." He nuzzled her neck and drew her in tighter against his body— and the erection that pressed against her ass.

A flash of heat lit up her body. "Quinn…"

"Hmm?"

"What're you doing? You're injured. You shouldn't be…"

"What? Hard as a rock after waking up with you in my arms?"

"Yes. That."

He laughed. "Sorry, babe. It's basic biology, as you well know. A hot woman who smells like a dream and feels like heaven leads to a natural reaction in the helpless man who can't seem to resist her."

"He can't resist her?"

"Nope."

"I need to get up and get going. I have to work today, and before that I want to go to the boat and get what you need. I can get a ride out with Kara on the launch, right?"

"Don't worry about it. Jared will do it for me."

"Are you sure?"

"Uh-huh. So does that mean you have time for more snuggling?"

"A little." She swallowed hard. "Maybe."

"Maybe or definitely?" His hand ducked under her T-shirt and left a heated path on the way to her breast, which he cupped as he ran his thumb back and forth over her nipple.

Mallory gasped and pushed back against him, her hips moving without her making a conscious decision to encourage him.

"I'll take that as a definitely," he whispered. He worked his other arm under her shoulders to hold her tight against him as his hand slid down the front of her into her pajama pants.

She sucked in a deep breath when he continued down, his fingers delving inside her panties. Mallory had to force herself to remain still so she wouldn't move wrong and add to his pain—not that he seemed to be worried about his pain at the moment.

"Turn onto your back," he said.

She moved carefully and found him propped up on an upturned arm, looking down at her with those brown eyes that she found so compelling.

"Mmm, much better."

In the new position, he could reach between her legs and slide his fingers through her slick heat.

Groaning, he dropped his head to her shoulder and drove two fingers deep inside her. "So hot and so sexy."

Between his words and the movement of his fingers, Mallory felt herself climbing toward the inevitable conclusion. Then he hooked his fingers, found her

G-spot and took her from climbing to soaring. She came hard, her hips rising as her internal muscles clamped down on his fingers.

"Ah, damn," he said gruffly. "I can't wait to feel that happen with my cock instead of my fingers."

Mallory shivered from the aftershocks as much as the promise she heard in his words. She couldn't wait either. When she'd recovered her composure, she reached for him, flattening her hand over his erection. "What about you?"

"You have to go to work. Can't be late on your first day."

"I won't be late." She tugged at the button to the khakis he'd slept in and unzipped him, moving carefully in light of the huge bulge that made unzipping difficult. Then she gave him a taste of his own medicine by caressing his bare chest and abdomen before letting her fingers wander inside his boxers to stroke his cock.

He gasped from the first contact of her skin against his.

Mallory took great pleasure in the feel of his long, thick, hot shaft as she stroked him and learned what made him shudder, and that was attention to the sensitive head, where she used her thumb to spread around a bead of fluid.

His fingers dug into the flesh on the top of her arm. "Ahhh, fuck, you're going to make me come so hard."

"Do it. I want to see that." She stroked him from base to tip, keeping a tight grip as she moved from top to bottom.

Keeping his eyes closed, he moved with her, pushing into her hand until he came with a sharp cry that made Brutus bark and both of them laugh. "Now look what you've done," he said a full minute later. "You've made a big mess."

"That doesn't count as a mess." She pressed a gentle kiss to his lips, mindful not to touch the cut on his bottom lip. "Don't move."

Feeling him watching her, she got up and went into the bathroom to retrieve a towel that she brought back to the bed to clean him up. Then she let Brutus out into the backyard, filled his bowl with food and got Quinn some pain pills and a glass of ice water.

"Thanks for taking care of me and Brutus."

"My pleasure," she said.

He took both from her with a grateful smile. "That was the best wakeup call I've had in years."

Mallory smiled down at him. "Me, too."

"I need to get hurt more often."

"Please don't. How about some more ice?"

"That'd be good. Thanks."

With her body still tingling from the orgasm, she refilled the ice bag, got him settled and then headed for the bathroom to shower and get herself together for her first day of work on the rescue. Mason had sent over a uniform that consisted of navy blue pants and a light blue button-down shirt with the Gansett Island Fire Department patch on one short sleeve and a paramedic patch on the other. As she buttoned the shirt and tucked it into the pants, her new job began to feel official.

After she dried her hair, she put it up into a ponytail and applied sunscreen and a light layer of makeup that included mascara. When she emerged from the bathroom, Quinn let out a low whistle.

"That is one sexy paramedic."

Mallory felt her face heat with embarrassment. "Stop."

"What can I say? I have a thing for a smart, sexy babe in a uniform."

"Any babe, or one in particular?"

He reached out a hand to her.

Mallory crossed the room to take his hand.

He brought her hand to his lips and brushed them over her knuckles. "Definitely one in particular. You'll be careful, right?"

"I hardly think there's anything to worry about around here, but I'll be careful."

"Good."

"You want me to make you something to eat before I go?"

"Nah, I'll be fine."

"Help yourself to anything in the kitchen. There's eggs, cereal, yogurt, fruit. Whatever you want. How about coffee? Should I make some?"

"I wouldn't say no to that."

"You got it." She bent over to kiss him. "Take it easy today. Let's get that leg healed so you can get back to normal, okay?"

"Yes, ma'am. Whatever my nurse tells me to do."

She waggled her brows at him. "That's good to know. I'll text you later to check on you."

"I'll look forward to that. What time are you off?"

"Four."

"I'll see you then."

Mallory started to leave the room, but then turned back. "Are you sure you'll be okay? I can tell Mason that today's not a good day—"

"I'm totally fine. I did the crutches for months before I was ready for the prosthesis. I'm used to them."

"Okay, then, but if you need anything, call me. I won't be far away."

"You got it."

Mallory left the bedroom, made the coffee and downed a container of yogurt before grabbing her keys and cell phone and heading for the barn with ten minutes to spare before her first shift began. As she left the house, she hoped Quinn would be okay on his own.

Lying in Mallory's bed, Quinn reached for his cell phone and dashed off a text to Jared. *I need a favor. Are you around today?*

*Sure, what do you need?*

*A run to the boat for some clothes, and then a ride to work?*

*You can take a day off, Quinn.*

*Mac is running through the final punch list today. I need to be there. You still have a key to the boat, right?*

*Yep. I'll head out there now and bring your stuff to Mallory's. It's off Ocean Road, right?*

*Yes.* He typed in the address. *Thanks.*

*No problem. See you soon.*

Quinn absolutely hated having to ask anyone else for help, but he knew his brother wouldn't mind, especially since he felt responsible for Quinn getting hurt on his property. Quinn sat up and reached for the dreaded crutches that he hated with a fiery passion. More than anything, he hated that he needed them and glared at the prosthetic leg and foot sitting next to Mallory's closet, almost mocking him with what he couldn't have today.

Because he didn't want to have to explain about his leg to everyone he encountered today, he would strap on the prosthetic after a shower, keeping it loosely affixed to his sore leg while he continued to use the crutches. It wouldn't feel great against the bruised stump, but it was better than having to deal with questions about his missing leg.

With Brutus following close behind him, he hobbled to the bathroom, where he broke open the toothbrush Mallory had left for him and put it to use. Next he headed for the kitchen, poured coffee into the mug she'd set out for him and filled it with the cream she'd placed on the counter to make it easier for him. She was a gem. He'd known that before he got hurt, and she'd only confirmed it for him with the way she'd come running to him last night and offered him a place to stay while he recovered.

Brutus sat on the floor looking up at him, his adorable face scrunched inquisitively, as if to say, *What's going on, Dad? Why do you need those sticks to walk?* Brutus had come into his life after he had the prosthetic, so he'd never seen Quinn on crutches before.

"Temporary setback, buddy," he said. "We'll be back to normal in a few days. At least I hope so." Because he couldn't manage the crutches and the coffee, he stood in the kitchen and drank his coffee, looking out the kitchen window to the backyard and the ocean in the distance. After he finished his coffee, he took a closer look at her home.

This really was an adorable little house that Mallory had rented from her sister, and in a very short amount of time, she'd put her unique stamp on the place with eye-catching art on the walls and bookshelves full of mysteries, thrillers, romances and nursing references. On the mantel, she'd placed photos of her with a woman who was probably her mom, a group shot with her siblings and cousins from Laura's wedding last year and another with her and her dad.

There were other framed photos of groups of women he didn't recognize. He'd have to ask her about them. He wanted to know the details, and that alone made her different from any woman he'd been with in a long time. When he'd been on active duty, most of his "relationships," such as they were, had been about sex. His relationship with Mallory was about so much more than that. They hadn't even had sex yet, and he was already more committed to her than he'd been to any woman.

He had no idea how long he stood there, looking at her pictures and thinking about her, before a knock on the door had him pivoting on the crutches toward the door to admit Jared. "That was quick."

Brutus greeted Uncle Jared with unbridled enthusiasm.

Jared squatted to give Brutus some attention. "Kara took me out and waited for me while I packed up a bag. Hope I got everything you needed."

"If you got clean clothes, I'm good."

Standing upright, Jared carried the bag into the house and put it in the bedroom. "At least now I know why you don't own a pair of shorts."

"I have shorts. I just don't wear them anymore."

"Because you didn't want anyone to know."

Quinn shrugged. "Something like that."

"Why does it matter? It's not like you lost your leg doing something stupid. You lost it serving your country."

"I don't know why it matters."

"Where the hell did you get all those muscles?" Jared asked, gesturing to Quinn's bare chest and arms.

"In the gym after I lost my leg. Upper-body strength was key to my recovery."

Sighing, Jared sat on one of the two barstools that had been tucked under the counter. "I wish you'd told me."

"Why? So you could swoop in and throw money at the situation and try to fix everything for me?"

"I wouldn't have done that."

Quinn raised a brow in disbelief.

"Okay, maybe I would've, but at least you wouldn't have been alone."

"I was okay."

"Lizzie told me I'm not allowed to be pissed with you, that this was your situation to handle as you saw fit."

"I really, *really* like your wife. She's probably way too good for you."

"She definitely is, because, left to my own devices, I'd probably say some things that couldn't be unsaid or unheard."

Quinn held his brother's gaze. "Thank goodness for Lizzie, then."

"Yeah, thank goodness for her." Jared looked down and then back up at Quinn. "I know you prefer to go it alone, but I hope you know you've got me, and you can count on me."

"I do know that, and I appreciate it. You and Lizzie have given me a whole new purpose by hiring me. You've already done more than you know."

"I guess that's something."

"It's everything, Jared. I'm going to grab a shower, and then we can head out to the site, okay?"

"Sure, whatever you want."

"Have some coffee while you wait."

"Don't mind if I do. You don't... Do you need help in there?"

"Thanks, but I've got it."

Quinn went into Mallory's bathroom, giving thanks for the tiny house that required very little effort to get around. He was used to showering on one leg, so that wasn't a problem either.

He moved slowly and carefully, because the last thing he needed was to fall again. With a towel wrapped around his waist, he went into the bedroom, sat on the bed, put on the sock he wore over the stump and wrangled the prosthetic into position, wincing when the padding made contact with his bruised and swollen stump. He secured it using the loosest possible setting and then got dressed, still sitting, the way he'd been taught to do in rehab. Everything was such a major production when one of your limbs was missing. Balance and coordination were nonexistent, and the simplest things became a struggle.

It took fifteen minutes to put on boxers, khakis and a button-down shirt that he left untucked because that was easier than standing and tucking it in while balancing on one leg and two crutches. He made his way into the living room, where Jared watched CNBC as he drank his coffee.

"You can take the boy out of Wall Street," Quinn said.

"But you can't make him ignore his portfolio," Jared concluded.

They shared a laugh that went a long way toward putting things back on track between them.

"Ready?" Jared asked.

"Yep." Quinn grabbed his keys and cell phone from the counter where Mallory had left them the night before and put both items in his pocket. "Hey, Jared?"

"Yeah?"

"I'm sorry if you were hurt by what happened last night. I never meant for that to happen."

Jared stared at him, incredulous. "*You're* sorry? Dude, I feel like shit because I knew that hole was there and never did anything about it. I'm the one who should be apologizing to you."

"Don't sweat it. Better me than someone who would sue Daddy Warbucks."

"Ha! That's true. It's getting fixed today. I called Alex to take care of it."

"Are you really so far gone that you can't fix a hole in your own lawn by yourself?"

"Nah, I just have better things to do today."

"Such as?"

"Drive my big brother around and make sure he's got everything he needs, such as breakfast. Did you eat yet?"

"Not yet."

"Let's hit the diner on the way to the office."

Realizing Jared intended to spend the day with him, Quinn made his way to the door, grateful for the time with his brother even if he hated the reason for it. "That sounds good. Thanks, Jared."

"Sure thing."

# CHAPTER 22

Mason greeted Mallory when she arrived at the barn for her first shift. She met the rest of the guys on her shift and memorized their nicknames—Shorty, Boner and Trip—rather than their real names. Shorty and Boner were firefighters, and Trip was the other paramedic.

She'd agreed to work day shifts on Monday, Tuesday and Wednesday for the summer, wanting to avoid the weekends when everything was a hundred times busier. As this was the Summer of Mallory, she planned to enjoy her weekends rather than deal with the partiers who invaded the island every weekend.

No, thanks. She was too old for that crap, or so she'd told Mason when he asked about her preferred schedule.

He gave her a tour of the small public safety building that housed both the police and fire departments, introduced her to everyone they encountered and set her up with a locker that was located inside the women's restroom.

After that, she received a handbook with department policies and procedures that Mason reviewed with her in detail in his office. Then he showed her where the supplies for the rig were kept and went over the routine that each shift followed.

It was a lot of information to absorb all at once, but he was patient in answering her questions and getting her oriented to their way of doing things. At ten minutes to eleven, he asked if she'd like to join him at the AA meeting.

"Are we allowed to do that?" She'd been resigned to missing meetings on the days she worked.

"As long as we take a radio with us, we're allowed."

"Good to know, and yes, I'd like to go."

"We can take my truck. If anything comes up, we can meet the others at the call."

"Sounds good."

In the truck, he said, "I'm sure you must have questions about everything we reviewed this morning. You can feel free to ask me about anything that isn't clear."

"I'll reserve the right to pepper you with questions once I've had more time to review the manual and work a couple of shifts."

"My door is always open. We're really glad to have you and to have the opportunity to learn from you."

"From *me*? I'm the low one on the totem pole."

"And you have the most experience in emergency medicine. We're all excited to have you on the team, even temporarily."

"Wow, that's nice to hear."

"I was hoping I might be able to talk you into doing some training while you're with us—anything you think we would benefit from. I'd leave the content up to you."

"I'd love to. Training was one of my favorite parts of my old job."

"Keep it up. You're already in the running for employee of the year."

Mallory laughed. "And it's only my first day. I think I'm going to love this job."

"I sure hope so," he said with a note of wistfulness that put her on alert. "You know, Quinn asked about you when you were back in Providence."

"I heard that."

"So you're seeing him?"

"I am."

"Oh."

After an uncomfortable silence, she said, "Mason…"

"Nah, it's okay. I get it."

*Ugh*, Mallory felt terrible. "I hope we'll be very good friends and colleagues this summer."

"Of course we will. Why wouldn't we be?"

That was his way of saying no harm, no foul, and she couldn't be more thankful for his acceptance of the fact that she had chosen to spend her time with Quinn. She and Mason were friends, nothing more. She hated to disappoint him, but better now than later, when it might make things awkward at work. "Good."

They attended the AA meeting, where Mallory missed seeing Quinn, and returned to the station to help prepare lunch. Her first call of the day came right after lunch when an elderly island resident called for help after a fall at home. With Trip's assistance, Mallory assessed the woman's injuries and determined she should be transported to the clinic for X-rays and further evaluation by Dr. Lawrence.

At the clinic, she briefed David and Katie.

"Let's get you comfortable, Mrs. Givens," Katie said after they transferred her to a bed in the clinic.

Mallory and Trip were on their way back to the rig when she ran into Maddie in the waiting room.

"Look who it is," she said to Hailey, who was with her. "Auntie Mallory."

She would never get tired of being called Auntie Mallory or grow immune to her niece's excited reaction to seeing her. After receiving a hug and sloppy kiss from the little girl, Mallory lifted her into her arms.

Hailey's brows furrowed as she studied the patches on Mallory's sleeves.

"You look great in that uniform," Maddie said.

"The pants make my ass look huge."

"That's not true."

"You're too kind. Everything okay with you guys?"

Maddie's smile faded ever so slightly, but Mallory noticed. "Just my weekly check-in with Victoria. After what happened last time, we're being extra cautious with this baby."

"Totally understandable, but I'm sure everything is fine."

"I won't truly believe that until he—or she—is sleeping in my arms."

Aware that Trip was waiting for her, Mallory handed Hailey back to Maddie. "Hang in there. You're doing everything right."

"Thanks. I'm sure I'll see you soon."

"I'm sure you will. No parties tonight?"

"Not that I've heard of, but the day is young and so are we."

Mallory laughed at the witty retort. "Yes, we are." She waggled her fingers at Hailey. "You girls have a nice day."

"You, too."

The rest of Mallory's first day flew by in a flurry of paperwork, training and bonding with the guys she worked with, all of whom were handsome and at least ten years younger than she was. Trip was even younger, having told her he had just turned twenty-five. She felt like a mother hen around them as they talked about their plans for the evening, which included women and beer.

"You guys have to work in the morning," she reminded them.

"We know, Mom," Boner said with a wink, and with that, Mallory had a nickname.

She left the station a little after four and drove the short distance home, wondering if Quinn would be there or if he'd gone to work. When she stepped through the door, she found Brutus there but no sign of Quinn, so she texted him.

*Just got home. Are you at work?*

*Yep, finishing up here soon.*

*How about a home-cooked dinner?*

*That sounds fantastic.*

*Do you need a ride home?*

*Nope. Jared has assigned himself to me. I've made him my bitch today.*

Mallory laughed at that and was glad to hear the brothers had spent the day together. *Go easy on the poor guy.*

*What fun would that be? Home soon.*

Mallory ran for the shower and took the time to shave her legs, among other areas. After what'd happened in her bed this morning, she fully expected things to progress tonight and couldn't wait for him to get home.

Maddie left the clinic with Hailey's little hand curled around hers. Ever since her daughter had begun to walk, she didn't want to be carried anywhere, which was fine with Maddie. This pregnancy was exhausting her in a way the previous three hadn't. The worrying took a toll. She knew that but couldn't seem to stop obsessing about all the things that could go wrong, even while doing everything in her power to ensure a healthy pregnancy.

Victoria had put her on a monitor for a full hour, during which no abnormalities had been detected. She'd determined the baby was active and thriving exactly the way he was supposed to. And without confirmation, Maddie was still certain the baby was a boy. During the test, Hailey had sat patiently on the bed with Maddie, looking through the books they'd packed for the outing.

Hailey let out a cry of excitement and pulled on Maddie's hand. That was when she realized her husband was leaning against the big black SUV he'd bought for her.

With no other cars in the lot beside their two, Maddie released Hailey to run to her daddy, who scooped her up and made the little girl shriek with laughter when he spun her around over his head.

"If she pukes on you, I'll laugh at you," Maddie told him.

"My little angel wouldn't do that to me, would you, Hailey?"

She filled her tiny fists with handfuls of Mac's thick dark hair. "Dadadadada."

"Don't give Daddy bald spots, angel." He freed his hair from her grip and turned his formidable blue-eyed gaze on Maddie "How'd it go?"

"Everything's fine."

She saw the relief cross his face before he schooled his expression. He was every bit as nervous as she was, even though he usually tried to hide it from her so as not to add to her worries. She loved him for that.

He held out his arm, inviting her to join the snuggle with Hailey. "My two best girls."

"Do you have room in these arms for one more?"

"Do you know something I don't?"

"Nope. Just wondering."

"I have room for as many girls as I can get."

"Hear that, Hailey? Daddy used to be a playboy in Miami before he came home to Gansett and knocked Mommy off her bike."

Chuckling, Mac held her tighter and nuzzled her hair. "Best day of my life."

"What're you doing here? I thought you'd be out at the job site."

"The job is officially finished as of thirty minutes ago."

"Wow! Congratulations on the biggest job yet for McCarthy Construction."

"Thanks, babe."

"I'm so proud of you, Mac. You've grown that business into something really special over the last couple of years." Sometimes she felt guilty for not contributing to the family coffers, but they'd decided she would stay home with the kids until they were all in school.

"What's that frown about?" He traced the outline of her lips with his fingertip.

"No frown."

"I saw a frown. How about we go home and get this little angel down for her nap, and then you can tell me what makes you frown before we celebrate the end of my biggest job yet?"

"I could be talked into that."

"I'll follow you home."

Mac strapped Hailey into her car seat, kissed her until she giggled and then kissed Maddie.

On the short ride home, she saw him following behind her in the big truck he used for work. She took the final turn onto Sweet Meadow Farm Road, the road to the home where they'd been so happy together. Except for a brief time after they lost Connor, their marriage had been as close to perfect as it was possible to get.

If they lost this baby, too…

"Stop, Maddie. Stop it right now."

"Stop, Mama," Hailey said from the backseat.

Maddie smiled at her daughter in the mirror. "Mama is being ridiculous. Victoria said everything is fine, and that's what we have to believe."

"Mama," Hailey said as she chewed on her fingers.

Maddie brought the SUV to a stop at the foot of the stairs that led to their gorgeous deck. Everything about this place they called home appealed to her, especially the man who'd made it all possible.

He came to get Hailey from her seat and carried her into the house. "I'll put her down while you get off your feet, babe."

"Thank you." She went to get a glass of ice water and listened to Mac talking to their little girl as he got her ready for a nap. Taking her water with her, Maddie went upstairs to their room to use the bathroom. She was standing at the sink washing her hands when Mac wrapped his arms around her waist and flattened his hands over their baby. "How's my baby mama doing?"

"Okay."

"Just okay?"

"Better after seeing Victoria but still anxious."

"I wish I could get a time machine to take us to the finish line now."

"I wish you could, too."

He took her hand and led her to their bed, encouraging her to lie down.

When she had stretched out, he took her feet onto his lap and began to massage them, pressing his thumbs into her arches.

"Feels good."

"Close your eyes, relax and tell me what had you frowning before."

Maddie closed her eyes, but her mind was too busy to allow her to fully relax. "Nothing really."

"Don't lie to me, Madeline. I know what I saw."

"Sometimes I feel bad that you work two jobs, and I don't work at all anymore."

He huffed out a laugh. "Are you for real right now? You're running after kids from the second you get up almost until the second you go to bed while taking care of everything having to do with the house. If that's not a full-time job, tell me what is?"

"It doesn't bring in any money."

"We have what we need, don't we?"

She nodded. "And then some."

"I couldn't do what I do without you here doing what you do better than anyone. Knowing you're with our kids gives me such peace of mind. Please don't think you aren't contributing, because you are. You make it all happen, baby."

"I sure got lucky the day Mac McCarthy knocked me off my bike," she said with a sigh of contentment.

"We both got lucky that day."

After a while, she felt Mac crawl up the bed and turned toward him, wanting his arms around her. Everything felt better when he held her. "I miss having sex with you."

"Don't say that word. I can't hear that from your lips right now."

"But I really, really miss it."

"Maddie… I'm begging you. Please don't talk about it."

"Do you want me to, you know, do something for you?"

The moan that came from him made it sound like he was being murdered rather than offered sexual favors. "That wouldn't be fair."

"I don't care about being fair. I care about you not getting what you need—"

"Maddie, sweetheart, the only thing I truly need is for you and our baby to be safe and healthy. Going without for a while is no sacrifice compared to that."

"I hope the next three months go by quickly," she said with a sigh.

"So do I."

"And then there's the six weeks after the baby arrives…"

He moaned. "Let's talk about something else."

"Like what?"

"Like how hot it's going to be the first time we get back in the saddle."

"Mac! That doesn't count as changing the subject."

"But you know it'll be hot."

She reached for him and brought his lips down on hers. "When is it not hot between us?"

He whimpered pathetically. "I'm never going to make it."

She laughed at his distress and then kissed him again.

# CHAPTER 23

Mallory made a quick trip to the grocery store to buy steak, potatoes and vegetables to make a salad. After returning home, she got the potatoes in the oven and the steak cooking on the grill Janey had left on the deck. While the steak cooked, she played fetch in the backyard with Brutus.

Quinn found her there when he came in with Jared.

Brutus let out a happy bark and charged up the stairs to greet Quinn. Thankfully, Jared was standing behind him, or the excited puppy might've knocked Quinn over.

"Careful, pal," Quinn said as he scratched Brutus behind the ears.

Quinn looked over at her, and his gaze collided with hers, heating her from the inside as memories of their encounter came rushing back to her.

"I put your bag in the kitchen," Jared said.

"Thanks for everything today," Quinn said.

"And that's my cue to get the heck out of here," Jared said. "You guys have a nice evening. I'll be back in the morning to take you to work."

"Thanks, Jared."

"See you, Mallory."

"Bye, Jared."

He bent to give Brutus a scratch before he took his leave.

"Alone at last," Quinn said when they heard the screen on the front door close behind Jared.

"So it seems. Are you hungry?"

He continued to stare at her when he said, "Starving."

Mallory moved from the yard to the steps that led up to the deck, where he stood propped on crutches, watching her every move. She came to a stop in front of him. "How're you feeling?"

"Fine."

"Your leg is better?"

"A little."

"That's good."

"Kiss me."

Taken aback by the gruffly spoken words, Mallory looked at him for a long moment before she laid her lips on his in a soft, sweet kiss that made her heart beat faster.

"I know for a fact that you can do better than that."

Never one to back down from a challenge, she flattened her hands on his chest, slid them up to his shoulders and looped them around his neck to draw him down to her for a real kiss, the kind with tongues and teeth and desire so sharp and so potent she nearly forgot her own name.

"Now that's more like it," he said when they resurfaced many minutes later. "What're you cooking?"

"Um, steak and potatoes?"

"Will it keep for a little while?"

Fully aware of what he was asking her, she didn't hesitate when she nodded and reached behind her to turn off the grill.

Tipping his head, he indicated that she should go ahead of him into the house.

Her heart pounded a rapid rhythm as she reduced the oven temperature and then turned to find him waiting for her.

"Brutus," he said, "go lay down like a good boy."

Brutus landed on the dog bed Mallory had put in front of the fireplace.

"For once, he finally minded me, and his timing couldn't be better." He nudged Mallory toward her bedroom.

Reminding herself to breathe, she stopped next to the bed and waited for him to catch up to her.

"I wish," he said, "that I could pick you up in my arms and carry you in here."

"I don't need that."

"I still wish I could." He maneuvered so he was sitting on the bed and propped the crutches against the bedside table. "Come here."

She took a few steps to close the distance between them.

Quinn wrapped his arms around her and rested his head against her belly. "It's been a long time since I wanted someone the way I want you."

She ran her fingers through his hair. "I feel the same way."

"You look so pretty," he said as he began to unbutton her blouse. "You always look so pretty. The first time I saw you, I wanted to talk to you and get to know you. I was so happy to see you again at the meeting after we met at the accident site. And now that I know you, I'm still hungry for more of you. That first day, after the meeting, when I saw you at the diner with Mason?"

"What about it?" Mallory asked, breathless.

"I wanted to punch him."

"We're just friends!"

"I still wanted to punch him, because he got to be there with you, and I couldn't be."

Her legs were feeling decidedly unsteady. "Quinn…"

He parted the two sides of her top and pressed his lips to the skin between her breasts, staying right there for the longest time, seeming to breathe her in. "That was the first time in my life I wanted to punch another guy because he got to be with the woman I wanted." Looking up at her, he said, "You did that to me from the very beginning."

Mallory bent to kiss him.

He wrapped his arms around her and fell back on the bed, bringing her with him, gasping when her leg knocked against his.

"Sorry," she whispered against his lips.

"That was my fault." Driving his hand into her hair, he brought her back to him for another of the kisses that made her brain cells fry and her body go haywire from an overload of desire. As he kissed her, he turned them so she was on her back and he was looking down at her. "I haven't done this since I lost my leg."

"I know."

"I'm not sure how it'll go."

She caressed his face, dragging her thumb over his wounded bottom lip, which didn't seem to be bothering him. "I don't care. Your leg is only one part of you. I know it's all you're thinking about, but I promise you it doesn't matter to me."

"That helps to know." He helped her out of her shirt and dragged a finger down the front of her, stopping at the clasp that held her bra together. Before he released it, he glanced at her face. "So we're on the same page here?"

"Same page, same paragraph."

Smiling, he released the clasp and helped her out of the bra.

She tugged on his shirt. "You're overdressed for this party."

"We can't have that." Rather than unbutton his dress shirt, he pulled it over his head and tossed it aside. Then he reached for her and drew her into his arms until her breasts were pressed against his chest. "Ah, God, that feels good. *You* feel good."

Mallory caressed his back and nuzzled his neck. "So do you."

"I want to go slow, but I'm not in a slow kind of mood right now."

"What kind of mood are you in?"

"The fast and furious sort."

"I can live with that."

His lips came down on hers while he tugged on the button to her jeans and unzipped her.

She did the same for him, releasing his belt and the button to his khakis.

They pushed and pulled until the most important parts were bare. His pants were wrapped around his thighs, his cock hard against his stomach.

Mallory reached out to stroke him.

"Fuck," he said on a low growl. "Condom."

"I'm clean if you are."

"I am, but are you also protected?"

She nodded. "All good."

"This is going to be even faster than expected."

Laughing, Mallory curled her arms around him as he made himself at home on top of her.

He gazed down at her, his fingers brushing the hair back from her face. Tipping his head, he kissed her with a kind of desperation he hadn't shown her before.

Keeping her hand wrapped around his cock, she guided him to where she wanted him most.

He entered her in increments, giving her time to adjust and accommodate him. The whole time, he watched over her, making sure they were still on the same page. "Good?" he asked.

"So good. Don't stop."

Releasing a gruff laugh, he said, "I may never want to stop."

After that, there were no more words, only intense pleasure that she felt everywhere as he moved inside her, touching off sensations she'd forgotten she was capable of feeling. The exceptionally tight fit ignited every nerve ending she owned.

Mallory smoothed her hands over his back to grip his ass, digging her fingers into the dense flesh as she pulled him deeper into her. She arched her hips into every stroke.

He drew her left nipple into his mouth, sucking on the tight tip as he pushed hard into her, triggering a screaming orgasm that she felt from the top of her head to the soles of her feet and everywhere in between.

"Oh, *damn*," he whispered, dropping his head to her shoulder and riding the wave of her release into his own. His fingertips dug into her shoulders as he let himself go before dropping down on top of her.

Her heart pounding and her body tingling, Mallory wrapped her arms around him and held on tight.

"I'm going to want to do that again very soon," he said.

She smiled, her lips curving against his neck. "Me, too."

"I'm crushing you."

"I like it."

"You like *me*."

"You're okay."

He took a bite out of her neck, making her squeal. "Admit it. You like me."

"I wouldn't be naked in bed with you if I didn't like you."

"You like me a *lot*."

Mallory snorted with laughter. "You're full of yourself."

He pressed his hips against her. "You're full of me, too."

"Ha-ha, very funny. How about you get your big self off me so I can finish making our dinner."

Lifting himself with his strong arms, he kissed her before he withdrew and moved to the side of her. He took hold of her hand and brought it to his lips. "You're amazing."

She leaned over to kiss him. "So are you."

"I have a feeling this could be something big between us. Do you?"

Mallory didn't hesitate when she said, "I do."

He surprised her when he gave her hand a tug, throwing her off balance and propelling her right back into his arms. "Well, look at that," he said, seeming exceptionally pleased with himself.

Before she could protest, he kissed her until she forgot all about dinner.

By the time they got around to eating, it was nearly eleven. Mallory wore his T-shirt, and he had put his pants back on, taking pains to ensure she didn't see his leg. She hoped that, in time, that wouldn't be a big deal to him, but she was on his timetable.

"I bet this steak was good five hours ago," she said, enjoying the view of him in the light of the single candle she'd placed on the table.

"But the potatoes wouldn't have been as crispy."

"Very true. I'm actually a much better cook than this meal would indicate."

"This is the best dinner I've had since the last one I had with you." He sat close enough to lean in for a kiss. "Thanks for cooking for me."

"You're welcome."

"And thanks for letting me stay here."

"You're very difficult to have around, but somehow I'll cope."

"Gee, thanks." He took another bite of crispy potato before he put down his fork and sat back in his chair to take a scrutinizing look at her.

"Do I have potato on my face or something?"

Quinn shook his head. "I just like to look at you." He reached for her hand and linked their fingers. "I meant what I said before."

"What in particular? Lots of things were said 'before.'"

"That this could be something amazing—and important. To me, anyway."

"To me, too. It already is."

"Why do I feel a gigantic 'but' lingering in the midst of it?"

"No buts."

Raising a brow, he said, "None at all?"

"Not for today or tonight or tomorrow. Beyond that, I don't know. I'm taking things a day at a time right now until I figure out a plan."

He rubbed his lips on the back of her hand, and that was all it took to make her want him again. "I hope you'll keep me informed of your plans."

"I will. I promise."

"I'm totally remiss in not asking how the first day at work went before now."

"It was good. I liked it."

"Any good calls?"

"Only one today, for an elderly woman who had fallen at home, but Mason said that's a rare day. We'll usually get at least two or three calls in a shift before the season begins in earnest, and then it's anyone's guess."

"They must be thrilled to have someone with your level of experience working with them."

"They are. Mason asked me to do some training for the team, which I'm happy to do."

"Mason this, Mason that. Are you sure you're just friends with that big guy?"

"You sound like a jealous boyfriend."

"Maybe I am."

"What? Jealous or my boyfriend?"

"Could I be both?"

"Do you want to be?"

"I could live without the jealousy, but I'd love to be your boyfriend."

"I haven't had one in a long time."

"That works out well, because I haven't been one in a long time."

"Have you ever been in love?"

"Twice. Once in college and once when I was first in medical school and thought I might get married."

"What happened?"

"The college romance fizzled after we graduated, and the medical school romance fizzled when she married someone else while I was deployed"

Mallory winced. "Ouch."

"That was a low point, but I learned a big lesson not to let myself get too involved with anyone, which was the beginning of another low point of too much sex and not enough humanity."

"I admire the way you talk so freely about your shortcomings. Not a lot of guys will do that, especially badass army trauma surgeons. Usually, there's more swagger than introspection."

His eyes sparkled with amusement. "And you've known a lot of badass army trauma surgeons?"

"A few here and there."

"If there's one thing I've learned from AA, it's humility. I'm a badass in the OR—or I was at one time—but when it comes to life, I've been somewhat of a fuckup. I'd like to think that phase is behind me now."

"No one gets to almost forty without a few hard knocks along the way."

"True." He continued to hold her hand and kiss the back of it and basically distract her with only his lips brushing up against her skin. "We ought to do something really cool for our fortieth birthdays. How often do you meet someone who was born on the exact same day as you?"

"Not very often. What would count as something really cool?"

"I don't know. Like a trip or a big party or… something."

"You'll be getting ready to open your facility around the time of our birthday."

"We could work around that. I'll make the time. Turning forty is a big deal. It ought to be celebrated."

"Ugh, do we have to? I'd prefer to forget all about it."

"One thing that surviving a serious injury teaches you is to enjoy every moment and celebrate the milestones."

"When you put it that way, forty doesn't look so bad. Ryan didn't even make it to thirty, so I guess I shouldn't complain."

"Being forty definitely beats the alternative, and besides, if you let me, I'll hold your hand through it and make it not so bad."

Mallory looked down at their joined hands and then up at his handsome face to find him gazing at her with true affection. "That'd be nice."

"See? You do like me. You want to keep me around until August."

"I never said that," she replied with a teasing smile.

"Yes, you did." He yawned dramatically and released her hand to stretch his arms above his head. "I'm exhausted. You'd better get me back to bed, nurse Mallory."

Rolling her eyes at him, she got up to see to the dishes and cut up the leftover steak for Brutus, who devoured the pieces she put in his bowl. She was standing at the sink when she felt Quinn behind her.

Propped on the crutches, he hooked an arm around her waist and kissed her neck, sending goose bumps down her spine. "Thanks for such a great night."

"Thank *you*."

"I didn't do anything."

"Um, I seem to recall you doing a few things."

His low laugh rumbled through his chest and vibrated against her. He pressed his cock against her back. "I might need you to refresh my memory."

She would be sore and tired tomorrow, but that didn't stop her from abandoning the dishes to follow him back to bed.

# CHAPTER 24

The following week, Quinn led Jared and Lizzie on a tour of the now fully renovated building that would open to patients in a few short months. He was finally off the crutches and walking, albeit carefully, on his prosthetic leg again. His stump still hurt, but not like it had at first.

"Everything looks so good," Lizzie said, taking in the new plaster, paint, tile, crown molding, doors and windows. "Mac and his company did a beautiful job."

"They certainly did. They were on budget and on schedule."

"Mac had the incentive of needing to be free and clear by the time the marina opened for the season," Jared said.

"Where are we with hiring?" Lizzie asked.

"I met with the recruiter last week, as you know, and I've offered the director of nursing position to someone we'd be very lucky to have."

"Anyone we know?" Jared asked.

"Maybe," he said, smiling as he thought of Mallory. After seven nights in her bed, he hadn't begun to sate the desire she stirred in him. He told himself the longing he felt for her had no resemblance whatsoever to the past, when he'd been all about the sex and had no regard for the women he did it with.

This was totally different because it was all about *her*. He didn't just love sleeping with her—and having sex with her. He also loved their conversations about life and loss and figuring out the way forward when your whole life had been upended. They had far more in common than their birthdays and their alcoholism, and he'd found comfort in being with someone who understood what it was like to stand at a crossroads and not know for certain that you were taking the right path. He liked that they were figuring it out together one day at a time, the way they'd been taught in AA.

"Are you going to tell us, or keep us in suspense?" Lizzie asked.

"I know better than to try to keep you in suspense."

"You're learning, bro," Jared said. "She's worse than a CSI investigator when someone holds out on her."

"I suppose that's better than when he says I'm like a dog with a bone," Lizzie said with a long-suffering sigh. "Now spill the beans, Quinn."

He smiled at her feistiness. "I asked Mallory if she'd be interested."

"Mallory, as in your girlfriend, Mallory, who you are currently living with?" Jared asked.

Quinn wasn't sure if his brother was expressing approval or disapproval, but he honestly didn't care either way. "One and the same."

"She'd be fantastic," Lizzie said. "I heard she ran the ER at one of the big hospitals in Providence for years."

"She did," Quinn confirmed. "Not only does she have management-level nursing experience, but she's also a medical school graduate and a certified paramedic. In fact, she's probably overqualified for the job."

"We can make it worth her while, can't we, Jared?" Lizzie asked.

"Of course, my love," he said indulgently. "Whatever you want."

"Seriously! We can't let someone like her slip through our fingers."

"I've made the offer, and she's asked for some time to think about it. She was laid off in May and is still getting her bearings while she works on the rescue for the summer. I'm trying not to push her to decide anything before she's ready."

That was true for their personal relationship, as well. In all the time they'd spent together recently, they hadn't once spoken of what would happen at the end of the summer. He kept thinking they had plenty of time to figure that out, but with every minute—and every night—he spent with her, he wanted more. He wanted to know that what they were building together was more than a summer fling. However, as much as he wanted those answers, he knew better than to push her to make decisions before she was ready.

*Patience*, he thought. This situation required more patience than he'd ever needed before, except for after he lost his leg and wanted to be back up and at it right away, even if that wasn't possible. He'd gotten through that and could be patient for her, because that was what she needed, but it wasn't easy. After so many years on his own, he'd finally found someone who made him not want to be alone anymore, and he wanted to go all in with her.

"How are things going with you two?" Lizzie asked in a deceptively casual tone.

"Careful, bro," Jared said as he wandered over to check out the view from one of the future patient rooms.

"Hush, Jared. I'm talking to Quinn, not you."

Jared chuckled under his breath, but they both heard him.

"It's going well, if you must know. I like her. She likes me. We have fun together."

"Is that all it is? Summer fun?"

Her question struck at the heart of his insecurities where Mallory was concerned.

"I guess we'll find out in September, won't we?"

"Quinn…"

"It's okay, Lizzie. I'm happy with it the way it is." *For now*, he thought. Mallory had been a great help to him at the meeting with the recruiter and had been an excellent sounding board for questions he had afterward. At some point, he'd have to hold her feet to the fire about the job—and what was happening between them. Neither had to happen today or even tomorrow. But he hoped he had answers sooner rather than later in both cases.

Mallory took the stairs to the second floor, where her uncle Kevin had rented office space over the South Harbor Diner to open his psychiatry practice. She'd called to see if he had time to chat since today was one of her days off from the rescue. He'd told her to come right over, which had set off a flurry of nerves. She'd expected to make an appointment for next week, but apparently family had head-of-the-line privileges.

She knocked on the door to his office, and he called for her to come in.

"Hi there," she said to her uncle, who was the youngest of Big Mac's two brothers.

He jumped up from his desk to greet her with a hug and a kiss. "This is a nice surprise." Ushering her to a seating area that included several easy chairs, he encouraged her to have a seat and then sat across from her.

Mallory was still getting used to the easy affection that her family members doled out, as if they'd known her all her life rather than just a year. "Thanks for squeezing me in."

"They're hardly lining up at the door—yet," he said with a chuckle.

"I'm sure they will be once the word gets out."

Kevin shrugged. "Either way, it's fine. I'm happy to be partially retired and working when I feel like it rather than because I have to."

"That sounds like an ideal existence."

"It is for me. I get to spend lots of time with Chelsea when she's not working and can pick and choose my hours here."

"So you're here to stay, then?"

"Looks that way. My ex-wife and I are selling our house in Connecticut, and I'm looking to buy something here. My brothers are here, my sons are here, my nieces and nephews are here. Why would I want to be anywhere else?"

"So Riley and Finn are planning to stick around, too?"

"Mac's construction company is keeping them so busy that they haven't mentioned going back to Connecticut in a couple of months now. I think the island is starting to feel like home to them."

"I'm beginning to feel the same way myself."

"Ohhh, your dad will be so happy to hear that."

"Don't tell him quite yet."

Kevin ran his fingers over his lips. "I would never repeat anything we talk about, Mallory. I hope you know you can trust me with anything that's on your mind."

She smiled at him. "So you've figured out this isn't a social call?"

"I had a sneaking suspicion. What can I do for you?"

"Linda actually suggested I talk to you a while ago about some unresolved issues I have with the way my mother handled telling me about my father."

"She told you in a letter after she died, right?"

"That's right."

"Had you asked her about him?"

"Only my entire life. I always wanted to know who he was, but she was evasive and said she'd tell me when the time was right. As I got older and busy with school and work and life, I asked less often, but I still wondered. There was always a huge hole where he should've been, you know?"

"I can imagine."

"She did everything for me. She was the best possible mother I could've had, and when I think of her now, I seethe with anger. It's like the anger is all that's left of her now that I've met my dad and all of you. Now that I know what I missed out on my whole life, I'm so, so *angry* with her for keeping me from him. And I hate myself for feeling that way toward her."

"You can't help the way you feel."

"I know, but it still makes me feel guilty when she's not here to defend herself."

"What do you think she'd say if she was here?"

Mallory thought about that for a moment. "She'd probably apologize."

"Would that help?"

"Not really. It wouldn't change anything."

"Why do you suppose she didn't tell you?"

"She was afraid I'd choose him over her, and she'd be all alone, or so I assume. Her family rejected her when she got pregnant, so it was really just her and me. I wouldn't have left her alone. I would've wanted both of them in my life."

"But she couldn't know that for sure, right? When you were say, ten, she might've thought, this would be a good time to introduce Mallory to her father, but what if she decides she'd rather live on Gansett with him and his family than here in Providence with me? Maybe I should wait a little longer..."

"How does a little longer become almost forty years?"

"That I can't tell you, and neither can she, thus your anger."

"I keep thinking I should get over it. We all know you can't change the past, and she did what she did for reasons that were valid to her. I get that. But every time I hear my siblings talk about things that happened years ago, the anger comes surging back to the surface again."

"Let's talk about that. You know that you wouldn't have been with them all the time. Even if your mom had told you about your dad sooner, they'd still have stories and family things that you weren't part of, right?"

"I suppose so."

"You would've been with your mom most of the time. You would've still missed out on much of what went on with your siblings."

"At least I would've *known* them," she said, blinking back tears. "I would've liked to have known them. And the rest of you, too, especially my dad."

"I know," he said gently, "and what I think might be happening is in addition to grieving the loss of your mother, you're grieving the loss of what you should've had with your dad and the rest of your family. Do you think that's possible?"

"Probably." She wiped away tears. "I tell myself that what I have now is enough. It's more than I ever could've hoped for when I came looking for my dad."

"And yet you're still angry."

Mallory laughed even as she wiped away new tears. "And yet I'm still angry."

"You know what might help? If you wrote her a letter and told her everything you're thinking and feeling about what she did. Maybe if you got it all out there and off your chest, you might be able to get past the anger."

"That's an interesting idea." Especially in light of her habit of writing things down, Mallory thought.

"It might also help you to know that you're not the only one who has had some anger with how this was handled."

Surprised to hear that, Mallory said, "Who else?"

"Who was the other person who should've been told?"

Mallory stared at him for a long, charged moment. "Dad?"

Kevin nodded. "He would never, *ever* speak poorly of your mother, not to you or anyone. But I know he's wrestled with why she didn't tell him. It's been hard on him, too."

"He's never said that to me."

"He wouldn't. He'd never burden you with something you had nothing to do with."

"He wouldn't be burdening me."

"That's how he would see it. He aches over what he missed with you, Mallory. Please don't think for one second that he doesn't. And I'm not speaking out of turn here. He's spoken to me about this as his brother, not as his doctor, and I'm telling you this as my niece, not my patient."

"I understand." She wiped her face with the tissue he handed her. "Is it normal, after something like this happens, to feel disconnected from your life?"

"It's normal, after losing your mother, finding your father and a family you didn't know you had and then losing your longtime job—all in one year—to feel extremely disconnected. Nothing about this new life resembles the old life, and it's only natural that it'll take some time for the new to seem normal to you."

"I've been offered a job here."

"On the rescue? I heard. That's wonderful."

She shook her head. "That's a summer job. There's no budget for the off-season. The job I've been offered is director of nursing at the healthcare facility Jared and Lizzie James are opening this fall."

"That's amazing! Congratulations."

"Thank you. It's nice to feel wanted after the way I was unceremoniously dumped by my former employer."

"Why do I sense there's more to this than you're letting on?"

"Because you're good at this, and because there is." Mallory sighed. "The offer came from the man I'm seeing, Dr. Quinn James, the facility's medical director."

"Ahhh, sticky."

"Right."

"Would he be your boss?"

"He says no, that we'd be colleagues and could set it up so I'd answer directly to his brother and sister-in-law."

"That would seem to negate any potential conflict of interest issues."

"It does."

"So what's the problem?"

"The relationship with him is new, and the worry becomes what happens at work if things go south between us. His brother owns the place. He's not going anywhere."

"Which is a reasonable concern."

"And?"

"And what?"

"I can tell there's more you'd like to say. Speak to me as my uncle and not a therapist."

"As your uncle, I'd remind you that you're a highly qualified professional with impeccable credentials who could probably land the job of your choice in any city in this country. If things go south with him personally, and it becomes untenable to work with him professionally, you leave."

"You say that as if it's simple."

"It is. You're still in that early career mind-set of having to hold on to a job at all costs because you might not be able to find another. We both know the shortage of qualified nurses would make you a hot commodity anywhere you chose to go. So go into the new job with the new man holding your own set of cards. Play them as you see fit."

"You're good at this. You might want to consider a career."

Kevin's ringing laugh made her smile. "If only I were as good at sorting my own crap as I am with other people's."

"Are things okay with Chelsea?"

"Things are great with her, other than everything being on hold until my divorce is final at the end of the summer."

"What then?"

"We're waiting to talk about it when I'm free and clear."

"And that's driving you nuts."

"Little bit. She's the *one*, you know? Took me more than fifty years to find her, and I worry all the time that I'm going to lose her."

"I've seen you two together. She's not going anywhere."

"Still… I'll be happy when we can make it official in some way or another. Stuff like this, what I have with her… When you live long enough, you know it doesn't come along every day, which makes it that much more urgent. Does that make sense?"

"It does. I've experienced some of that myself in recent weeks."

"With your doctor friend."

She nodded.

"So it's something special with him?"

"Could be. I'm taking baby steps."

"If I could give you one piece of advice, it would be to grab something that feels special and hold on with everything you've got. I spent thirty years in a mediocre relationship that I don't regret because I got my amazing sons from it and we had a good life. But I can tell you there's absolutely nothing like the real thing."

Mallory already knew that to be true and had begun to realize that her feelings for Quinn were similar to what she'd felt for Ryan. He hadn't been gone so long that she'd forgotten the thrill of being truly in love. "Thank you for your wisdom," she said as she got up to leave.

He stood to give her a hug. "I'm here for you as a therapist or an uncle or a friend, any time you need any of the above."

"That means the world to me. You have no idea."

"We're all happy to have you as part of our family, Mallory, and I'm a big believer that things happen for a reason. Maybe if you'd known your dad as a child, you wouldn't be here now, and you wouldn't have met Quinn. It's possible this was how it was always meant to be."

"You've given me plenty to think about."

"Then my work here is finished."

"I'll see you at Dan and Kara's wedding?"

"Yes, you will." He walked her to the door and opened it for her. "Be kind to yourself, sweetheart. You'll figure out the path that works for you when the time is right."

She gave him a kiss on the cheek. "Appreciate it."

"My pleasure."

# CHAPTER 25

Mallory went down the stairs and walked slowly through town, taking in the sights and sounds of the bustling ferry landing and enjoying the heat of the warm sunshine on her face. The town was decidedly less busy now that Race Week was over, but islanders expected busy weekends and weeks of madness once school let out.

She crossed the street to a bench that overlooked South Harbor and watched one of the big ferries arrive with a small number of people onboard, but it was full of cars as well as fuel and mail trucks.

From her vantage point looking down at the harbor, she could see that Joe was at the controls of the arriving ferry, and she watched, fascinated, as he turned the huge vessel around in the small harbor and backed it into port.

"Quite somethin' to watch, t'isn't it?" Ned Saunders asked as he took a seat next to her on the bench.

"I could never do that."

"We all have our gifts. That's one a' Joe's."

"What are his others?"

"Painting."

"What kind of painting?"

"Landscapes. He's got a gift fer it."

"Every time I think I've heard it all, there's something more to learn about my family," Mallory said with a sigh.

"Yer doing just fine, gal."

"You really think so?"

"Course I do or I wouldn'ta said so."

She smiled at his adorable bluster. "I feel like I'm constantly playing catch-up. I don't get the jokes. It's like being the new kid in a school full of kids who grew up together."

"Ya'll catch up. Gonna take some time, but ya'll git there."

"I hope so."

"Yer daddy is tickled pink that ya're here for the summer. Got his heart set on keepin' ya here for longer."

"Does he?" Mallory asked, amused and pleased to hear that.

"Ya know it. Ya probably got him figured out by now. A big softie, he is."

She couldn't think of a better word to describe her father. "For sure."

"Best guy I ever known. He woulda been there fer ya. Every step of the way. Hope ya know that."

A sudden lump in her throat made it impossible to do anything more than nod.

"Fer what it's worth, I hope ya stick around, too."

"That's very nice of you to say."

"Ya can't be in on the joke if ya ain't where they are." Seeing that people were beginning to disembark from the ferry, Ned stood. "Gotta get back ta work." He gave her shoulder a squeeze. "Have a nice day now."

"You, too, Ned."

She watched him walk away, whistling as he went, and thought about what he'd said about how she couldn't be in on the jokes in her family if she wasn't *with* her family. Between what Kevin had said and Ned's words of wisdom, it was abundantly clear that her move to Gansett Island needed to be longer term than just the summer. Three months wouldn't be long enough to learn the tiny details she yearned to know about each of her family members.

Mallory wanted to know them the way they knew each other and learn to speak their language. Janey had told her she could rent the house for as long as she wanted and had hinted that she hoped it would be longer than the summer.

She had a home, a job offer, her wonderful family all around her and a guy who wanted her to stay. Mallory laughed out loud at the simplicity of her decision when framed in the proper context. She'd asked for the summer to make up her mind, and here it was, early June, and she already knew what she was going to do.

Rising from the bench, she headed home, eager to tell Quinn the news.

Blaine and Tiffany took the three-o'clock boat off the island for the meeting with Jim. They'd brought Blaine's truck and would drive to the state attorney general's office in Providence, where the meeting would take place. It had taken a couple of weeks to hammer out the conditions for the meeting.

At first, Jim had refused to meet with Tiffany if Blaine was with her. Blaine had been adamant that she not go alone. They'd compromised, agreeing that he would accompany her to the meeting but not be in the room when she spoke to Jim. Blaine had agreed reluctantly, and things had been tense between them ever since.

Tiffany totally understood why he was upset, but all she could think about was trying to put this situation to rest for Ashleigh's sake. Protecting her daughter was her only goal.

Blaine stood by her side at the rail as the ferry approached the breakwater at Point Judith. "If he touches you in any way, I'll be through that door so fast, he won't know what hit him." Those were the first words he'd spoken since they left the house.

"Okay," Tiffany said, knowing it was pointless to object. He had to feel like he could protect her, or he wouldn't be able to handle being relegated to the observation room.

Blaine wrapped his much bigger hand around hers. He didn't say anything else, but the tight squeeze of his hand said everything for him. When the ferry pulled into port on the mainland, he led her down the stairs and helped her into the truck. After he was settled in the driver's seat, he reached for her hand again and held it all the way to Providence.

Sam Rhodes met them in the lobby and escorted them upstairs to the room where the meeting would take place. He showed Blaine the door to the observation area where he'd be able to see and hear everything.

"I'll give you a minute," Sam said to Tiffany. "When you're ready, you can join us."

"Thank you," Tiffany said.

Sam stepped into the conference room and shut the door.

Tiffany looked up at Blaine, noting the dark circles under his eyes and tension that clung to him. She reached up to caress a pulsing muscle in his cheek. "I love you."

"I love you, too." He rested his hands on her shoulders. "Protect yourself in there, Tiffany. Don't let him say or do anything to harm you. I mean it."

"He'll be on his best behavior with the prosecutor in there, and I'll be fine because I know you're right outside the door, watching out for me." With her hand on his neck, she brought him down for a kiss. "Let me get this over with so we can get on with our lives, okay?"

Nodding, he returned her kiss and let her go with what seemed to be tremendous reluctance.

She smiled reassuringly at him and left him in the observation area. Outside the door to the conference room, she took a deep breath, steeling herself for whatever might happen. Jim meant nothing to her. Not anymore. But he was and would always be Ashleigh's father, and there was nothing Tiffany wouldn't do for her little girl, including face off with the man who'd disappointed her so profoundly.

Tiffany had taken care with her appearance, and the effort paid off in the wistful way in which Jim studied her as she walked into the room and sat next to Sam, across the table from Jim and his attorney. Jim wore a light blue dress shirt, and unlike the last time she'd seen him, he was well groomed, the way he'd always been before he went off the rails.

Tiffany folded her hands and made sure her diamond engagement and wedding rings from Blaine were prominently displayed.

"You asked for this meeting," Jim said in the snide tone she'd become accustomed to from him in the last few years of their marriage. "What do you want?"

"I would like for you to consider accepting a plea to spare your daughter the humiliation of a trial."

He snorted. "She's four. What does she know about humiliation?"

"She'll be five soon and going to school with other kids whose parents will be talking about how, in a drunken stupor, you pulled a knife at an engagement party and assaulted Dan. Is that what you want your daughter to be confronted with on the playground in kindergarten?"

To his credit, Jim had the good sense to seem chagrined. "No, that's not what I want."

"Take the plea, Jim. Spare her the embarrassment and ridicule of having your sins thrown in her face. We live in a very small town. This will stick to her forever as it is. Why make it worse than it already is?"

"What about your sins? Will those stick to her, too?"

Tiffany stared at him, determined to remain calm and not take the bait. "I've never committed a felony or been intoxicated in public."

"No, you just sell dildos for a living."

"Jim," his attorney said, the warning clear.

"Which is perfectly legal," she said, remaining calm.

The two of them stared at each other across the table, and in that uncomfortable silence, Tiffany made a decision. "Could we have a minute alone, please?" she asked the lawyers.

"Umm, that wasn't the plan," Rhodes said.

"I need one minute," she said.

Jim nodded to his attorney, who got up and left the room with the prosecutor.

Tiffany knew that Blaine would be furious, so she spoke quickly. "I'd like to ask you one more time to tell me what it was that I did so wrong that led to all this.

And I want to be clear that I'm asking for Ashleigh's sake. Someday my daughter is going to ask me what happened between Mommy and Daddy, and I'd like to be able to tell her, because I don't have the first clue."

Jim stared mulishly across the table, his jaw set in the stubborn expression she knew all too well.

"I was a good wife to you, Jim. I worked two jobs to put you through law school. I took care of everything so all you had to do was study. When we moved home to Gansett, I ran two businesses while keeping our home and taking care of the beautiful daughter I gave you. I'd really like to be able to tell Ashleigh something other than I don't know, not *if* she asks, but *when* she does."

He was quiet for so long that she didn't think he was going to answer her.

Tiffany was about to give up on him when he finally said, "It wasn't anything you did."

"Then what was it?"

"It was me," he said with a sigh. "I was dissatisfied with everything once we got back to Gansett. I don't know why, but things changed for me after we moved home. It was… a letdown to be back there where nothing ever changes."

Tiffany stared at him, her mouth agape. "So you threw away your marriage and family and the career we'd both worked so hard to give you because you were *bored?*"

"Not bored so much as disappointed. I kept asking myself, is this it? For the rest of my life? *This* is all there is?"

Wondering if she'd ever known him at all, she sat back in her chair and folded her arms. "You're a fool."

His eyes flashed with emotion. "Do you think I need you to tell me that? I've had nothing but time to think about the many ways I fucked everything up."

"So you get now that it was *you* who fucked it all up? Not me or Dan or anyone else. It was *you*, Jim."

"I get it," he said on a low growl.

Hearing him take responsibility for the mess he'd made was, she realized, the best outcome she could've hoped for. "You took everything we had when you left. Why did you do that?"

"I was so angry."

"At me?"

"At you, at myself."

"I did everything I could and more than I probably should have to keep our family together. I deserved better than to be treated that way, Jim, and so did Ashleigh." After a long pause, she said, "Take the plea and make it go away for all of us. Do the right thing for once." She got up and headed for the door.

"Tiffany."

Stopping, she took another breath and turned around. "What?"

"I love Ashleigh. She's the most important person in the world to me. I want to be better for her so I can be part of her life."

"I want that for her, too." With nothing left to say, Tiffany exited the room and ran smack into her husband, who'd been standing right outside the door. She curled her hands around his arm. To Sam Rhodes, she said, "I did what I could."

"Appreciate you coming in. We'll be in touch."

"Let's go," she said to Blaine, desperately wanting to avoid an altercation between her current and former husbands. Judging by the tightness in Blaine's muscles, it wouldn't take much to provoke him. She gave his arm a tug to get him moving in the right direction but didn't breathe easy until they were in the parking lot on the way to his truck.

Blaine opened the door for her and held it until long after she was settled in her seat.

"Blaine."

His gaze shifted to her.

"Talk to me."

"I… When you were alone with him… All I could think about was him swinging that knife at you, and I…"

Tiffany turned in her seat and wrapped her arms around him.

He buried his face in the curve of her neck.

When she realized her strong, fearless husband was actually trembling, her eyes filled with tears that slid down her cheeks. "I'm so sorry you were scared."

"I was afraid he'd try to hurt you, and there'd be no one in there with you."

"I'm okay, and it's all over now." She ran her fingers through his hair for a long time, until the trembling finally stopped.

He raised his head off her shoulder and kissed away her tears. "Is he going to take the plea?"

"I don't know, but I got some badly needed answers. At least I know now that what happened had nothing to do with me. He was dissatisfied with his life, if you can imagine that."

"No, I can't, because I get to be married to you, and I'll never be dissatisfied a day in my life because I have you."

"I'm so happy to be married to you. I'd go through hell all over again if it meant I got you in the end." Holding his face in her hands, she kissed him.

He responded with the pent-up emotion that followed weeks of tension, until they were half reclined in the front seat of his truck.

Tiffany laughed at their loss of control.

Blaine leaned his forehead on hers. "I love you so fucking much. I never knew it was possible to love anyone the way I love you."

"I love you just as much."

Tiffany's cell phone rang, and she saw Sam Rhodes's name on the caller ID.

"He's agreed to plead guilty to a misdemeanor assault charge and serve six months in jail, but he'll retain his law license, which was critical to him."

"Thank goodness." She flashed a thumbs-up to Blaine. "Thank you so much for letting me know."

"Thank *you* for convincing him it was the right thing to do."

She said good-bye to Sam and hugged Blaine. "Thank God it's over."

"Let's go home," Blaine said.

"Yes, please."

# CHAPTER 26

Mallory arrived home shortly before five and dug her ringing cell phone out of her purse. She didn't recognize the local number but still took the call.

"Hey, Mallory, it's Sydney Harris. How are you?"

"Hi, Syd. What's up?"

"I got your number from Janey. I wanted to let you know that Luke and I are doing a bonfire on the beach tonight if you'd like to join us."

"I'd love to. Thanks for the invite."

"Great. Plan on dinner, too. Luke built a grill on the beach this spring, and he's been dying to use it."

"That sounds great. What can I bring?"

"Not a thing other than a friend, if you wish to."

Mallory laughed. "Is that a subtle attempt to get me to admit to dating someone?"

"I might have heard a rumor. Or two."

"I'll see if he's available to join us."

"I'll look forward to seeing you both."

"Thanks again, Syd."

Mallory ended the call, feeling excited to see Quinn, to tell him her news, to invite him to come tonight and to be her plus one at Dan and Kara's wedding. Kara had told her it was casual and to bring someone if she wanted to.

Her talk with Kevin had really helped to clarify things, and she was ready to dive in headfirst with Quinn as well as her new life on Gansett. She took a shower, dried her hair and changed into jeans and a T-shirt, but grabbed a sweater that she knew she'd need when the sun went down. Even in early June, the nights on Gansett were still chilly.

As she waited for Quinn, it occurred to her that she'd like to have a glass of wine. There were times, such as this, when she was in a happy mood and looking forward to socializing with friends and family, that she wished she could have an occasional glass of wine. If only it were that simple. But she'd learned her issues with alcohol were anything but simple and that it was in her best interest to refrain from drinking.

She told herself she had so many things in her life to be thankful for these days that she didn't need the comfort she'd once taken from overindulging. Now she could find comfort in the new relationships she was forging with her family members as well as Quinn, and the new friends she was making on the island.

However, all the positive thoughts in the world didn't quench her desire for that glass of wine. The decision not to drink, not to give in to the almighty temptation, was a daily decision she made for herself. And like most days over the last decade, today she chose her sobriety over the temptation.

She checked the time and saw it was nearly six, which was late for Quinn to get home, so she sent him a text:

*On the way home?*

As soon as she sent it, she worried that maybe she sounded too much like a wife rather than a girlfriend or whatever she was to him.

Mallory kept an eye on her phone for a few minutes, but he didn't reply. She fed Brutus and let him out into the yard.

An hour later, she'd begun to worry that something had happened to him, so she called him.

No answer.

What if something had happened at work and no one was there to help him? Her stomach began to ache as a host of unsettling scenarios occurred to her.

A couple of days ago, Jared had texted both of them to invite them to dinner. Mallory hadn't asked how he'd gotten her number. She assumed Quinn had given it to his brother. Now that she needed it, she was happy to have Jared's number.

He answered on the second ring.

"Jared, hi, it's Mallory. I'm just wondering if you've spoken to Quinn."

"Not since this morning. Is everything okay?"

"I'm sure it is, but he's usually back to my house by now, and I can't reach him. I thought he might be with you."

"No, he isn't."

"Maybe I should go to his office…"

"I'll do it. It's dark as hell and deserted this time of day. I wouldn't want you out there by yourself."

"I hate to bother you."

"It's no bother. I'll call you in a few."

"Thanks, Jared."

Mallory took the phone with her to the sofa, where she sat to wait. Brutus curled up next to her, his head on her leg so she could scratch behind his ears. With every passing minute that went by with no word from Quinn, her anxiety quadrupled.

Darkness surrounded him. Where the hell was he? And why did his head hurt like a motherfucker?

Quinn reached up to touch the area on his forehead that radiated pain and encountered wetness. "Shit." He tried to sit up and immediately regretted it when his head spun and nausea burned his throat. "Ugh."

Then he realized his bad leg was at an awkward angle and the prosthetic had been wrenched—again.

He groaned. Fuck, fuck, *fuck*. The memories came rushing back to him. He'd been about to leave the office when he heard an odd noise coming from the basement. The last thing he remembered was reaching to turn on the light. Had he fallen down the stairs? How long had he been there? And where was his phone?

A quick inspection of his pockets yielded nothing. And then he heard it ringing and saw it light up about ten feet from him.

*Mallory.* Crap, she was probably wondering where he was and worried about him as she tried to find him. Damn it.

Forcing himself into a sitting position, he brushed away the blood on his face and fought through an urgent need to puke. He had to get to his phone, even if he had to crawl to it.

Closing his eyes, he took deep breaths to fight back the nausea and inched himself forward, hissing from the pain that came from his head and leg. Just when he'd been on his way back to what now counted for normal, this had to happen. Despair swept over him, reminding him of the awful days after he'd first lost his leg

Quinn moved slowly and painfully, his head swimming and his leg throbbing. He was about halfway to the phone when he heard Jared shout for him from upstairs.

"Down here," he said, relieved to have help.

"Quinn!"

"Basement," he called.

"What the… Oh my God!"

A sudden flood of light had Quinn closing his eyes tight against the pain.

Jared came pounding down the stairs. "Jesus, Quinn. You're bleeding like crazy. Are you okay? What happened? Oh shit! Your leg."

"Shhh, not so loud."

"Crap. You're hurt bad." Jared withdrew his phone from his pocket and called for the rescue.

Quinn was in too much pain to object.

"What were you doing?"

"I heard a noise coming from down here and decided to investigate. That's the last thing I remember before I woke up down here."

"Mallory's worried. I'm going to tell her to meet us at the clinic."

*Mallory.* Quinn sighed. She deserved better than this, better than him. She'd spent her entire adult life taking care of people. She needed someone who could take care of her, not a broken-down wreck of a man who needed constant care from her. The thought of not seeing her gorgeous face every day crushed him, but he needed to be fair to her.

Jared encouraged Quinn to lean against him while they waited. "How did this happen?"

"Not sure. I reached for the lights and came to down here. Must've made a wrong move somewhere."

"You could've been killed."

"That might've been better than dealing with this shit."

"Shut the fuck up. That wouldn't have been better. It was an accident. Could've happened to anyone."

Jared was trying to make him feel better, but what he said wasn't true. It wouldn't have happened to someone with two good legs who could instinctively tell that the next step was going to be a bad one.

Quinn didn't have the energy or the fortitude to argue the point.

"Should I check this noise you heard?" Jared asked.

"I don't hear it now."

"I'll check it out in the morning."

Paramedics arrived a few minutes later, along with Mason Johns, the fire chief. He was the kind of guy Mallory should be with—big, strong, commanding and in possession of all his limbs.

"What're we looking at here?" Mason asked him.

He appreciated Mason's acknowledgment that Quinn already knew what was wrong. "Probably a severe concussion in addition to the laceration on my forehead, and I wrenched my leg."

Mason glanced toward his leg, and Quinn saw the realization register with him. "You're an amputee."

"I am."

Mason directed his team to carefully carry Quinn up the stairs, where they had a stretcher waiting.

Jared followed them, carrying the prosthetic that Quinn had removed.

Quinn wanted to grab the thing out of his brother's hands and fling it across the room. He vibrated with rage and despair. Every step forward led to two steps backward. Just when he thought things were moving in the right direction—new job, new home, new lady—he was served a heaping dose of reality, reminding him once again of what'd been lost.

"I'm going to follow so I have my car," Jared said as they loaded Quinn into the ambulance. Quinn raised a hand to let his brother know he'd heard him.

At least he could be thankful for the small favor that Mallory was off duty when her coworkers had to rescue him.

Mallory rushed into the clinic and ran toward Katie Lawry, the first person she saw. Jared had told her only that Quinn had gotten hurt at work and was being transported to the clinic. "Katie, I'm looking for Quinn James. The rescue brought him in?"

"Right this way, Mallory." Katie led her to a cubicle, where Quinn was in bed and Jared stood by his side.

The sight of Quinn's bloodstained face and the evil cut on his forehead stopped her short. "Oh my God! What happened?"

"Wrong move on the basement steps," Quinn said.

"Did you fall down them?"

"Yep."

"Oh no. Are you hurt anywhere else?"

"Just the usual place."

"No…" Her heart broke for him. Right when he'd been back on his leg again. "What're they doing for you?"

"They called in David Lawrence," Jared said. "He's on his way."

Mallory took hold of Quinn's hand and had to hide her surprise when he pulled free and crossed his arms, his face set in a mulish expression she'd never seen before.

She glanced at Jared and noted he seemed as concerned as she felt. Something else had happened to Quinn at the bottom of those stairs, something far beyond his physical injuries.

Katie began to clean the cut on Quinn's head while they waited for David, who arrived a short time later and quickly assessed Quinn's injuries. "I'd like to get a scan of your head, just to make sure."

"I can already tell you it's a concussion," Quinn said.

"You know as well as I do that you can't tell me if you're bleeding on the inside, and we need to rule that out." To Mallory and Katie, he said, "I've heard it said that doctors make the worst patients."

"No comment," Katie said, smiling.

Mallory forced a small smile, but she couldn't work up anything more than that when Quinn was going out of his way to distance himself from her.

"We'll be quick," David said. "I promise."

They wheeled Quinn's bed from the room, leaving Mallory alone with Jared, who looked as shell-shocked as she felt.

"He fell down the full set of stairs?" she asked in a small voice.

Jared nodded.

"God."

"I know. He could've been killed."

Mallory crossed her arms and took a deep breath to ward off the emotional firestorm she felt brewing. This felt all too familiar, bringing back memories of the day her young husband had died so suddenly. That same thing could've happened to Quinn and right when she'd decided she wanted everything with him…

Jared startled her when he put his arm around her. "He's fine. Pissed off and banged up. But fine."

Lizzie came rushing into the room, looking undone and frazzled. "Where is he? Is he okay?"

Jared held out his hand to her, and she came over to him. "He fell down the basement stairs at the building. They think he has a concussion, and they're scanning him to make sure that's all it is. He's banged up but okay."

She sagged against her husband. "Thank God you called Jared, Mallory. Who knows how long he would've been there otherwise."

The thought of him alone and injured in the basement of that dark building made Mallory shudder. They waited in uneasy silence until Katie wheeled Quinn back into the room.

"David will be in shortly," she said. "Can I get you anything, Quinn?"

"Some ice water would be good."

"Coming right up."

Mallory immediately noticed that Quinn had bled through the gauze Katie had placed on his forehead. Acting on instinct, she went to the sink to wash her hands, pulled on gloves and, making use of the supplies Katie had left on a nearby tray, got busy replacing the dressing. At first, Quinn leaned away from her, but she didn't let up. If he thought he was going to push her away now, he was about to find out that she wasn't easily pushed.

"Hold still," she said sternly.

Katie returned with the water. "Oh, thanks, Mallory. It helps to have an extra set of qualified hands around here."

"Try telling that to my patient," Mallory said.

"I'm not your patient," Quinn said in a testy tone that again took her by surprise.

"All yours, Katie," Mallory said. She removed the gloves and trashed them on her way out of the room. Clearly, he didn't want her there, so she'd wait until the time was right to ask him what the hell was going on. She wasn't about to do that with an audience.

She sank into a chair in the waiting room and put her head back against the wall.

"He's upset that he got hurt again," Lizzie said when she joined her. "That's all it is."

"If you say so. Feels like more than that to me."

Lizzie sat next to her. "I don't know him very well. You probably know him better than I do, but the one thing I know for sure about him is that he's fiercely independent, and relying on others doesn't come easily to him."

"I think I might love him."

Lizzie gasped. "Really?"

Mallory nodded. "I haven't felt this way for anyone since I lost my husband thirteen years ago."

"Oh. I didn't know. I'm so sorry."

"Thank you."

"I think," Lizzie said tentatively, "he might love you, too, and he doesn't want you to have to deal with his… limitations."

"When I look at him, I don't see limitations. I see resilience and determination and perseverance."

"At some point, possibly very soon, you might have to tell him that."

Mallory looked over at Lizzie, offering a small smile. "Do me a favor?"

"Anything."

"Don't invite him to your house when they release him."

Lizzie returned her smile. "He is *so* not welcome at my house."

# CHAPTER 27

Two hours later, after five stitches to close the head wound and declaring the scans to be clear, David released Quinn with instructions to take it easy for the next couple of days.

"Thanks for coming in at night," Quinn said.

"No problem. I do it all the time. In fact, I might want to talk to you at some point about backing each other up so we can actually take vacations once in a while."

Quinn shook his hand. "I'd be down for that. Sounds good."

Katie wheeled Quinn to the door where Mallory waited with her car to take him home.

"I can go with Jared and Lizzie," he said.

"Oh, um, we've got the guest room all ready for your parents when they come," Lizzie said, glancing at Jared.

"Could be any time now," Jared said. "You want Mom falling all over you?"

Mallory held her breath, waiting to hear what Quinn would say.

"No, I don't want that." He looked up at her. "You sure you don't mind?"

"I don't mind, and Brutus is waiting to see you."

He gave a short nod, which was the only indication she got that he was coming with her.

She sent Lizzie and Jared a grateful look.

"Call us if you guys need anything," Jared said.

"We'll be fine," Mallory assured him.

With Jared's help, Mallory got Quinn settled in her car, and Lizzie discreetly placed the prosthetic leg in the backseat.

"Call me if you need me," Jared said again.

"Thank you, Jared."

"Good luck."

"Thanks. I fear I'm going to need it."

He gave her shoulder a squeeze, and then he and Lizzie headed for their cars.

Mallory wiped her damp palms on her jeans and got into the car. The brief drive home occurred in total silence. She pulled into the driveway and cut the engine. "I'll get the crutches."

Brutus met her at the door, and she took a second to give him some quick attention.

"Be careful with your daddy. He's hurt and feeling bad."

Brutus whimpered and followed her into the bedroom, where Quinn's crutches had been propped in the corner for a couple of days now. Knowing how much he hated them, it pained her that he had to use them again, even temporarily.

"Stay," she said to Brutus when she went back out the front door to help Quinn.

He took the crutches from her without a word and got himself out of the car, pausing when the concussion fought back against the movement. Closing his eyes, he took a couple of shallow breaths.

Mallory watched over him but kept her distance, knowing he'd want to do this himself. However, she stayed closed enough to grab him if he stumbled.

Quinn moved slowly up the walk to the stairs, which he took one at a time while Mallory followed.

Brutus lost his mind when he saw Quinn, but didn't jump on him.

"Hey, buddy," Quinn said to the puppy as he made his way to the sofa, where he landed with a wince and a long exhale.

Brutus jumped up on the sofa to give Quinn a full sniffing, focusing on the forehead wound.

Mallory went into the kitchen to get them both some water and to give herself a minute to figure out her next move. He'd come with her because he hadn't had a choice, but she couldn't believe the guy she'd been so happy with over the last couple of weeks wasn't still in there somewhere under the veil of despair and dejection over this latest setback.

Resolved to be strong for him and to fight for them, she took the water to the living room, handed him a glass and sat next to him on the sofa.

Her phone chimed with a text that she saw was from Mac.

*Are you coming to the bonfire? Syd thought you might.*

*I can't make it tonight. Tell her I'm sorry to miss it.*

*Everything all right?*

*Quinn had an accident, but he's fine. Will check in with you tomorrow.*

*Sorry to hear that. Let me know if you need anything.*

*I will. Thanks.*

"Are you supposed to be somewhere?" he asked. "You don't have to babysit me if you've got stuff to do."

"I don't have anything to do."

"But you had plans?"

"We were both invited to a bonfire at the Harrises'."

"I'm sorry you had to miss it."

"I'm sorry you got hurt."

"Again."

Mallory shrugged. "Shit happens."

He took a drink of his water and put the glass on the table. "This is the Summer of Mallory. You don't need to be taking care of an invalid."

She snorted out a laugh.

"You think this is funny?"

"Only the part about you being an invalid. Clearly, you don't have much experience with invalids if you think you are one."

"You know what I mean!"

"I know that you've had two recent setbacks that have you thinking this is how the rest of your life is going to unfold, and surely no reasonable woman would want to be part of that."

He stared at her, seeming taken aback that she'd zeroed in on the heart of the matter so quickly.

"What happened to you, in both cases, were freak accidents that could've happened to anyone. Does it occur to you that if you'd never lost your leg, you might still have stepped in that hole in the dark and maybe torn your ACL or MCL and needed surgery to fix it? The prosthetic probably saved you from a more serious injury, and yes, a week on crutches was a drag, but it wasn't the end of the world as we know it. In fact, that week gave you a good excuse to stay here with me, and if I'm not mistaken, that week was pretty great. Or maybe I was the only one who thought so."

"You weren't the only one."

"Then why are you pushing me away rather than pulling me closer when you need me?"

With his jaw set in the now-familiar mulish expression, he glanced down at his hands, which were flat against his thighs. He looked as if he wished he could get the hell out of there but knew that wasn't possible. "I'm not good at needing anyone."

"No kidding. Really?"

His gaze shifted toward her. "Are you laughing at me again?"

"Maybe just a little."

"That's not nice," he said with a glint of humor in his eyes that she eagerly welcomed. "I'm an injured veteran trying to navigate life post-injury and fucking it up every which way."

Mallory inched closer to him, hoping he would welcome her rather than push her away. "Not every which way."

"No?"

She shook her head. "I was really, really worried about you earlier when I couldn't get in touch with you."

"I'm sorry to do that to you."

She placed her hand on top of his. "All that matters is that you're okay."

He turned his hand up and linked their fingers. "I need you to do something else for me."

"Whatever you need."

"Remind me why I can't get rip-roaring drunk right now when I want to so badly."

"Because we both know that'll only make things worse rather than better, and you've worked too hard to create a life that doesn't require alcohol and drugs."

"It was easier when I could numb the pain."

"Believe me, I know."

"Keep reminding me of that?"

"Any time you need to hear it."

With his palm pressed against hers, Mallory felt like she could truly breathe again for the first time in hours. "I'd also like to point out that the fact someone actually cares about you is the only reason you're not spending a long, uncomfortable night in a dark, creepy basement."

He huffed out a laugh. "True." Giving her hand a gentle squeeze, he said, "You didn't sign on to be my nurse."

"I love being a nurse. I love taking care of people, especially the ones I love."

His body went taut, and she swore he stopped breathing. "Does that include me?"

"What if it does? Are you going to run away from me screaming?"

"I'm not sure if you've noticed that I can't exactly run at the moment."

"Figuratively speaking."

"I don't want to be a burden to you."

"You're not. What you've been to me is so much more than that, and I'd like to think that if I ever fall down the stairs or wrench my knee stepping in a hole, maybe you would take care of me until I was back on my feet again."

"Of course I would."

"Then consider this a down payment on all my future needs."

His gaze locked on hers. "All of them?"

"Only if that's what you want, too."

He raised his free hand to her face, running his thumb over her skin and igniting a firestorm inside her. "I want you. As you well know, I've wanted you from the first instant I laid eyes on you, and I'm beginning to suspect there'll never be a time when I don't want you."

"Ditto." She leaned in close enough to place a gentle kiss on his lips. "Let me take care of you. Let me care about you. Let's do this together. There's nothing you could throw at me that I couldn't handle except losing you. Don't make me have to go through that again."

"I won't. I promise."

"How about we get you settled in bed where you'll be more comfortable."

"Only if you come with me."

"Nowhere else I'd rather be."

She helped him up and held him until he was steady.

"My head hurts like a son of a bitch."

"I'll get you something for that." She helped him to the bathroom and waited outside the door to give him some privacy. This day had not turned out the way she'd planned, but they'd still taken a huge step forward, which was what she'd wanted.

He hobbled into the bedroom, where she helped him out of his shirt, running her fingers over the bruises on his ribs. "Does it hurt?"

"Not too bad. My head is the worst of it."

When she reached for his belt, he stopped her.

Mallory looked up at him. "If we're going to make a go of this, I'm going to see it every day."

After a long pause, he lifted his hand, giving silent permission for her to proceed in removing his pants. She unbuttoned and unzipped him carefully, noting the bulge that had formed there. Glancing up at him, she smiled.

"Can't help it. The sexiest babe in the world is undressing me. I'm concussed, not dead."

"And thank God for that." She slid the pants down over his hips and lower still, until his stump was revealed.

Wearing only his boxers, he sat on the bed. "There it is in all its purple glory."

Mallory saw fading bruises from the earlier injury and new ones from tonight. "I'll get some ice."

"I'm having déjà vu."

Mallory settled him against the pillows and pulled a light blanket over him. "Comfy?"

"Sort of."

"What do you need?"

"You've given me this new ache that needs tending to."

She laughed. "Not tonight, stud. Your head would explode."

"That's the whole idea."

Smiling, she tapped her index finger on the uninjured side of his forehead. "This one."

Scowling playfully, he said, "Oh, well, that wouldn't be good."

"Behave. I'll be back with some ice and pain pills." When she returned to the room a few minutes later, he had his head back and his eyes closed. She laid a towel over his leg and placed the ice bag carefully.

"Thanks, babe," he muttered.

"You're welcome." She brushed the hair back from his forehead and kissed him. "You want to take some meds?"

"Yeah."

She helped him with the pills and water. "Get some rest. I'm here if you need me."

Without opening his eyes, he patted the other side of the bed. "I need you right here."

"Give me one minute." She went into the bathroom to change into pajamas and brush her teeth. Then she let Brutus out one more time. He lay down on his bed by the fireplace while she went to join Quinn in her bed.

He reached for her hand and gave a tug to bring her closer to him.

Mallory rested her head on his chest and sighed when he put his arm around her to keep her there. "Are you in pain?"

"Everything is much better now."

"The pills will be kicking in."

"That's not why. It's you. You make everything better."

"You do the same for me."

He ran his hand up and down her arm, his touch igniting her the way it always did.

"Hey, Quinn?"

"Hmmm?"

"I got invited to a wedding this weekend, and I get to bring a date. Will you be my plus one?"

He kissed the top of her head and held her even tighter. "I'd love to be your plus one this weekend and every weekend."

On the day before Dan and Kara's long-awaited wedding, Mallory asked her dad and Linda if she could bring lunch to their house. When they happily accepted, Mallory picked up lunch from the grocery store deli and headed to the White House.

Parked in the driveway behind her dad's truck, she gathered up her bags and headed for the front door. As always, she hesitated before walking in, but they'd told her not to knock on their door. Their home, they said, was her home.

"Hey," Big Mac said in his big booming voice when she walked into the kitchen like she belonged there. "Let me help you!"

"I got it," she said, smiling at him, because how could she not? The sight of him made her happy. Then he made it even better by kissing her cheek and peeking into the bags to see what she'd brought.

"Ohhh, you got that chicken salad I love."

"She knows the way to your heart is through your stomach," Linda said when she joined them. She too gave Mallory a kiss and a quick hug before she smacked her husband's hand. "Don't be rude."

"Am I being rude?" Big Mac asked Mallory.

"Not at all."

He gave his wife a smug look. "I'm starving, and my daughter brought food."

"Dig in," Mallory said, amused by him as always.

"He probably had a dozen doughnuts this morning, and he's still starving."

"It was only three, and I'm a growing boy."

"You're going to be growing in all the wrong ways if you keep eating so many doughnuts."

"She tries to put me on a doughnut diet every spring, but it never works," he said as he broke open the bag of rolls Mallory had brought and made himself a sandwich. "It's her fault I'm addicted to them in the first place. They're her mother's recipe."

Mallory pulled a knife from the butcher block on the counter and sliced a tomato.

He put two slices on his sandwich and took a big bite. "Mmmm, that's good. Thanks, hon."

"You're welcome," she said, laughing as Linda handed him a plate with a long-suffering glare.

"She loves me," he said, his mouth full.

"I keep hoping he's going to grow up one of these days."

Big Mac winked at Mallory. "She likes me just the way I am."

Mallory and Linda made sandwiches and joined Big Mac at the table, where they chatted about Dan and Kara's wedding, among other topics. When Mallory thought about the reason she'd wanted to see them, her appetite waned and her throat tightened with emotion. She took a sip of her ice water and tried to get herself together.

Naturally, Big Mac noticed right away. "What's on your mind, sweetheart?"

She took a deep breath and said to Linda, "I took the advice you gave me a couple of months ago to talk to Kevin about my mother."

"Did it help?"

"Tremendously."

"He's the best at what he does," Big Mac said.

"Yes, he is."

"What about your mother?" he asked.

"I've had a lot of unresolved feelings about her keeping you from me until after she died."

"Oh."

"I'm sure you share many of those feelings, but you'd never say so out of respect to my mother—and me."

"I won't lie to you," he said. "I've had my struggles with it, but I'm trying to focus on the here and now rather than dwelling on things in the past that I had no control over."

"I'm finding that's easier said than done."

His lips curled into a small smile. "Me, too."

"Kevin suggested I write her a letter to put it all out there and get it off my chest."

"What do you think of that idea?" Linda asked.

"I liked it enough to actually write the letter in the middle of last night, and since I can't read it to my mother, I hoped I might read it to you guys. If you're willing to hear it, that is. No obligation."

Big Mac reached over to put his hand on top of hers. "We'd love to hear it, and we're honored you'd want to share it with us."

Linda nodded in agreement. "Absolutely."

"Okay, then." Mallory went to retrieve the folded pages from her purse and returned to her seat at the table. "Here goes."

# CHAPTER 28

Mallory cleared her throat and prayed for the courage to get through this. "Dear Mom,

"I can't believe it's already been a year since I lost you, and so much has changed for me in that time. Before I say anything else, I want you to know how much I miss you and love you and appreciate everything you sacrificed to make sure I had a wonderful childhood and life. You always used to say the two of us were a team, and I loved being on that team with you.

"After you died, I found the letter you left where you knew I would find it, finally giving me my father's name and telling me where he was. I spent a few days reeling from the contents of that letter, and trying to understand your fears about what might've happened if he'd known about me. Then I went to Gansett Island, hoping to have the chance to meet him and let him know I existed. I had no plan beyond that, but then again, I hadn't met him yet. How could I know what would happen after he knew about me?"

Mallory glanced at Big Mac, who hung on her every word. "What can I say about my father other than he's quite possibly the most amazing person I've ever met."

"Ah, damn," Big Mac said softly.

"From the minute we met and I shared your letter with him, he has made me part of his life and his family. And what a family I have through him. Four brothers, a sister, four sisters-in-law, a brother-in-law, two nephews, a niece, two uncles and four cousins, not to mention a wonderful stepmother who has willingly and happily accepted me into their family. I have gained twenty-one new family members, counting my cousin's three kids, and we're expecting two new arrivals soon. I found out I look exactly like my father's mother did at my age. Can you begin to understand what that means to me? To finally know, at age thirty-nine, where my dark hair and brown eyes come from?

"I've spent a lot of time with my new family over the last year and have gotten to know each of them. My brother Mac is the clown. He's forever coming up with new ways to get himself in trouble while making me laugh so hard, I forget to breathe. I already know that if I ever need him for anything, he'd drop everything and come running to help me out. Grant, a writer, is quieter but just as funny as Mac when he wants to be, and so smart about everything. Adam, the family's technical expert, is loyal and sweet and devoted to his family, but he also loves a good laugh and gets right into the scrum with his siblings. Evan, the musician, continues to surprise me with his many talents. Just when I think I've seen the full extent, he picks up a banjo and blows me away all over again. Janey is the baby of the family and plays the role to the hilt, driving her older brothers, who call her 'Brat,' crazy with the way she needles them. She's sweet and kind and crazy about animals of all sorts, especially the special-needs animals no one wants."

Linda wiped at a tear. "They sound so wonderful when described through your eyes."

"They are wonderful," Mallory said, wiping at her own eyes. "My stepmother, Linda, runs the entire show with a fierce love for her family. Nothing gets by her. They call her Voodoo Mama because she always knows what her kids are up to, even now that they are adults. She has been so good to me from the first time we met, and I am thankful to have her in my life. My uncles, Frank and Kevin, my father's brothers, and their adult kids Laura, Shane, Riley and Finn, are like the frosting on a very nice cake, not to mention the wide circle of family friends who have accepted me into their ranks and made me feel so at home with them. I am blessed beyond all belief to be part of this incredible family and the community that surrounds them.

"And yet, I have struggled with anger and sorrow over what I missed out on. I don't get a lot of their jokes. I wasn't there to help make the childhood memories they created together and cherish as adults. I'm one of them, but I'm not one *with* them. Despite their warm and loving welcome, the decades we should've had are lost, and we can't ever get them back."

Mallory paused for a moment before she continued. "Now that I've met him and gotten to know him, I'm certain that my father would've been there for me when I was growing up, even if it meant traveling from his beloved island to be with me in Providence. He would've come for parent-teacher conferences, softball games, basketball games, my proms and my graduations. He would've been there for me when Ryan died so suddenly, and he would've held my hand when I was losing you. He would never have tried to take me from you. That's not who he is, and I can't believe you didn't know that for sure, because you knew *him*."

Big Mac used his napkin to dab at his eyes.

"You denied us both the opportunity to be there for each other, and it's very difficult for me to forgive you for that. But I'm going to try, because if I don't, I fear the bitterness will swallow me whole. I refuse to carry that kind of burden with me for the rest of my life. I can't possibly know what you were thinking or feeling when you made the decision to keep him out of my life. In the last year, I've accepted that I'll never know why you made the choices you did or why you thought I was better off without my father. Now that I've had the chance to say these words out loud, I'm going to do my very best to let it go, to build a bridge and get over it. We can't change the past. We can only live for right now, and I can't let my present and future be clouded by a past I had no control over. While I wish you'd given me my father sooner, I will remain thankful forever that you gave him to me when you did. Better late than never.

"I pray every day that you are resting in peace and watching over me like you promised you would. I hope that you know how happy I am to have my father and his family in my life, and I'm sure you're keeping a close eye on what's happening between me and Quinn. I'll love you always. Mallory."

She folded the pages and laid them on the table.

"That's a beautiful letter, Mallory," Linda said. "Do you feel better now that you've written it down and spoken the words out loud?"

"I do. The process of having to think about what I would say and then writing it down was very therapeutic."

"I would've done all that," Big Mac said gruffly. "I would've been there for everything."

"I know that."

"I'm so sorry, Mallory. It makes me crazy to know you grew up without me when it didn't have to be that way."

She put her hand over his. "You have nothing to be sorry about."

He turned his hand to grasp hers. "You're a daughter that anyone would be proud of, and I love you very much."

Mallory blinked back the sudden rush of tears. "I love you, too. Both of you. And I'll never have the words to adequately thank you for the way you've welcomed me into your family."

"*Our* family," he said. "Yours, too, and what you said about how you're one of us but not one with us?"

Mallory nodded.

"It might feel that way, but you are absolutely one with us. You should never feel otherwise."

"I'll work on that."

"In the meantime," he said, "I'd like to hear more about what's going on with this Quinn fellow."

"Mac!" Linda said, rolling her eyes.

"What? She's my daughter, and she's got a new guy. I have questions."

"You wanted a father," Linda said, laughing.

"Are you bringing him to the wedding?" Big Mac asked.

"I am."

"Excellent. He and I can have a conversation."

"A conversation?"

"That's what I said."

"Be careful what you wish for," Linda said. "You're about to see a *whole new* side of your dear old dad."


Quinn was determined to dance with Mallory at the wedding—and to make love to her afterward. Sleeping next to her every night but not being able to touch her the way he wanted to was far more painful than the concussion.

He'd been back on his leg for two days, and while it wasn't entirely comfortable yet, it beat the hell out of the crutches.

Quinn checked his watch. Where the hell was Jared? Just as he had the thought, a knock sounded at the door. He left the bedroom and walked carefully to the front door to admit his brother, who carried a suit bag over his shoulder.

"Come in."

"You're getting around well."

A week ago, it would've bugged him to feel like Jared was assessing his mobility. Now he had bigger things to worry about. "Let me see the suits."

"Yes, sir," Jared said with a grin. "Like I said on the phone, your shoulders are broader than mine."

"No, they're not. We're the exact same size."

Jared produced handmade suits in gray, navy and navy pinstripe. Having a billionaire for a brother had its advantages.

Quinn gravitated to the gray one and put the jacket on over his T-shirt. "See? I told you. Perfect fit."

"Lizzie told me to bring shirts and ties, too, because if you don't have a suit, you probably don't have the shirt or the tie either."

"I have them. I just don't have them *here*."

Jared sat on the other sofa and watched as Quinn chose a shirt and tie to go with the gray suit. "Good to see you off the crutches."

"It's good to be back on two feet again."

"How's the dome?"

"Still hurts if I move too quickly, but better than it was. Sorry for all the time out of work. I'll make it up to you."

"Don't be ridiculous. I don't care about that."

"And don't worry," Quinn said with a grin for his brother, "I'm not going to sue you for the shitty basement stairs, either."

"You're a pal."

Quinn held up a light blue shirt with a navy-blue-and-silver-striped tie. "What do you think?"

"Works for me."

"Thanks for the loan."

"No problem. I sure as hell have no use for suits these days, except when Lizzie puts me to work at weddings."

"What're you hearing from Mom and Dad?"

"Dad has a cold, so they're postponing their trip to July. You're off the hook for another month."

"I'm going to talk to them about my leg."

"When?"

"Soon. I've been a little busy recovering from a concussion."

"Just tell them and get it over with. What do you think they're going to say? They'll be sorry you didn't tell them sooner, and they'll want to know how you are. Beyond that, you're making a mountain out of a molehill."

"You're right, and I'll tell them in the next few days."

"How's it going with Mallory?"

"Great."

"That's it? Just great?"

"Just great."

"Are you moving back to the boat or staying here?"

"I'm not sure yet. I need to talk to Mallory about that. Brutus likes it here."

"Brutus does, huh?"

"Uh-huh."

"You're a pain in the ass, you know that?"

"Why? Because I don't feel the need to share every detail of my life with you?"

"Yes, exactly."

Quinn snorted out a laugh. "Tough shit, little brother."

"Lizzie and I are trying to have a baby, and it's not happening," Jared said.

Still wearing the suit jacket, Quinn sat across from his brother. "Oh, um…"

"After the wedding this weekend, we're going to New York for a few days to see a specialist."

"I'm sorry to hear it's come to that."

"Don't let on that I told you. She's really tender on this topic."

"Of course. No worries. Will you let me know how it goes?"

"Sure."

When Mallory came breezing through the door, her face flushed from being in the sun, Quinn couldn't help the smile that stretched across his face. God, he loved the way her eyes lit up at the sight of him and how she didn't try to hide her feelings from him. There were no games with Mallory. What you saw was what you got, and he found that incredibly refreshing.

"Hi, Jared," she said as she bent to kiss Quinn.

"I've got your wedding date set up with proper attire," Jared said.

"I like it," she said. "Will you be there, too?"

"Yep. Lizzie's running the show, and I'm her faithful servant."

"AKA bitch," Quinn said.

Jared laughed. "That, too." He stood to leave. "I'll see you there."

"Thanks again, Jared."

"Any time."

Quinn stood and took a second to get his balance. The pain radiating from his head and leg was better than it had been, but he was frustrated to still be dealing with both a week after his fall.

"I like the way this looks on you," Mallory said, running her hands down his arms. "Very sexy."

He hooked an arm around her waist and brought her into his embrace. "I like the way everything looks on you, but I'm a particular fan of the way absolutely nothing looks on you, too."

"Are you flirting with me, Dr. James?"

"Yes, definitely."

Mallory laughed and pressed a kiss to his jaw, which was prickly with stubble. "How was the lunch with your folks?"

"It was great."

"What did they think of the letter?"

"They liked it a lot."

"It's a good letter. I'm glad they liked it. How do you feel now that you've shared it with them?"

"Unburdened."

"I'm happy to hear that."

"The Summer of Mallory is turning out far better than I ever could've hoped for."

"Is that so?"

She made herself right at home in his arms. "Mmm-hmm."

"Have I mentioned that I'm feeling a *lot* better? Like ninety-nine percent better?" As he said the words, he rubbed his erection against her belly.

"That much better, huh?"

"You know what would make me feel even more better?"

She chuckled at his terminology. "I can't imagine."

"Spending the rest of this afternoon naked in bed with you."

"Are you sure you're up for that?"

He pressed against her again. "Positive."

"I'll only agree to this plan of yours if I can do all the work."

Quinn's brain went completely blank except for a series of images that featured her naked and on top of him. "I'm completely fine with that."

She laughed as she took him by the hand to lead him into the bedroom that had become theirs over the last week. His laptop was on her desk, his sweatshirt hung from a hook behind the door, and his shoes were on the floor by the bed. He liked having his stuff mixed in with hers. He liked the way it felt to spend all his spare time with her, and he loved, absolutely *loved*, the way she looked at him with such affection.

"Hey, Mallory."

After closing the blinds, she turned to him. "Hmm?"

"Thanks for everything over the last week."

"Having you here has been a terrible hardship," she said with a teasing glint of humor in her eyes.

"I'll be out of your hair soon." Only because he was watching her so closely did he notice her face fall with disappointment.

"Really?"

"Brutus and I don't want to outstay our welcome."

"That's not possible. I like having you guys here. In fact... If you want to stay indefinitely, that would be fine with me."

"Would it?"

"Yes, it would." She helped him remove the suit jacket and laid it carefully over a chair. Then she dragged his T-shirt up and over his head. "I could look at this sexy man chest every day and never get tired of the view. You wouldn't want to deprive me of my favorite view, would you?"

"I wouldn't want to deprive you of anything."

"Good answer." She ran her hands from his well-developed pectorals to his broad shoulders. "You and Brutus are fun to have around. I'd be sad if you left."

"We can't have that."

"Unless you miss living on the boat and would rather be there. The star-gazing is so much better out there."

He looked down at her. "The overall view is way nicer here."

"So you'll stay?"

"I'll stay."

# CHAPTER 29

Quinn kissed her softly at first but with increasing urgency as she responded with the same sense of desperation he felt. As he kissed her, he raised her shirt up until he had to stop kissing her to remove it. Reaching behind her, he unhooked her bra and sucked in a gasp when her hands brushed against his abdomen as she unbuttoned and unzipped his pants.

He kicked them off, no longer giving a shit if she saw his leg or any other part of him, for that matter. She made him so crazy with desire that he couldn't be bothered worrying about things that now seemed trivial when stacked up against his need for her.

"Sit," she said, giving his chest a gentle push.

He did as she asked and watched as she knelt to remove his pants and boxers, working them carefully over his leg. "On or off?" she asked of the prosthetic.

"Off," he said, and leaned back to watch her move quickly and efficiently to remove it. What would've been inconceivable to him only a week ago was now no big deal, thanks in large part to the matter-of-fact way she approached his disability. She didn't care that he was an amputee, so why should he? "Hey."

She looked up at him with big brown eyes that just did it for him.

"Thank you."

Her brows furrowed. "For what?"

He gestured to his leg. "For making it no big deal."

"It is no big deal to me. I get why it is to you, but when I look at you, that's the very last thing I think of."

"You have no idea how much that means to me." He encouraged her to stand and removed her white shorts, leaving her in only a pair of tiny white panties. "Mmm, so sexy."

"You like them? I stopped by Tiffany's store yesterday."

"I love them. I'll have to stop by there myself to see what else she has that would look good on you."

She wrapped her arms around his neck, and Quinn nuzzled her belly, loving the way she trembled in his arms. "I'm supposed to be doing all the work."

Quinn released her and fell backward onto the bed. "Don't let me stop you."

"Scoot up to the pillows."

He arranged himself to her liking and waited with breathless anticipation to see what she would do. For the longest time, she only looked at him, her hungry gaze making him so hard, he ached. Then she placed her hands on his inner thighs, making him nearly launch off the bed and then groan with frustration when she moved them up, making a wide circle around his groin.

Laughing softly, she continued her journey up to his abdomen and chest, leaning forward so her soft breasts pressed against his erection as she kissed the fading bruises on his ribs.

"You're torturing me, but of course you know that."

She looked up at him, the picture of innocence. "What am I doing?"

He released a sound that was part laugh, part groan. "Feel free to move things along."

"Like this?" she asked, kissing a path straight down the center of him until her lips were a heartbeat away from the head of his cock.

Quinn held his breath, anticipating her next move.

She ran her tongue over the full length of him and then wrapped her hand tight around the base as she took him into the heat of her mouth.

*Fucking hell...*

She took him deep while continuing to stroke him.

He gripped handfuls of her silky hair, holding on for dear life. "Babe, hang on... Mall— *Mallory... Fuck...*" Ignoring his warnings, she stroked him to a searing release that made him cry out from the power of it.

Brutus began howling in the next room, which made them both laugh.

"He thinks I'm hurting you."

With his hands still buried in her long hair, he sat up to kiss her. "I love when you do all the work."

"You've only begun to see my bag of tricks."

"I'm not sure I'll survive this."

Mallory glanced down at his cock, which was still hard even after the epic orgasm. "We'll see about that." She straddled him, the heat of her sex against his cock as the silky panties rubbed him until he was as hard as he'd been before. "I thought he might agree with my way of thinking."

"He's a slave to your way of thinking."

She laughed, and watching her as she moved so seductively on top of him, her breasts swaying, her face flushed from desire, he couldn't contain the emotions she roused in him.

Taking hold of her hands, he brought them to his lips, kissing one and then the other. He looked up at her. "I love you, Mallory."

She faltered, and he took advantage of the opening to tug her down on top of him, wrapping his arms around her. "You..." Her voice faltered.

"Love you."

"I love you, too."

They stared at each other for a long, charged moment in which everything inside him settled, finally. Years of turmoil and hard work to put his life back together had led to her, and he couldn't be happier to have found her.

"I want to be inside you more than I want my next breath," he whispered.

She trembled in his arms. "Let me go so I can make that happen."

He released her and watched as she removed the tiny scrap of fabric that stood between them. Then she stopped his heart when she straddled him and made quick work of giving him what he'd said he wanted.

*Holy shit...* He squeezed her buttocks as she began to move, taking him quickly to the edge of madness. Eager to slow things down, he sat up and drew her nipple into his mouth while anchoring her hips with his arm tight around her.

"Quinn," she gasped.

Her internal muscles fluttered madly, squeezing him so tightly, he saw stars. He stopped trying to fight it and let her go so she could ride him until they came together. His fingers dug into the flesh on her hips as he rode the waves of release.

She came down on top of him, and he gathered her up, holding her as their bodies twitched and cooled.

"Holy cow," she whispered.

"Mmm, seriously."

Her lips moved softly on his chest, right above the heart that beat for her. "Quinn?"

"Hmm?"

"About that job you offered me."

He hadn't been expecting that, not now anyway. "What about it?"

"If the offer is still on the table—"

"It is."

"Then I'd like to accept."

"Really?"

She nodded. "I talked to my uncle Kevin about it, and he made a good point. If it doesn't work out, I can go anywhere I want with the credentials I have. We're both professionals, and we can separate our work life and our personal life."

He held her tight, his heart full from knowing she was going to stay after the summer, that they would live and work together to make a go of the facility—and their relationship. "It's going to be great, and you're not going anywhere. I need you far too much here with me."

She raised her head off his chest and gazed into his eyes. "So we're really going to do this, huh?"

"We're really going to do it." Holding her tight, he rolled them over so he was on top. "Starting right now."

# EPILOGUE
## MR. & MRS. TORRINGTON
## A GANSETT ISLAND SHORT STORY

Kara hadn't been kidding when she referred to her family as a shit show. The Ballards had descended en masse onto Gansett Island two days before the wedding, and now Dan was at the police station to retrieve three of her brothers who'd been arrested after the rehearsal dinner.

Blaine Taylor greeted him, a grim expression on his face. "Quite a crew."

"How bad are we talking?"

"They busted up the Rusty Scupper," Blaine said. "The owner is determined to press charges."

"I'll reach out and see if we can make it go away."

"They're leaving after the wedding, right?"

"First boat out on Sunday."

"Excellent."

"Sorry about the trouble."

"Certainly not your fault." Blaine led him into the hallway that housed the island's single cellblock, where Kara's brothers Keith, Kieran and Kyle had spent the night. Keith and Kyle had sleeve tattoos, earrings in both ears and chips on their shoulders a mile deep. Kieran was slightly more tolerable when he wasn't under the influence of his older brothers.

"Gentlemen," Dan said, using the term loosely. He often wondered how the oh-so-prim-and-proper-country-club maven Judith Ballard had managed to raise a bunch of hoodlums.

"Aren't you supposed to be a hotshot lawyer?" Keith asked. "Get us out of here, will ya?"

"Happily, but there're conditions. Chief?"

"Make restitution to the Scupper, or he's going to press charges," Blaine said. "Stay out of trouble, or I'll put you on the next boat to the mainland, wedding or no wedding. Am I clear?"

Keith didn't like being told what to do, that was obvious, but he nodded nonetheless. "We'll take care of it."

"I'll expect to hear from Pat at the Scupper within the hour, or I'll be rounding you up again." Blaine unlocked the cell, and the three brothers filed out. "Good luck," he said to Dan under his breath. "You're going to need it."

"Thanks for calling me and not Kara. I'd hate for anything to ruin this day for her."

"No problem. See you at the wedding."

Dan's future brothers-in-law were in the parking lot when he emerged into the bright sunshine, dropping Ray-Ban Wayfarers from the top of his head to cover his eyes. "Let's have a little chat, boys."

"We're all set," Kyle said.

"Yes, I can see that by the way you spent the night before your sister's wedding in jail," Dan said.

"What'd you want?" Keith asked, hands on hips.

"Keep it together for Kara today and tonight, or you'll deal with me, and I can be a royal pain in the ass when I want to be. We clear?"

"All good," Keith said tersely. To his brothers, he said, "Let's go."

They headed toward the Sand & Surf Hotel, where they were staying. No doubt Laura and Owen would have a few stories to share after the weekend. "You're welcome for getting your sorry asses out of jail," Dan said to their retreating backs.

Dan got into his Porsche and drove home to the house he shared with Kara. She was at the Chesterfield, where the four-o'clock wedding would be held. He checked his watch. Right about now, Chloe would be doing her hair and makeup. She'd left that morning with everything she needed for the rest of the day, kissing him and telling him not to be late.

As if he'd be late for the most important event of his life. He'd almost done this once before. On the short drive home, he thought about catching his best man fucking his future wife the night before their wedding. What had once been one of the most traumatic things to ever happen to him, second only to losing his brother in Afghanistan, he now listed as one of the great blessings in his life.

If he'd married her, he never would've met Kara, and that would've been a tragedy of epic proportions. He wouldn't have known how lacking his earlier relationship had been because he wouldn't have had Kara to show him the way it should be.

Dan missed his brother, Dylan, today, but that was nothing new. He missed him every day. He ran his hand over the steering wheel of the car that had belonged to his brother. Having the car kept Dylan close, but on days like this, his absence was a physical pain that nothing could soothe.

He pulled into his driveway and parked beside his best man's car. As Dan emerged from his car, Grant McCarthy came out to greet him.

"You got one hell of a day to tie the knot," Grant said of the gorgeous sunshine.

"We sure did." June weather on Gansett was a crapshoot, but it could be pouring rain for all he cared.

"Where you been?"

"Getting Kara's brothers out of lockup."

Grant's mouth fell open. "Seriously?"

"Serious as a heart attack."

"What'd they do?"

"Busted up the Scupper."

Grant wrinkled his nose. "Why are they hanging out in that dive?"

"Your guess is as good as mine. What're you hearing from Stephanie?"

"Everything is going well and right on schedule."

"Excellent. I'm going to grab a shower, and then we can head over there."

"A little eager, much?" Grant teased.

"You have no idea."

Kara stood before the mirror, taking a critical look at herself in the casual yet elegant dress she'd chosen for her big day. The ivory silk hugged her curves in a way that Dan would appreciate, but it wasn't so sexy that she'd be uncomfortable in it. Tiffany had helped her pick it out, and as usual, her friend had been spot-on in her suggestions.

She wore her long auburn hair in an elaborate updo that left her shoulders bare, and had gone with just enough makeup to appear dressed up and to ensure that Dan would actually recognize her when he saw her. She couldn't wait to see him in the navy sport coat and khakis they'd chosen for him and Grant to wear.

At the thought of him waiting for her downstairs, the tension and strain of the last few weeks slipped away. Kara had followed his advice and kept her contact with her mother to a bare minimum, which had infuriated her mother. Not that Kara cared. She refused to be sucked into her family's never-ending drama on this of all days.

No, today was about her and Dan, and she was determined to make it the best day of her life.

Stephanie came into the room, wearing a navy blue, tea-length dress that showed off her spectacular legs. The two women had become even closer friends during the winter they'd spent together in LA, and having Grant and Stephanie as their only attendants had been an easy choice for her and Dan.

"You look amazing." Stephanie had brought Kara's bouquet of white hydrangeas, and Stephanie would carry the same bouquet in blue.

"Thank you. I feel pretty amazing today."

"Your handsome groom has arrived along with mine, and the guests are taking their seats."

"Glad to hear he actually showed up," Kara said with a smile.

"Wild horses couldn't have kept that man away from you today. Your dad is in the hallway, and Lizzie says we're ready whenever you are."

Kara took a deep breath to calm the butterflies in her belly. She never had liked being the center of attention, but even that couldn't detract from her joy at marrying Dan, the absolute love of her life. "You can send him in, and Steph? Thank you so much for being my matron of honor."

Stephanie squeezed her hand. "My pleasure. See you downstairs."

Kara's dad, Chuck Ballard, came in dressed in the same blue blazer and khaki pants that Dan and Grant were wearing.

"Sweetheart," he said, "you look lovely."

"Thank you, Dad." She had debated whether she wanted him to give her away. After her family had acted like it was no big deal that Kelly had basically stolen her boyfriend, Kara had been fed up with the lot of them, including her parents, who threw an elaborate wedding for Kelly and Matt. But she had only one father and would have only one wedding, so she'd asked him despite her reservations.

"I want you to know how thrilled your mother and I are that you've found someone who makes you so happy. We're very proud of you, and we love your Dan." He hesitated, as if considering whether he should say more. "We handled things badly with Kelly, and you were hurt by it. I'm sorry for that."

Stunned to hear him admit to being wrong about anything, Kara had no idea what to say.

"What she did was wrong, and I've told her so. I've also told her she's to stay far, far away from this island today. This is your day, and she doesn't belong here."

Overwhelmed, Kara hugged him. "Thank you."

"Now, let's forget all that nonsense and get you married." He extended his arm.

She slipped her hand into the crook of his elbow.

He covered her hand with his. "I love you, Kara, and I wish you and your new husband the very best of everything."

"Thank you, Dad. I love you, too."

Dan thought he was prepared for whatever she might have in store for him. He was dead wrong. She blew him away with her simple elegance, her embarrassment at being the center of attention and the way she kept her gaze firmly fixed on him while she made her way to him on the arm of her father.

The ceremony was being held on the lawn of the former Chesterfield estate that Jared and Lizzie James had turned into a wedding venue.

Dan's heart felt like it might explode from the emotional overload of this moment. With his parents and sisters seated in the front row and Grant standing by his side, Dan took a step forward to meet his bride.

Chuck shook Dan's hand and kissed Kara's cheek before taking a seat next to his wife and family on the other side of the aisle.

Dan kissed Kara. "You're beautiful."

"You don't look too bad yourself."

He smiled at the predictably saucy reply. He couldn't wait for a lifetime of her particular brand of sauciness.

Grant's uncle Frank, a retired Superior Court judge, presided over the brief ceremony in which Dan and Kara exchanged traditional vows and rings. Knowing his bride hated the spotlight, he'd agreed to keep it short and sweet.

Ten minutes later, Frank gave him permission to kiss his bride.

Dan was careful not to embarrass her too much when he kissed her.

"It's my great pleasure," Frank said, "to introduce for the first time as Mister and Missus… Dan and Kara Torrington."

While their guests applauded enthusiastically, Dan escorted his wife down the aisle and ducked into the secret garden inside the hedges to steal a better kiss. Surrounded by fragrant flowers, Dan took her into his arms and kissed her passionately, thrilled to finally be married to the woman he loved more than life itself.

"*Finally*," he whispered against her lips. "There's no getting rid of me now."

"Oh damn, really?"

"You knocked the cover off the ball with this dress, babe. I mean seriously—*wow*."

"I'm glad you like it."

"I *love* it. I'll never forget how you looked as you came toward me today. Best moment of my entire life."

"Mine, too."

He kissed her forehead and held her in his arms, hoping they wouldn't be missed for a few more minutes. "You think anyone would notice if we split?"

"Probably. We are the hosts, after all."

"We should've let your parents do it."

She looked up at him with horror, and they lost it laughing.

He took hold of her hand. "Let's get this over with so we can get to the good stuff—the wedding night and honeymoon." He'd surprised her with two weeks in Ireland followed by a week in England. They were leaving the island on the noon boat tomorrow.

"I'm with you, Counselor."

He tucked her hand into his elbow. "Yes, you are."

They emerged from the garden to find Lizzie waiting for them, pretending to check her phone.

"Right this way." She gestured for them to follow her to where their photographer waited to take the family photos Judith had insisted on.

They went through the motions, posing with both families as well as Grant and Stephanie, and then headed up the back stairs to the Chesterfield, where the reception would be held in the big rooms downstairs as well as on the back veranda.

"It looks amazing, Lizzie," Kara said.

"Couldn't agree more," Dan added.

"I'm so glad you're happy with it."

A theme of navy blue and white had been carried throughout the big rooms full of friends and family who'd come to celebrate their new life together, including the entire McCarthy family, Alex and Jenny Martinez, Paul and Hope Martinez, Luke and Sydney Harris, David Lawrence and Daisy Babson, and even Slim Jackson and his fiancée, Erin Barton, had returned to the island for the wedding after spending the last few months in Florida.

"Is Mallory seeing Quinn James?" Dan asked Kara.

"From what I hear, they've moved right past the seeing-each-other phase and into the living-together-at-her-place phase."

"Wow, good for them."

Lizzie led them to the dance floor for their first dance as husband and wife. "Ladies and gentlemen," Lizzie said into the portable microphone she carried along with her clipboard. "Please direct your attention to the dance floor! Dan and Kara have chosen their friend Evan McCarthy's new single, 'Can't Stop,' for their first dance as husband and wife. Here to perform his new hit is our own Evan McCarthy!"

As Evan played the first notes of the song they'd loved the first time they heard it, Dan took Kara into his arms and let the rest of the world slip away as he focused on the woman who was now his wife.

*Look how far we've come*
*Look at all that we've become*
*Look how high we've flown*
*Your heart has always been my home*

*Listen to the rhythm of the rain*
*Wash away our tears and then we start again*
*Listen to a whisper in the wind*
*It's calling me, it's calling me*

*I can't stop wanting you for the rest of my life*
*Holding you in the middle of the night*
*Falling in love with you*
*All over and over again*
*I can't stop wanting you for the rest of my life*
*Holding you in the middle of the night*
*Falling in love with you*
*All over and over and over and over again*

*Found the beauty of*
*A timeless, endless love*
*So much left unknown*
*But my heart will always be your home*

*Listen to the rhythm of our hearts*
*They beat as one no matter how far we're apart*
*Listen to the echo of a dream*
*It's calling me, it's calling me*

*I can't stop wanting you for the rest of my life*
*Holding you in the middle of the night*
*Falling in love with you*
*All over and over again*
*I can't stop wanting you for the rest of my life*
*Holding you in the middle of the night*
*Falling in love with you*
*All over and over and over and over again*

The song ended with a rousing round of applause for Evan as well as Dan and Kara. Dan kissed Kara and took her by the hand to lead her from the dance floor.

Lizzie handed the microphone to Grant, who cleared his throat dramatically.

"Oh jeez," Dan said, groaning. "Don't give him a microphone."

Lizzie ushered them to their seats at the table they would share with Grant and Stephanie as well as their parents. Thankfully, Chuck and Judith Ballard had hit it right off with Dave and Nancy Torrington, and the two couples were already like old friends after knowing each other a couple of days.

As he held the chair for his wife, Dan took note of his new brothers-in-law, who were hitting the open bar hard. He wouldn't hesitate to shut them off if they started to get unruly, which was another benefit to being the host of this shindig.

"As Dan's best man, it's my job to thoroughly embarrass the bride and groom," Grant said, drawing laughs from their guests. "But since Dan usually does a pretty good job of embarrassing himself—and Kara—I'll leave that to him."

Dan glanced at Kara to find her nodding in agreement. Traitor.

"From the first minute Dan met Kara, he had his heart set on her. It took some convincing and some cajoling and a bit of blackmail, but he finally won her over to his way of thinking."

"A lot of blackmail," Kara said, smiling at him.

"Raise your glasses to Dan and Kara," Grant said. "We wish you a lifetime of love and happiness."

Much later, as the party began to wind down, Dan was relieved that Kara's brothers had behaved for the most part. As he was half drunk on champagne himself, the last thing he wanted to deal with was unruly in-laws. Thankfully, that wasn't going to be his problem tonight.

He and Kara were talking to Slim and Erin when Judith and Chuck approached them.

"Welcome home, you guys," Dan said to their friends. "So glad you could be here today."

"We wouldn't have missed it," Erin said.

"It's good to be home," Slim said, putting his arm around Erin to lead her away.

"This was a lovely day," Judith said. "Well done."

While Kara stared at her mother, seeming dumbfounded by the unexpected compliment, Dan answered for both of them. "Glad you enjoyed yourselves. We're going to say our good-byes, and we're leaving in the morning, so we won't see you." He shook Chuck's hand and kissed Judith's cheek. "But we'll see you again soon."

"I hope you'll come to Bar Harbor to meet our friends at some point."

"Sure, we'll see if we can make that happen."

Kara hugged and kissed her parents. "Thanks for coming."

"So happy for you, sweetheart," Chuck said.

Hand in hand, Dan and Kara made a trip around the room to say their good-byes. As soon as he possibly could, he guided her out of the room toward the stairs that led to the honeymoon suite where they'd spend their wedding night.

"You just basically told everyone we know that you can't wait to have sex with me," Kara said as they went up the stairs from the second to the third floor.

"So? We're newlyweds. That's what we're supposed to do."

"You don't need to be so obvious about it."

He stopped on the third-floor landing and scooped her up and into his arms. "Why can't I be obvious about how crazy I am about my new wife?"

"You're more than welcome to be obvious about it from here on out."

"Excellent." He opened the door to their room and swept her inside, kicking the door closed behind them. "Alone at last." The first thing he did was pull off his tie, unbutton his shirt and remove the sport coat, tossing it over a chair in the elegantly appointed room.

"Feel better?" Kara asked him, amusement dancing in gorgeous brown eyes with the flecks of gold that made them sparkle.

"Much, but I'll feel way better when you tell me how to get you out of that stunning dress."

"It's really simple," she said. "Up and over."

"I can handle up and over, but come here first and let me take another good long look. I won't want to forget a single detail."

She took his outstretched hand and let him bring her closer.

"You're beautiful every day, but today you were…" His throat tightened, and for once, he didn't have the words.

"I wanted to be beautiful for you."

"Mission accomplished, my love." He kissed her softly, giving her all the love and tenderness he felt for her. He'd give her the stars and the moon if she'd let him. "You own me, Kara Torrington. Heart and soul."

"I was thinking today about the day you found out Kelly was here and planning to confront me." As she spoke, she released his belt and undid his pants. "How you ran to me while still badly injured from the boat accident, and took me away so she couldn't find me. Remember?"

"How could I forget? That was the day you agreed to marry me."

"You've owned my heart and soul from the very beginning, but that day… That was it for me. You're it for me."

"I should certainly hope so now that I've shackled myself to you for life."

Smiling, she kissed him with such sweetness, he wanted to drown in it. "How about you do that up-and-over thing now."

"Yes, dear. Whatever you want." He squatted to grasp the hem of her floor-length gown and rose to bring it up and over her head, blinking several times to get his brain around what she was wearing under it. "Holy *shit*," he whispered. "Are you kidding me?"

Kara laughed at his befuddled reaction to the sexiest lingerie he'd ever laid eyes on—ribbons and bows and hooks and skin, lots and lots of lightly freckled white skin.

Dan placed a hand over his chest. "Am I having a heart attack?"

"I really hope not, because I have plans for you."

"Mmm, suddenly I'm feeling much better." He ran his hands over the lace and silk that covered her. "What's the secret to removing this thing?"

She turned her back to him so he could see the laces that held it together.

"How'd you get this on?"

"With a little help from my matron of honor."

"Remind me to thank her the next time I see her." He finished unlacing the contraption and revealed the rest of her magnificence. With his hands on her shoulders, he turned her to face him and took a long look at his beautiful wife. "I wonder every day what I did to get lucky enough to find you, but today..." He leaned his forehead on hers. "The word 'lucky' doesn't begin to describe it."

With her hands inside his shirt, she pushed the two sides off his shoulders and wrapped her arms around him, her soft skin brushing against his making him crazy with desire for her. "I think all the time about how lost I was until you found me."

"Thank God I found you." He held her tight, probably too tight, but he couldn't bring himself to let her go. Not now or ever. Slowly, he began backing her up to the bed, letting his pants fall as he went. They fell onto the bed together, him on top of her, her body opening to welcome him. He usually prided himself on his finesse, but he had the rest of his life to worship her. Tonight, he just needed her.

"Dan..."

"I'm right here, baby, and I'm dying to make love to my wife."

"Then please do, because your wife loves you so much."

He gazed down at her, brushing the hair back from her face as entered he for the first time as her husband. "I love you, too. More than anything else in this world."

Kara wrapped her arms around him and held on tight as he set out to show her how much she meant to him.

"A whole lifetime of this," he whispered. "Can you believe we get a whole lifetime of this?"

"I can't wait for every minute of it."

Kissing her, he said, "Me, too."

\*\*\*

Thank you for reading *Light After Dark*! Join the Light After Dark Reader Group (https://www.facebook.com/groups/LightAfterDark16/) to chat about the book with other readers with spoilers allowed and encouraged. Watch for release week prizes in the group too! Also, make sure you're a member of the Gansett Island Reader Group (https://www.facebook.com/groups/McCarthySeries/) where you will find more than 10,000 other fans of the series. The series group is usually the first to hear of big news and other announcements, so don't miss out! Join the group today! Also, make sure you're on my email newsletter list at marieforce.com for notification of preorders, free books, appearances and other events in your area.

I hope you enjoyed your visit to Gansett Island. My fictional island has become such a huge part of my life—and yours—over these last five years, and I've created so many characters who speak to me between books and during the writing of new ones. I can't possibly give them all a new story in every book, but I still have so much to say about all of them.

With that in mind, I'll be launching a new "Gansett Island Episodes" series in 2017, featuring shorter stories about past characters who readers love and want more of. Mixed in with these episodes will be at least one full-length book a year. So we'll have plenty more from our favorite island, with new stories for past characters as well as all-new stories, too. I'm looking forward to this new adventure and hope you'll take the ferry to Gansett for the new episodes! I expect that Riley McCarthy will be the next character featured in a full-length book, but I reserve the right to change my mind about that!

Featured in *Light After Dark* are original songs by two talented songwriters. The first, "Smells Like Nostalgia," was written and performed by my daughter, Emily Force. You can listen to the song here: http://www.cdbaby.com/cd/emilyforce In the short story, Mr. and Mrs. Torrington, my friend David Sardinha's song, "Can't Stop" is featured as Dan and Kara's wedding song. You can listen to the song here: http://www.cdbaby.com/cd/davidsardinha3. Thank you so much to Emily and Dave for sharing their work with me and the Gansett Island family.

My thanks as always go to my amazing HTJB Team: Julie Cupp, CMP, Lisa Cafferty, CPA, Holly Sullivan, Isabel Sullivan, Nikki Colquhoun, Cheryl Serra, Ashley Lopez and Courtney Lopes. I so appreciate everything you ladies do behind the scenes to keep things running smoothly while I write the books. Thank you to beta readers Anne Woodall and Kara Conrad for their help with every book, and my editorial team of Linda Ingmanson and Joyce Lamb. Full credit for the amazing cover goes to awesome designer Kristina Brinton. A special thanks to my friend Sarah Spate Morrison, Family Nurse Practitioner, who fact checks the medical details for me—this time on a very tight turnaround. Thank you, Sarah!

A big, huge thanks goes to the readers who continue to ask me every day for more Gansett. I can't tell you how much I appreciate your enthusiasm for my fictional island. I couldn't do what I do without your support. A million thank-yous would never be enough.

xoxo

Marie

*Turn the page for a sneak peek at, Gansett Island Episodes, Episode 1: Victoria & Shannon, available now!*

# GANSETT ISLAND EPISODES

## EPISODE 1: VICTORIA & SHANNON CHAPTER 1

Desperate times called for desperate measures, or that was what Victoria Stevens told herself as she took an early lunch break for an errand she'd put off long enough. She had tried everything she could think of to get her boyfriend, Shannon, to open up to her without success, and there was only one person on this island who could help her figure out what to do next.

On paper, Victoria was one half of a perfect relationship. Together nearly a year, she and Shannon O'Grady enjoyed a lot of the same activities, TV shows and friends. They'd lived together for almost a year, laughed often, hardly fought and had the hottest sex she'd ever had with anyone almost every day. Though she told herself it couldn't be better, that was a big, fat lie. It could be better. It could be a *lot* better.

What they had, she'd finally been forced to acknowledge, was a lovely, wonderful surface relationship that lacked the kind of true intimacy she craved. She saw what she wanted for herself every day in the couples she worked with as a Certified Nurse Midwife, and refused to settle for less in her own life. So even if her relationship with Shannon seemed perfect on the surface, the foundation was shaky.

For one thing, they never talked about anything important beyond their work schedules, what was for dinner or whether they should go to a party they'd been invited to. In some ways, she felt like she didn't know him any better now than she had the day she met him, and that was a problem she couldn't continue to ignore as much as she might want to.

Five years ago, she would've ignored it. She would've told herself to stop being melodramatic and enjoy what she had. The future would take care of itself. But staring down her twenty-ninth birthday had her taking stock of where she'd expected to be by thirty—and it was *not* in a go-nowhere relationship with the hottest guy she'd ever met, let alone dated.

She'd waited until Shannon, a deckhand for the Gansett Island Ferry Company, departed on the eleven o'clock boat to the mainland. As she walked into town from the clinic where she worked, she saw the boat he was on way off in the distance. That meant the coast was clear for her trip to the ferry landing, which bustled with activity on a Friday in late June.

This was the right thing to do, or so she told herself. If she allowed in any other thought, such as the propriety of asking Shannon's cousin questions she probably ought to ask Shannon himself, she might chicken out, and that was not an option. Outside the door to the ferry company's main office, she took a deep breath and knocked on Seamus O'Grady's open door.

He was on the phone and waved her in.

Victoria went into his office and took one of the chairs that sat in front of his desk.

"I understand," he said in the lyrical Irish accent that was so familiar to her after a year with his cousin. "I appreciate the call. I'll have a talk with him tonight and get back to you tomorrow. Very good. Thank you." Sighing, he ended the call and placed his cell phone on the desk. "Sorry about that."

"Everything okay?"

"Jackson is having a few challenges at summer camp," Seamus said of one of the two brothers he and his wife, Carolina, had taken in after their mother died of lung cancer. "Getting into some scrapes with the other kids and 'acting out,' or so the director says. I'll admit to being out of my league with things like this."

"You're doing great, and you'll figure out what to do."

"I hope you're right, but you didn't come by to talk about my woes, did you?"

"No," she said with a smile, "I came to talk about *my* woes."

His brows knitted with concern. "What's wrong?"

"Shannon."

"What about him? I thought things were going great for the two of you."

"Things *are* great." Victoria paused and shook her head. "No, that's not true. It *could* be great, but it's like there's this gigantic brick wall standing between us, and I can't get around it or over it or through it no matter how hard I try."

"Ahhh," Seamus said, nodding. "I see."

"I hope you know… I'd never bother you with this if I wasn't feeling sort of desperate about what to do."

"First of all, love, you're never a bother. We're friends, aren't we?"

"I'd like to think so." She and Shannon spent a lot of time with Seamus and Carolina and now their boys, too. The four of them regularly went out to dinner, played cards and spent holidays together.

He stood. "Take a walk with me. This isn't a short conversation."

Victoria got up to go with him, eager to hear what he had to say even if part of her was afraid, too.

They walked to the pier where the fishing boats came and went, bringing in fresh catch-of-the-day that was sold to island residents and restaurants. In the middle of the day, the pier was mostly deserted, with many of the boats out on the water.

"Has he told you about Fiona?" Seamus asked after a long silence.

"Who?" Victoria immediately thought of the woman who worked with Grace McCarthy at the pharmacy, but clearly Seamus meant someone else.

"I didn't think so."

"Who is she?"

"She was his first love back in Ireland." He rested his arms on one of the pilings and stared out at the ocean. "It's still hard to talk about her even after all these years."

Suddenly, Victoria was sorry she'd sought him out and particularly sorry she'd asked questions she had no business asking. "I, um, maybe it would be better if I didn't know."

"Would it?"

He was giving her an out, and Victoria wanted to take it because she sensed that whatever he was about to tell her would change everything. Was that what she wanted? To change everything? "I... I don't know."

"You want to understand him, right?"

She nodded.

"Then you need to know about Fiona."

Resigned to hearing the story, Victoria leaned against the next piling, needing the support it provided.

"I can't remember a time when they weren't together. They met in school and were inseparable from then on. After they finished school, they moved to Dublin so she could pursue a career as a model. Shannon got a job as a bartender to help make ends meet so she could focus on her career, which was really taking off. She had a top agent and a couple of photographers who loved to work with her."

Victoria wanted to run away from whatever was coming next. "Wh-What happened?"

"I'm only going to tell you this much, love. She was murdered."

Victoria felt like she'd been punched. "Oh God," she whispered.

"I'll leave it to him to share the details, if he chooses to. I've already said more than I should have. He's intensely private on this topic. He doesn't talk about her at all."

Her heart ached for Shannon. Tears flooded her eyes, spilling down her cheeks.

"As you can imagine, he's never been the same since she died. For a long time afterward, we worried he'd take his own life rather than have to live without her. So we made sure someone was always with him the first year. We watched him around the clock. The second year, he started drinking and spent most of that year and the next drunk. By the time he finally snapped out of that stage, we were about to send him to rehab. But one day, he got up, took a shower, got dressed and went back to work at the bar, as if nothing had happened. That's what he did for years—got up, went to work, did what he had to do to survive. Then, eight years after he lost Fiona, he came here and met you, and he's been different."

"How so?" she asked, her voice scratchy. "How has he been different?"

"He smiles again. He laughs. He participates. You have no idea what a huge improvement those things are from the way he was for so long."

Using her sleeve, she tried to mop up the tears. "I've wondered," she said haltingly, "why it seemed he was willing to go only so far with me. Now I know it's because he isn't capable of more."

"A year ago, I would've agreed with you. Now, I'm not so sure that's true."

"Why do you say that?"

"I've spent a lot of time with the two of you. I've seen the way he looks at you and watches you when you're in the room, looks for you when you're not. He's as invested in you as he's able to be, even if he doesn't say so."

"I'm not sure what to do with this information, Seamus." She'd gotten way more than she'd bargained for from Shannon's cousin.

"What do you want to do with it?" he asked.

"I want to find him and hold him and tell him I love him and I always will even if he's not capable of loving me back."

"He's capable. He just doesn't know it yet. You'll have to lead him to it if you're interested in a future with him. Is that what you want, Vic? A future with him?"

"I think so," she said softly. "But I can't compete with her. I feel awful even saying that."

"I understand, and you shouldn't feel awful. For what it's worth, I see the way he is with you, and I think he cares for you more than either of you realize."

"Do I tell him what I know?"

"That's up to you, love. I can't tell you how to play this. I wish I could."

"Will he mind that you told me?"

"If he does, that's between the two of us. Don't you worry about me. I can fight my own battles. I told you what I did because I like you for him. I like you two together, and I wanted to help. My intentions were pure, and that's what I'll tell him if it comes to that."

"I really appreciate this, Seamus."

He held out his arms to her, and she walked willingly into his embrace. "He's lucky to have you in his life, and he knows it. Have some faith in that."

"I'll try," she said, smiling up at him. "Your wife is lucky to have you, too."

"Aye, I tell her so every day."

Victoria laughed at the predictable comment. "I'll see you later." She walked back to the clinic lost in thought and grief-stricken over what Shannon had been through losing his first love in such a horrific way. So many things made sense to her now that she knew what'd happened to him.

Most of the time, he came off as a happy-go-lucky sort of guy. However, every so often, the darkness would swoop in, and he'd punch out of their relationship for a day or two, even if he never physically left the home they shared. Victoria had learned to give him space during the dark moods, even as she wondered what caused them. Now she knew, and understood, for the most part anyway. If only she could figure out how best to use the information Seamus had given her to improve their relationship.

In her heart of hearts, she believed they had what it took to make this the kind of love story that lasted a lifetime. But that could happen only if they both wanted it. She couldn't do it on her own. She was still pondering her predicament when she walked through the main doors to the clinic. Dr. David Lawrence stood at the registration desk, speaking with Katie Lawry, their nurse practitioner, and Anna, the receptionist.

"Oh, there you are," David said. "I was about to call you."

"Why? What's up?"

"Tiffany Taylor is in labor in Exam Three." He took a closer look at her. "Have you been crying?"

She shook her head. "No."

"Vic… What's wrong?"

"Let's talk about it later." As her colleagues looked at her with concern, Victoria took Tiffany's chart from David and went through the double doors to the exam rooms, knocking on the door to number three. "Hi there," she said to Tiffany, owner of the Naughty & Nice boutique, and her husband, Blaine, the island's police chief. "What's this I hear about labor?"

"We were in bed, and she woke up in a puddle," Blaine said, seeming incredibly stressed.

"Any contractions?"

"Over the last day or two, I've had like a rolling ache that comes and goes pretty regularly, but since it didn't feel like the labor pains I had with Ashleigh, I thought they were Braxton-Hicks contractions. Not the real thing."

"Let's take a look." Victoria washed her hands and put on gloves before helping Tiffany into position. As this was Tiff's second child, she knew the drill.

Victoria performed an internal exam and discovered Tiffany was fully dilated and effaced. "You work fast, Mrs. Taylor. You're about to have this baby."

"Right now?" Blaine asked, sounding panicked. "She's not due for another week. This was supposed to happen on the mainland."

"Well, it's happening right here and now."

"What if something goes wrong or she needs a C-section?"

"We have everything we need if that should happen." After David had delivered his ex-fiancée Janey Cantrell's baby by emergency C-section last year, they'd taken steps to bring in the proper equipment to perform emergency surgery, if necessary. They never again wanted to be unprepared for an emergency of that magnitude. "The best thing you both can do is relax and breathe. Tiffany had an easy labor with Ashleigh, and there's no reason to believe this one won't be routine, too."

As she said the words, Tiffany's face tightened with obvious pain. "I'm feeling the need to push." She clung to Blaine's hand. "Can I push?"

"Not quite yet. Let me get everything ready, and then we'll get that baby out." She left the exam room to round up help.

"What's going on?" Katie asked.

"She's ready to deliver now, and I think it's going to be quick. Can you give me a hand?"

"I'm all yours in five minutes. I've got to move a few things around."

"Ask Anna to clear my afternoon, will you?" In Victoria's world, nothing took precedence over a mom in labor.

"You got it." Katie went to speak to the receptionist.

"You're sure you're all right?" David asked when they met up in the hallway.

"Can we talk after work? I've got a baby to deliver."

"Of course."

"Thanks." David was one of her closest friends, and there was no one else she'd rather talk to about what she should do with the information Seamus had given her.

Victoria put her long dark hair up in a bun, donned a gown and thoroughly washed her hands. Right now she needed to focus on the new life that Tiffany was about to bring into the world. She'd have plenty of time later to figure out what she was going to do about her own life.

**Get *Episode 1: Victoria & Shannon* now. Order**
**a signed copy from Marie's Store at *marieforce.com/store.***

# OTHER TITLES BY MARIE FORCE

**Other Contemporary Romances Available from Marie Force:**

*The Gansett Island Series*

Book 1: Maid for Love *(Mac & Maddie)*

Book 2: Fool for Love *(Joe & Janey)*

Book 3: Ready for Love *(Luke & Sydney)*

Book 4: Falling for Love *(Grant & Stephanie)*

Book 5: Hoping for Love *(Evan & Grace)*

Book 6: Season for Love *(Owen & Laura)*

Book 7: Longing for Love *(Blaine & Tiffany)*

Book 8: Waiting for Love *(Adam & Abby)*

Book 9: Time for Love *(David & Daisy)*

Book 10: Meant for Love *(Jenny & Alex)*

Book 10.5: Chance for Love, *A Gansett Island Novella (Jared & Lizzie)*

Book 11: Gansett After Dark *(Owen & Laura)*

Book 12: Kisses After Dark *(Shane & Katie)*

Book 13: Love After Dark *(Paul & Hope)*

Book 14: Celebration After Dark *(Big Mac & Linda)*

Book 15: Desire After Dark *(Slim & Erin)*

Book 16: Light After Dark *(Mallory & Quinn)*

Book 17: Victoria & Shannon (Episode 1)

Book 18: Kevin & Chelsea (Episode 2)

A Gansett Island Christmas Novella

Book 19: Mine After Dark *(Riley & Nikki)*

Book 20: Yours After Dark *(Finn McCarthy)*


## *The Green Mountain Series*

Book 1: All You Need Is Love *(Will & Cameron)*

Book 2: I Want to Hold Your Hand *(Nolan & Hannah)*

Book 3: I Saw Her Standing There *(Colton & Lucy)*

Book 4: And I Love Her *(Hunter & Megan)*

Novella: You'll Be Mine *(Will & Cam's Wedding)*

Book 5: It's Only Love *(Gavin & Ella)*

Book 6: Ain't She Sweet *(Tyler & Charlotte)*


## *The Butler Vermont Series*
## *(Continuation of the Green Mountain Series)*

Book 1: Every Little Thing *(Grayson & Emma)*

Book 2: Can't Buy Me Love *(Mary & Patrick)*

Book 3: Here Comes the Sun *(Wade & Mia)*


## *The Treading Water Series*

Book 1: Treading Water *(Jack & Andi)*

Book 2: Marking Time *(Clare & Aidan)*

Book 3: Starting Over *(Brandon & Daphne)*

Book 4: Coming Home *(Reid & Kate)*


## *Single Titles*

Five Years Gone

Sex Machine

Sex God

Georgia on My Mind

True North

The Fall

Everyone Loves a Hero

Love at First Flight

Line of Scrimmage

## The Erotic Quantum Series
Book 1: Virtuous *(Flynn & Natalie)*

Book 2: Valorous *(Flynn & Natalie)*

Book 3: Victorious *(Flynn & Natalie)*

Book 4: Rapturous *(Addie & Hayden)*

Book 5: Ravenous *(Jasper & Ellie)*

Book 6: Delirious *(Kristian & Aileen)*

Book 7: Outrageous *(Emmett & Leah)*

## Romantic Suspense Novels Available from Marie Force:
## The Fatal Series
One Night With You, *A Fatal Series Prequel Novella*

Book 1: Fatal Affair

Book 2: Fatal Justice

Book 3: Fatal Consequences

Book 3.5: Fatal Destiny, *the Wedding Novella*

Book 4: Fatal Flaw

Book 5: Fatal Deception

Book 6: Fatal Mistake

Book 7: Fatal Jeopardy

Book 8: Fatal Scandal

Book 9: Fatal Frenzy

# About the Author

Marie Force is the *New York Times* bestselling author of contemporary romance, including the indie-published Gansett Island Series and the Fatal Series from Harlequin Books. In addition, she is the author of the Butler, Vermont Series, the Green Mountain Series and the erotic romance Quantum Series. In 2019, her new historical Gilded series from Kensington Books will debut with *Duchess By Deception*.

All together, her books have sold 7 million copies worldwide, have been translated into more than a dozen languages and have appeared on the *New York Times* bestseller list 29 times. She is also a *USA Today* and *Wall Street Journal* bestseller, a Speigel bestseller in Germany, a frequent speaker and publishing workshop presenter as well as a publisher through her Jack's House Publishing romance imprint. She is a two-time nominee for the Romance Writers of America's RITA® award for romance fiction.

Her goals in life are simple—to finish raising two happy, healthy, productive young adults, to keep writing books for as long as she possibly can and to never be on a flight that makes the news.

Join Marie's mailing list for news about new books and upcoming appearances in your area. Follow her on Facebook at *https://www.facebook.com/MarieForceAuthor*, Twitter *@marieforce* and on Instagram at *https://instagram.com/marieforceauthor/*. Join one of Marie's many reader groups. Contact Marie at *marie@marieforce.com*.

Made in the USA
Middletown, DE
01 September 2018